I0598200

The Dream Collection

The Verbecks of Idaho

by
R.E.S. TIDMORE

RUTHLESS WRITERS
PUBLISHING

Ruthless Writers Publishing & Design
Book formatting by R. W. Publishing & Design

Printed ISBN: 9780989524391
Ebooks ISBN: MD 97809895243, DD 9780989524360, and UD 9780989524384.

Other Titles

The Awakener Series
Awaken
Oblivion
Torn

Managing Mayhem
Bliss

Coming Soon

Book 4 in the Awakener series
Redeemed

The Dream
Collection

Dedication

꧁♥꧂

To my father-in-law, you inspired this story and series with your infectious mischievous good humor and determined spirit to push through any challenge and come out on top.
Thanks for being you.

Midnight's Dream

Chapter One

"Listen here, boy," Harold Miller complained to his son's back. "You may be running my cattle ranch and taking care of this sad bag of bones, but you can at least pretend to listen to me."

Logan continued to ignore his father, back to him, while he repaired the dilapidated fence surrounding the white, two-story farmhouse, paint curling and flaking off like a river sunburn. The house, and most everything around it, was in poor condition. The flower beds had stick-like carcasses protruding through weed infestation. The flower beds had once been his mother's pride and joy. It was difficult to see them like that. It stirred an anger inside Logan he didn't wish his father to see. Since Logan's mother died ten years ago, his father worried less and less about the house, and was only interested in the day-to-day workings of his ranch. For Logan, it was a crushing blow to his mother's memory.

But now, with his father ill and unable to handle even the most mundane task, the Glade—one of Idaho's most known ranches other than the Verbecks—had become Logan's sole responsibility. It was a Herculean task, and his to-do list was a mile long. He had barely made a dent since coming home.

Logan turned around and eyed his father as he moved closer. He heard his weary groan and spied him looking up at the sun. It was nearing ninety-five degrees on this dry and hot summer day, although it wasn't anything a little shade couldn't fix. There was no breeze wrestling through the flat, open mouth of the Miller land today. Not a single pine needle could taunt the wind into bending the tall evergreens standing watch at the edge of the land. Logan blew out a breath, wiped his brow, and went back to hammering a nail into the fence.

The smell of cattle infused the air around them, heavy and strong. Harold's eyes swept the landscape. One hundred head of cattle grazed the northeast pasture. He shook his head at Logan. "When did you bring the herd in from the back mountains? I didn't hear you bring them in."

Logan clenched his jaw but remained calm. He'd just started going through his list since he returned home after a twenty-two-year absence. It felt odd to be here. His parents had come to visit him at least once a year while he lived with his uncle in Elk Creek after his best friend, Joel Verbeck, died when he was twelve. However, once he went away to college and his mother died, there was no point in coming back here. Until now.

He wanted to yell at his father to get his ass back in bed and to stop bothering him, but every man has his pride. So, he bit his tongue and drove the final nail home, gave the fence a vigorous shake, and then turned to lean against it, facing his father. Sweat trickled down his face.

"I'm not ignoring you, Pop. Max, John, and I brought the herd in last night because it was cooler outside," he said, brushing his hair away from his eyes.

"Oh, well, that makes sense." Harold scratched at his two-week-old gray beard, looking a bit lost.

"Pop, I have a lot to finish today. Can you please go back to bed and stop worrying about things? Uncle Clay taught me to run a ranch better than you ever did." He wanted to smile when fire ignited in his father's dark-brown eyes at the mention of his brother, Clay. It was amusing to get his father's blood boiling once in a while. It showed him that the cancer wasn't winning.

"I'll go to bed when I'm done giving you the what-for, young man, and not a second before!" Harold straightened and pointed. "Don't you be talking to me about your uncle. If it weren't for me, that man wouldn't know anything about cattle, let alone running a ranch." His hollowed features hardened with contempt.

Logan saw the vein in his father's forehead pop out. There was something on his father's mind, and it wasn't his uncle. That vein never surfaced unless he was intent on a fight.

"You've been back on the Glade for six months, and I haven't seen you leave the ranch once other than to help round up some cows with John and Max. Why don't you go out and meet some young women?" Harold eyed Logan.

Logan didn't know how to take that, so he waited, dissecting his father closely. He wasn't smiling, and the corners of his mouth didn't twitch like they did when he'd joked with Logan as a boy. Logan cursed under his breath. His father was dead serious. This conversation wasn't going to be fun.

Harold went on. "You know, you're not as young as you used to be."

Unable to resist, Logan threw his head back and howled with laughter. He wasn't having this conversation. He went on with his work, inspecting the rotting boards on the next section of the fence. He loved physical labor, even though he hadn't done this type of work in a long time. He held a law degree from Berkeley. His work as a defense attorney for nine years had not been as satisfying as using his hands or breaking his back to get a job done right.

Smacking his gloved hands on his jeans, Logan couldn't stay still. The constant battle to keep his anxiety over his father's illness at bay was emotionally and physically draining. He had the dark circles under his eyes to prove it. Since he had come home, sleep had been elusive. Work was his therapy.

As he bent down to grab the new wood fencing lying beside his foot, someone grabbed him around the waist and dragged him backward. The force shocked him. Startled, Logan set one leg back shoulder-width apart from the other, bent both legs and pulled his elbows tight against his ribs. He was ready for a fight. He'd known it was only a matter of time before Cole Verbeck, Joel's oldest brother, came for him.

Logan spun around at his assailant and was stunned to see it was his father dragging him back like an errant dog. The hidden strength within his father surprised and pleased him. Harold and Logan were an even match, standing over six feet, both with thick shoulders.

He glanced around. There was nothing but open fields for miles. Not a car in sight. He was relieved that Cole Verbeck wasn't on his property looking for revenge. Cole blamed Logan for the death of his brother, Joel. But that was twenty-two years ago. Logan could only hope that Joel's ghost didn't haunt Cole as much as he haunted Logan.

"Pop, what's your problem?" Logan asked. "I was ready to knock your head off. You know I'm on edge waiting for Cole to find out I'm back in town."

"He will come around when he comes around. I'm tired of you turning your back on me. There's nothing on this ranch that needs to be done so badly that you have to turn your back on me."

"Like you did to me after Joel died? How does it feel, Pop?" he lashed out. Resentment seeped through his pores.

Hurt flashed in Harold's dark eyes, but he said nothing.

Angry with himself for opening his mouth, Logan knew this wasn't the time to reopen old wounds. Taking a deep breath, he relaxed and refocused. Women . . . his father wanted him to meet some women.

"Pop, you may believe this or not, but I don't want or need to meet any women."

"Why? You got one roped in and ready to brand?" Harold sneered.

Logan's mouth turned down. "No, Pop. I don't. What's going on in your head, anyway? Is the chemo killing brain cells instead of cancer cells?"

Harold threw his hands high in the air like an angry child, causing Logan to step back.

"Well, why the hell not? You're a Miller. I want to watch some grandkids grow up before I die."

So, there it was!

He tried not to squirm under his father's blunt honesty. Guilt hit Logan like a brick, hard and square in the chest, deflating him. His father was worried he wasn't going to beat the cancer. Though they'd trudged along a rough road in the past, Logan couldn't imagine a world without his father in it. He was the only family he had left. He rubbed his chest and swallowed hard.

Logan didn't know what to say. Harold failed to grasp that even though Logan was home for now, he still wasn't sure if this was the life he wanted. He still had his condo in California and a job waiting for him to come back to if he wanted it. Before Logan had been sent away at the age of twelve, ranching had been the only life he'd ever known, but that was a long time ago. Things had changed. More importantly, he'd changed.

"There's too much to do around the ranch and this

house to think about adding a woman to the mix."

His father paled, turning pasty under the intense heat of the sun. Logan decided it would be best not to argue with him further. He felt uneasy seeing the apparent weakness his father fought to suppress. He tried to give him what he wanted.

"Listen, you stubborn old fart. If you want grandkids, how about you go back to bed? Then I can scratch a few more things off my list today. Then maybe I'll go into town with Max tomorrow. I'm sure he will be able to find some women."

Logan grabbed his father's shoulder and squeezed. "If by some miracle I get lucky, it takes nine months before a baby comes out. So take your sad-looking self upstairs and get some sleep."

Harold snorted at him but stalked off toward the house. Logan tried not to laugh as he heard his father shout over his shoulder:

"It's not miracles that make babies. It's sex. Have some. It works!" Harold was mumbling something about having ten women buzzing around him when he was young and how they'd all wanted his babies. The screen door slammed shut.

Logan stood there for a while in the heat. His father wanted grandkids.

He smacked his gloved hands together again and scowled. This was when a brother or sister could have come in handy. But he didn't have any, so he was screwed. He picked up the fence board and went back to work.

Chapter Two

It had taken Logan a week to manage a night out on the town. Ian's Bar was buzzing with people, none of whom Logan recognized. After twenty-two years, he honestly hadn't expected to. Pulling out a sketchy-looking barstool, he rested his weary body, feeling much older than his thirty-four years. Max Turner slapped him on the shoulder, tilting his bristly chin toward the back of the bar where pool tables and a dance floor resided. His blue eyes were dancing with amusement.

"Women," Max said, giving Logan a playful shove. "Sitting on your ass doesn't attract the right kind of woman."

Logan didn't reply, reluctant to burst Max's fantasy. A bar was never a place to find a decent woman, at least not from his personal experience.

Max went on. "You have to get up and dance. Women love a man who can dance. It's sexy." He did a little side-step twist and was off. Logan shook his head, amused.

Max was what most women called a giant teddy bear. As big as an ox and as tough as a John Deere. He was the nicest, kindest, hardest-working man Logan had met in an awful long time. Max needed a raise.

Spinning around on the stool, he turned to observe the people in the bar. Everyone seemed preoccupied, unaware of his critical analysis. Once upon a time, he'd only seen trouble here. However, things had changed. Now he only saw ordinary people looking for an escape from the harsh daily life this community bathed in. Could he find his place among them?

"What can I get you?" an aged voice said from behind. Logan swung back around to meet a sour-faced bartender.

"Budweiser," he replied, running a hand through his shaggy hair, still not used to the feel of it. In his old firm, shaggy hair wasn't an option. Here, he could grow it down to his butt and no one would care. It was liberating, in a way.

The bartender gaped at him. "You Harold's boy?" he asked, scrunching up his face.

Logan returned his gaze questioningly. "Why do you ask?"

"You look like him. When he was young, I mean. But your eyes look like Sue's. She had the most beautiful, green eyes I'd ever seen." Remembrance twinkled in the bartender's own eyes.

Logan interrupted the daydream. "That she did." He wasn't sure where the conversation was leading. "Is there a problem I should know about? I mean, with my father, that is."

The bartender threw down the rag that was resting on his shoulder. "Why, yes, there is. Tell your old man that Ian Smith still has a score to settle with him, so he better not be dying just yet."

Logan watched the bartender's back as he wandered off, steam shooting from his ears. A moment later, he returned with a Budweiser. Obviously, the grumpy-faced bartender was Ian Smith, the owner of the bar.

Ian plopped the beer down in front of Logan and glared at him. "That man stole Sue from me thirty-eight years ago. Thought he was my friend back then. He took her right from under my nose. That rogue never stepped foot in here after that." The sour-faced man snorted and went to take the order of a man sitting three stools down.

Logan thumped the wood counter, amusement spiking his veins. His father was a thieving scoundrel, stealing his mother away from this grumpy old man. That was a hoot. He'd have to ask his father about that one—see if he could get a rise out of him once more.

Logan's happy mood suddenly shifted into reverse. His brows creased and his shoulders sagged. He realized that he didn't know anything about his father's youth. He'd never asked him. Never thought to ask him. His father had been forty when Logan was born. To Logan, his father had always seemed old, strong, and unbending, like iron. He never thought of him as weak in any way . . . until now.

The chemo had stopped working, and Logan was afraid. The uncertainty and hopelessness he felt overwhelmed him at times. He'd already lost his mother when he was twenty-two and in his first year of law school. She had been his one ray of hope breaking over the mountain ridge that was his life. If he lost his father too, there would be nothing left to tie him to the ranch other than a deed of ownership.

He felt powerless. He was just starting to get to know his father again. He had to find a solution somehow. He couldn't just wait and watch him die. Maybe there was a new breakthrough in one of the cancer research centers. He took a long pull off his beer. The future seemed bleak.

Chapter Three

Licking her lips, Emma Verbeck tasted the sharp bitterness of the Budweiser and grimaced. Yuck. How did people drink this stuff? The bottle thunked onto the table she was sitting at. She tried not to fidget with the hem of her black cotton blouse. She could feel the collective glancing at her. The horror of it, their hometown doctor drinking at a bar in hooker-red shoes that matched her new red lipstick. She wiggled her toes in the heels and peeked under the table at them. But they were so stinking cute and went perfectly with her faded skinny jeans. She didn't care if the townspeople watched her, judged her. It felt good to be out of scrubs. Her heart-shaped face scrunched; she couldn't even remember the last time she wore heels. These poor hooker shoes had been in the box for at least four years. She sighed.

Since she had decided to come home to Havencrest three months ago to start her family practice, she would see them in her office at some point and learn all the townspeople's secrets. That thought made her smirk impishly at the crowd, calming her nerves. She was here to get a break from work and to pretend to have a life because she was single and almost twenty-nine years old, and not being married was a crime in Havencrest. She loved her hometown but she really wished their archaic way of thinking could be put to death; not like a bury you in the ground kind of way, more like put you in the freezer and be the next school term of med students' cadaver.

She didn't know why she'd told Peter to meet her here for a drink. She wasn't a drinker or a talker, but Peter already knew that. Hell, he'd helped make her that way. She could never get a word in with three older brothers bossing her around. Her time at college, med school, and her residency had been just the break she needed to become her own person. That was the hard part about family; they always saw the person you used to be, never the person you had become.

The crowd was loud, and people were bumping into her table. She scooted over in the booth, wanting as much space as she could get. Maybe coming to Ian's bar was a poor choice for a break from work. She had been feeling nostalgic when Peter called to check and see how her office was running after Mrs. Sturt crashed the computer system for the third time that day, not having been to Ian's since Cole and Peter took her there when she visited after graduating from med school. Not to mention she wanted to see Ian, the owner of the bar. He'd had a heart attack a few weeks ago and she wanted to check on him. It was a two-birds-one-stone kind of thing.

She gritted her teeth, feeling like an idiot sitting there all by herself. At the booth next to her, three women were doing shots and squealing with laughter.

Where the heck was Peter? He was such the ladies' man, she couldn't believe he would miss the opportunity to schmooze on a Friday night. That was it. She was calling him. She didn't have all night. She'd told Mrs. Foster she would swing by and take a look at a cut on her leg since she couldn't make it to the clinic.

She pulled out her phone and hit Peter's number. With the phone to her ear, she waited for him to answer, going against every impulse to evade conflict. This was her brother, and the only way to be seen as strong and independent was to act like it. It went to voice mail. "Listen here, you pain in my ass. You were supposed to meet me here thirty minutes ago. You better be out there serving and protecting because if you're not, I'm going to start a rumor about a very suspicious rash you have near your nether regions. And there just so happens to be a group of very attractive women in the booth next to me where I can start said rumor. You have fifteen minutes to show up or call. The clock is ticking." Emma hung up the phone and smiled. *That should do the trick.*

When Peter's fifteen minutes passed and Emma was on the verge of jumping ship, ready to let her brother fend for himself, she turned toward the entrance and saw Max Turner shoving a devilishly handsome outsider into the bar. He was gorgeous. Golden-blond hair, sun-kissed skin, and a lean, hard body. Her heart hammered against her breast. She leaned back, admiring the new visitor. He carried himself well, a man who knew what he was worth. A single eyebrow hitched; she was intrigued. Maybe she could stay a little while longer.

Max slapped the man on the back, then danced off toward his waiting female followers. She rolled her eyes. Max was a hopeless flirt, and all the girls knew it. The stranger sat on a barstool and watched the townspeople milling about with a razor-sharp stare.

She sank into the corner of the booth, nervously concealing herself from his roaming eyes. *Really, you're hiding like a child.* She wrinkled her nose. Shyness ruled the majority of her life. She'd found that if you kept to yourself, others rarely noticed you. That was how she preferred it after Joel died and her mother left. Now, however, she was a doctor, and the time for shyness was over. She was working on it, a little—maybe barely—fine, not at all. To be real, she had only been working on it with her brothers. *Let's not mislead ourselves.* She frowned.

Cautiously, she peeked at the outsider from around the corner of the booth. He faced off with Ian. She studied the mirror that hung on the bar wall. A careful look captured his distinct features as his interaction with Ian was cut short. His beautiful, emerald-green eyes were dark . . . haunted even. A secret lurked behind them, and pain. Compassion and curiosity urged her to go to him.

Chewing her lip, Emma put on her Dr. Verbeck facade, locked away her shyness, and held fast to her barely scraped-together courage. She stood, convincing herself this would be good practice, talking to a stranger. In her three-inch, red, hooker heels, she flipped her long curls over her shoulder and casually strolled toward the empty barstool next to the stranger.

About three steps from the barstool, Emma's courage faltered and she veered off toward the door. Then she thought about how Peter would react when he strolled in and saw her next to the attractive outsider. He would probably grumble at having to drink his beer by himself. The idea was immensely satisfying. She halted and then swung around. Rebelling against her brothers never failed to motivate her. If only she felt more confident than she pretended to be.

Sliding onto the barstool next to the man, she found herself drawn to him in a peculiar way. Her pulse pounded in her ears. She was so far out of her comfort zone that she didn't know how to get back. Oh, but my, he was handsome.

❦

The scent of wild sunflowers floated around Logan, washing away the stench of cigarettes and stale beer. He inhaled deeply, closing his eyes in rapture. It had been years since he'd smelled anything that reminded him of his mother. He turned toward the source. Lost in thought, Logan hadn't noticed when the gorgeous midnight's dream had sat down beside him.

He paused, unable to breathe. A splash of freckles sprinkled her straight nose and high cheekbones. Ebony-black ringlets framed her heart-shaped face, enhancing the beauty of her porcelain skin. She was magnificent. And she was watching him take her in.

He felt apprehension. Did she like what she saw as he did, or did he fall short of the wants of such a creature?

A smile pulled at her full lips and her wheat-colored eyes sparkled. He returned the smile of the exquisite stranger.

A nervous laugh escaped her lips and the color of her cheeks deepened.

"You looked lonely. Do you mind if I finish my beer with you before I head out to check on one of my patients?" she said, smiling weakly.

He had a feeling this young woman didn't do this sort of thing—this talking with strangers. He welcomed the risk she took.

He gave her a small salute with his beer and eyed her curiously. She reminded him of someone, though he couldn't put a finger on it. There was a memory attached to her eyes. He took another sip of his beer as he tried to work it out in his head.

They sat in silence. His mind thought of a thousand things he could say to her, but none came out of his mouth. He was on the verge of cursing up a storm when she spoke.

"Are you new to the area, or are you just passing through?" she asked.

"I was born here in Havencrest, about ten miles south in the back country. But I've been gone for most of my life."

Her face was an unreadable mask, yet Logan saw a hint of surprise in her eyes.

"Really? Why don't I recognize you? I've lived in Havencrest my entire life. Well, except for my escape to go to college and med school. What's your name?" she asked, her voice velvet-edged and strong.

He avoided the question, wanting to remain anonymous for as long as he could. "Medical school? I take it you're a doctor."

Her eyes sparkled with pride. "Yes, just opened the family practice clinic on Main Street down the road about three months ago."

"Havencrest does need a doctor, but it is a small town."

She tipped her head to the side, studying him. "You didn't answer my question. What's your name?"

He took a pull of his beer, eyed her and gave in. "Logan Johnson," he said, giving his mother's maiden name. There were plenty of Johnsons in town and in neighboring communities to hide his lie. That was, as long as Ian Smith stayed at the other end of the bar. "I work at the Glade with Max." He pointed to his friend swinging a tall blonde around like a joyous rag doll. Logan was trying to keep a low profile since he was back in town. He wasn't ready to deal with Cole Verbeck.

She stiffened. Logan didn't know if it was at the mention of the Glade or Max. Then she relaxed her shoulders and smiled warmly as she looked in the direction of Max.

"You work with Max. That must be a hoot. He's a funny guy."

Taking a swallow of his beer, Logan eyed the dark beauty. Did she grow up with Max? If she did, Max could blow his cover. The idea chafed his hide.

"May I ask what your name is?" he said, turning to face her. She didn't move. Her legs stayed crossed, her upper body leaning into the bar. She wore faded jeans with a pair of sexy red heels and a cotton blouse buttoned to the middle of her chest, exposing the tops of full, round breasts. His eyes lingered and his mouth watered. He averted his eyes as he felt his body heat and harden.

Everything she wore fit like a glove—a glove he wanted to wear. She was slender, but not skinny.

She stood, black ringlets skimming her back.

"Emma," she answered.

"You leaving already?" he asked, surprised. "Can I buy you another beer?"

"No, thanks. I'm not much of a drinker. Just came down to meet someone and to check on Ian." She tapped the counter where she stood, getting the grumpy old man's attention.

"Ian, thanks for the beer, love. I'll come and check on you again in a day or two. Don't go crazy with salt or your blood pressure is going to go through the roof. Try and rest as much as you can." Then she blew a kiss to the sour-faced man.

Interesting, a doctor that made bar calls. He was intrigued. Most doctors wouldn't see patients outside their office.

Jealousy sprang to life in Logan. For one fleeting moment, he wanted to be that old man. Jumping to his feet, he blocked Emma's escape. "Can I walk you to your car?" he offered with fingers crossed.

She appeared thoughtful for a moment, made her decision, and grabbed her purse. "Sure, but we'd better get out of here," she remarked, looking nervously at her watch. "Mrs. Foster may get irritated if I show up after dark."

Logan noted the strained expression on Emma's face. The instinct to protect this newly found creature flared within him. Even if it was from a grumpy Mrs. Foster.

They weaved their way through the crowd and stepped outside. Logan's senses were heightened by the warm summer breeze, carrying with it a hint of pine and fresh-cut hay. He sighed. Emma turned to look at him. One of her heels caught on the edge of a pothole and she stumbled forward.

꒰ ❤ ꒱

She was going down. *That's what I get for wearing heels.* Then she felt her fall halted by an iron grip around her waist. She sucked in a breath as Logan pulled her against his granite body. Tilting her head to the side, she peered at his face. His lips were a kiss away. She felt the heat from his body and she softened like a breathless girl of eighteen.

"Careful, I don't want you to hurt yourself," he whispered, his breath hot against her ear.

It caused a liquid heat to waltz down her spine and make tight, exquisite circles in her core. Her knees went a little weak. She cleared her throat, pretending not to be affected by his nearness. "Thank you. That's what happens when you're a flats kind of girl, not heels." Stepping out of his embrace, she shuddered. She opened her purse to retrieve a pair of black cotton flats. Swiftly, she stepped out of the pretty heels and into the practical flats, praying her flushed cheeks would cool down.

"You don't have to show me to my car. I don't have one here. It is over at my clinic. I just didn't have the heart to turn you down." She smiled sheepishly, peering at him from under her lashes. He smiled at her in a masculine way that set her heart racing. He was something. No one had ever aroused her so fast in her life. It was a bit unsettling to have a stranger touch her so profoundly. To be safe, she took a step back, thinking it better to keep some distance though she gazed at him, trying to figure out why there was some familiarity in his eyes. Logan Johnson. There were plenty of Johnsons in Havencrest. He said he was born ten miles south of town in the back mountains. That was by her family's ranch. He strongly resembled Harold Miller in the face and build. However, there was a quiet sadness in Logan's appearance. But he couldn't be Harold's son. She had been six years old when Joel died and when Harold sent his son away. What was his name . . . Leroy, Leonard? What did it matter?

"If you wouldn't mind walking with me to Mrs. Foster's house, I'd enjoy the company. It's just up the road. She has a cut I need to look at," she blurted.

"That's too bad," he said with compassion.

It was a warm evening and the sun had disappeared, casting the sky in a pinkish hue. As they strolled down the road, Emma was taken back to a time in between sophomore and junior year, when she'd snuck out of the house one summer evening to take a stroll like this with Sam Blacken, the varsity captain of the basketball team. Man, she'd had such a crush on him. Yet they never dated because she was too afraid of what her brothers would do to him once they found out.

"If you don't mind me asking, what kind of doctor are you? You said you started a family practice. So, I assume a family doctor," Logan said.

"Yes. I finished my residency in Boise. I'm not one for the city, but Boise is nice. But I love it here more. I like helping the people I knew while growing up, though it has its drawbacks." She gazed down the narrow, two-lane road with a railroad track cutting through it.

"How so?" He edged a little closer, brushing shoulders with her.

Her eyes narrowed, but she didn't move away. "Many of the people in this town, and neighboring ones, have known me almost all my life. So, when it's time to treat them for something, they tend to disagree with me and treat me like the child they've always known. And seeing the people I know getting old and sick . . . it just breaks my heart."

"I know what you mean. It's hard seeing people you love suffer," Logan said.

"How's Mr. Miller doing over at the Glade?" she asked.

"You know him?" he replied quickly. "Are you his doctor?"

She shook her head. "He's a stubborn man. He didn't want a child as a doctor." She shrugged.

"I'm sorry. He's a hard man to deal with," Logan said.

"Yes, yes, he is."

They fell into an easy silence. Small, rolling hills hugged the left side of town and houses stacked upon the rise and fall of them. Tall pine trees poked out of every open space in between the homes. But to the right was a flat, open plain reaching to the Payette River. With this cotton candy sky, it was something to see.

Emma listened to the crunch of rocks beneath their feet as they turned off of Main Street and headed toward a small, tired, blue house with a white front porch at the base of the nearest hill off Pine Street.

"Why did you become a doctor?" Logan asked, kicking a rock, sending it flying down the road.

"My father had a heart attack when he was out working in one of the fields on our ranch. My brother was with him and called for help. I ran out to him, but neither one of us knew what to do. It was the most helpless I've ever felt. I knew then and there I never wanted to feel like that again." She shrugged. "After that, I knew I wanted to be a doctor."

"I know what it's like to feel completely helpless; it's terrible."

Emma walked up to the porch. She saw that same sad look coat Logan's face that she'd seen in the bar. She couldn't help but wonder where it came from.

"Thank you for walking with me," she said shyly, stopping in front of Mrs. Foster's door.

"You're welcome. Maybe I'll see you around sometime," he said, grabbing her hand to lift it to his lips. He kissed her palm gently. Blood rushed to her cheeks once more, and pleasure slid like silk down her spine. It was a lovely gesture.

She gazed after him for some time on Mrs. Foster's front porch. The warm night air played with her curls. It was delightful talking to someone who didn't see her as the little sister of the Verbeck brothers. For as long as she could remember, that was all she was: the quiet, shy sister. She sighed, then hugged herself happily. *Holy hayfield!* She spun around on her toes and knocked on Mrs. Foster's front door. The memory of today was a keeper.

Chapter Four

Emma passed the Miller ranch at the end of her work-day. The ranch was also known to the town as the Glade. It was one of the most breathtaking plots of land in Idaho, with its gently rolling hills covered with tall grass feeding into the thick evergreens that lined the property. She paused and soaked it in as the sun was getting lower. The Miller ranch and her family's ranch touched on the west pasture, and they shared the bumpy dirt road she passed on her way home.

She squinted against the light and tried desperately to see out into the fields. She just wanted a peek at Logan and then she would be happy. Three dreadful days had passed, and she hadn't seen him once. She was beginning to think that Logan had lied to her. *Stop it. Stop it right now.* She didn't want to act like her older brother Cole, who ran their family ranch: suspicious of everyone and every word people said.

As she passed the Millers' driveway, she saw Logan on the porch fussing with the screen door. Her heart tripped over with excitement. Should she stop? No, too desperate. She peered at her watch and then back at Logan. He looked as though he would be there a little while. Emma gassed it and headed for home. It was a great day for a run. Right past Logan.

Rushing to the house, Emma flung open the front door

and made a beeline for her old room. Living at home with her two single older brothers at her age wasn't ideal and she'd prefer not to. However, it took all her savings and a small loan to buy the clinic building in town and get her practice started. So, here she was, starting from scratch to save and move out.

She caught a glimpse of Peter sitting at the kitchen table in his sheriff uniform reading the newspaper. Apparently, he was in no rush to help Cole with the work on the ranch, as usual.

"Damn, someone lit your ass hairs on fire!" he exclaimed.

Emma ignored the comment like she always did when Peter was trying to be funny and slammed and locked her bedroom door behind her. With two brothers, it was better safe than sorry. Peter and Cole were always pulling pranks on her. After years of being tortured, she was pretty good at evading them. She knew she had about three minutes before Peter would come knocking on her door, his curiosity piqued by her lack of interaction with him.

She untied her scrub bottoms, pushed them down, and then tugged off her scrub top as fast as her fingers would allow. She dashed over to her dresser. She grabbed a pair of running pants and a tank top. She had two minutes. She caught herself smiling like a crazy person. Footsteps came from the hall. Just as Emma tugged the tank over her head and snatched her socks and running shoes from the closet, a knock sounded on her door.

"What are you in a rush for?" Peter asked in a muffled voice. *Right on time.*

Emma wanted to laugh. She could see his shadow trying to peek into her room from under the door. She had one minute left before he would jimmy the lock like he had in high school to prank her by dumping a bucket of crickets in her room. It had taken her a month to find all the little bastards and get rid of them.

Dressed and with her shoes on, she unlocked the window and pushed it open. Emma had one leg out of the window when her door swung open. Peter was standing there with a surprised look on his face. She laughed hard and dove out of the window. Her brother had never caught her sneaking out in broad daylight. But after ten years of being away from home, it was time to turn a new leaf and give her brothers hell like she'd always wanted to.

She took off, laughing so hard that she stumbled twice. She looked over her shoulder and saw Peter in complete shock, slack-jawed, eyes bulging from her bedroom window. It was a good look for him.

"What the hell is your problem?" Peter yelled with a hint of amusement in his tone, leaning out the window.

"I'm going for a run. I'll be back in an hour or two!" she shouted.

"You could have just said so, you know!"

"And play fifty questions? No thanks!" she said, spinning around trying not to trip.

Peter crossed his muscular arms over his wide chest. "If I weren't so tired, I'd come after you."

"Yeah, right. See you later!" she yelled, waving back at him as a smile tipped the corner of his lips.

"You know I could if I wanted to!"

She laughed. "Your track days are long gone, big brother." She heard the window slam shut and she laughed again.

Emma sprinted out of the driveway. She didn't run into Cole and was glad for it. He was way harder to handle than Peter.

It took about a half a mile before she hit a good pace. She stretched out her legs and picked up her speed. She loved to run. It was her time to think . . . to dream. Right now, she was dreaming about a blond-haired, green-eyed god, and she was headed his way.

Because of her brothers, dating in high school was impossible because they never liked anyone she was interested in. When she was working on her undergrad degree at San Diego State University, she'd dated Matthew Phillips for two years. They met in her Abnormal Psych class, and she really fell hard for his cute dimples and blue eyes. She thought maybe they would get married, but when she'd gotten into the University of Washington for medical school, he'd broken up with her because he didn't want to leave California. It had taken her a little bit to get over him, yet when med school started, she didn't have time to think about him—or any other boy, for that matter. She could now though, and she was excited.

It was three miles from her driveway to the Millers', and she made it in record time. Twenty-three minutes. She stopped, bent over, and fought the light-headed feeling that threatened to overwhelm her.

"You okay?" she heard someone ask from not too far away. She couldn't look up for fear of passing out. She held up a finger to signal "just a minute." After a few deep breaths, she stood up and walked off the cramp that was building in her right hamstring, then she looked over.

Logan was there, a stone's throw away and jogging toward her. She fidgeted with her hair, realizing she hadn't put it in a ponytail in her great escape. Brushing her fingers through it quickly, she tried to unknot the curls before wiping the sweat from her forehead.

She was a hot mess. It was clear she hadn't thought through this whole scenario very well.

"I'm fine. I was pushing too hard to beat my PB," she said, trying to make it sound as though she did this regularly and that she hadn't come to spy on him.

"PB? What's that? I've heard the term before, but I can't remember off the top of my head," Logan said, stepping up beside her with an easy smile.

"Personal best."

"Oh right, that would make sense."

Logan was shirtless, and his jeans hung low on his narrow hips. Emma tried not to drool. She and Logan glanced back and forth at each other. It was obvious neither one knew what to say. She pointed at the screen door.

"Making repairs on the old house?" It was more of a statement than a question, but Logan took the bait.

He peered over his shoulder and then back at her. "Yes, the whole thing is held together by very old nails. And that screen doesn't seem to want to get fixed." He held out his hand. "Pinched me about five times. I was about to cut it into pieces when I saw you coming from down the road."

Putting on her doctor face, Emma gently took his hand and inspected the red patches of skin. She brushed a thumb over them and sparks of heat went off as though someone had lit fireworks under her skin. He flinched ever so slightly at her touch. She hoped she hadn't hurt him, and she regretfully let his hand slide from her fingers.

"It looks like you'll live," she declared in her professional voice, hiding the breathless feeling he caused within her.

Logan nodded, his features suddenly tight. "I was hoping to see you again. I mean, I wanted to see you again." His eyes scanned her face, dropped to her shoulders, then to her breasts, and finally to her hips. The fire she saw there made her squirm. She'd forgotten how fitted her running gear was, but his interest filled her with joy nevertheless. *He liked what he saw . . .*

A shy smile pulled at her lips. "I was hoping to see you again as well." She tucked a rogue curl behind her ear as Logan pulled in a deep breath. He reached out as if he were going to take her in his arms. She held her breath, her heart drumming. Then he shoved his hands into his pockets.

Dang!

"Would you like to have a glass of tea with me on the porch?" he asked.

Emma glanced at her watch. She had about an hour before Cole would be done working and wonder where she was. The last thing she wanted was Cole coming to look for her. She understood after Joel died, her mother abandoning them, and their father dying that Cole had taken up the father role. He was fearful of losing Peter and her, which caused him to be a little overbearing. Yet it didn't take the sting away from the embarrassment it brought from time to time. *Oh, look, my brother has come to get me like I am five.* She didn't know what bothered her more, that she understood why Cole would come looking for her, or that she would get in the truck like a good little sister when he found her because she didn't want him to worry. *Ugh.*

"Sure, that would be great, as long as Mr. Miller doesn't mind. But only for a few minutes. I have to fin-ish my run," she said, hoping that little bit of time was enough to tide her over until she saw him again.

"He won't mind."

Logan walked her up the steps to the Miller home and gestured for her to sit in a rocking chair. Then he disap-peared inside. Emma sat there with her knees bouncing. Her anxiety grew as the seconds ticked by. Even though she'd escaped her brothers to seize this moment, she was afraid they would somehow mess this up with Logan. Taking a deep breath, she reminded herself that she was a grown adult. Her brothers would just have to accept that and let her date whoever she wanted to.

Logan poured two glasses of tea, his mind torturing him with visions of Emma sitting on his porch alone. He'd fought the urge to touch her again. Between those tight, black running pants, that snug, blue tank top, and that hair, he was coming unglued. He couldn't believe he'd almost grabbed her, wanting to taste her full, pink lips. It was such an uncontrolled urge, and so unlike him. He was a damn defense attorney. He took pride in his unwavering control. What was happening to him? He'd never wanted his ex like this.

Honey Cantrell had been another defense attorney like him, though she'd been with the firm a year prior to his arrival. She'd been all long legs, red hair, and business suits. She prowled the office like she was a dying man's last meal. He'd never seen anyone carry themselves with such confidence. It had been intoxicating. She'd pulled him in so tight he forgot what it was like to breathe. He'd thought he loved her and that she felt the same; that was, until he walked in on her having sex with one of the partners in their office on their desk. He'd frozen, stunned at what he was seeing. He'd dropped the file he was carrying to the floor and she smiled at him. He did the only thing he could. He walked out, went to his condo, grabbed all her stuff, and went back to the office and set it all on her desk. He never talked to her again unless they were working on a case together. Which he made sure never happened, until one of the partners made him.

He'd never felt so betrayed. Of course, other than by Cole Verbeck when he accused him of killing Joel, his best friend. That betrayal had cost him years of his life on a ranch that wasn't his father's.

He left the kitchen and made his way to the front door. His body was so tight he could hardly move. He prayed she wouldn't notice. He pushed open the screen with his back, strolled over to Emma, and handed her a glass of tea. His goal, to get to know her better. To get her talking and spend a little more time with her. He sat on the swing across from her on the porch. He watched her lips press against the glass and saw her throat move as she swallowed her drink. He wanted to kiss that throat. He had to think of something else fast to distract him.

"Do you run over here often? I mean, if you do, maybe we could run together. I always wanted to be a runner. I just never had the time when I was working on a case. I used to run occasionally with a friend in college; Daisy. We both sucked at it."

Emma blinked at him wide-eyed. He wasn't sure what he'd said to get a look like that out of her. But he clearly had said something.

"Case? What do you mean, when you were working on a case? What did you do before you came here?"

And there it was. He'd incriminated himself. Look at that, six months off and he was slipping. He cleared his throat. "I used to be a defense attorney."

"What? No way. Why on earth would you come to work in Havencrest if you could do that?"

He pushed back on the swing and then lifted his feet to get it swinging. "Needed a break. I was an attorney for quite a few years and I never took a vacation. I was working myself to death trying to make partner. One day I got a phone call and everything changed. And here I am." He slapped his jeans and dust puffed out of them in a cloud. "I get to play in the dirt like a real man."

She wrinkled her nose. "You mean, like a real smelly man," she said with a laugh.

The corners of his mouth tipped. "You got jokes. I see." He liked it. Emma made house calls to grumpy old people, and she had jokes. Compassion, humor, and beauty. He wasn't likely to survive this without some kind of wound to his heart.

Then Emma's eyes darted around, picking at her pants. "I ran a lot when I was doing my residency. It was the only way to stay sane from the lack of sleep." She looked around. "I run this way from time to time," she said, looking guilty of something, but he didn't know what.

"The next time you do, come by. It would be an agreeable change for me."

Her eyes sparkled. "That would be nice. Having someone to run with," she agreed before standing up and finishing her drink. "I'm sorry, I have to go. I still have to run through town and back before it gets too dark."

Logan stood and walked her to the edge of the porch. "Do you want to go to Cascade Lake on Friday? Maybe go swimming and have a picnic?" The thought of her saying yes thrilled him.

She bounced down the stairs, and shot him with her amber eyes and a bright smile. "I would love to. Friday at six o'clock. I'll meet you at the Van Wyck Campground. You'll have to bring the food. My last appointment is normally at five thirty, so I won't have time."

"It's a date."

Without another word she took off, her long legs increasing the gap between them. She ran with a natural grace, something he knew he would never have. She was beautiful. It was only Tuesday. This was going to be the longest week of his life. At least she'd said yes, and now he had something to look forward to.

He finished his tea and strolled back over to the screen door he'd been fixing. "Now you listen here, be nice to me. I have a date in a few days, and I can't be getting all covered in pinch marks."

He grabbed the screen and opened it. It groaned and popped.

Chapter Five

Logan leaned against his pop's old, white Ford pickup waiting for Emma to arrive. He'd parked near the turn-in for the parking lot to make sure he wouldn't miss her, since he had no clue what she was driving.

He peered up at the sun; not a wisp of a cloud in the sky. He wiped the sweat running down the side of his face. He couldn't have picked a better day to go for a swim. It had crested a hundred and two degrees by three this afternoon. With a navy tank top, Hawaiian board shorts, and flip-flops on, he was feeling very Cali. The only thing throwing off the vibe was his straw cowboy hat. He pressed his lips, realizing he hadn't thought much about California over the past six months he'd been back in Idaho. He didn't miss the suits. He didn't miss the late nights in the office. And he sure as hell didn't miss the microwave dinners he'd been surviving on. But he did miss Ramberto's Taco Shop down the street from his condo. Lord, they had the best carne asada burritos. His mouth watered thinking about them. He would almost make a trip to Cali for them.

He glanced at the cab of the pickup, with a literal picnic basket sitting on the seat filled with his sad little PB&Js, Ruffles chips, fruit salad, and soda pop. It was a far cry from burritos. He hoped Emma would forgive his lack of cooking skills. He was a bit rusty at this wooing thing. After what happened with Honey, Logan didn't have much of an appetite for women. He focused on making partner with his firm and couldn't remember the last time he had been on a date—or had met anyone that he wanted to go on a date with.

Emma came bouncing down the road in an old, yellow 1970s Chevy pickup. How had he not noticed that beater before now? The radio was blasting with the familiar voice of Kelly Clarkson. She swung in and parked next to him. He strolled over to the door and with a loud creak and then a bang, it opened for her. Emma hopped out radiating happiness. She took his breath away with a white cotton dress that he could see through to her curves.

"Ready to do this?" she said, pushing back her own cowboy hat, long curls carrying on the wind, smiling up at him, eyes telling him everything she was feeling.

"Been waiting on you." He pulled out the picnic basket from the cab of the truck and held it up for her to see. "It's official. We're having a picnic. You pick the spot."

She giggled, spun toward the lake, and with an adventurous toss of her head she cried, "Onward!"

He laughed, sincerely amused with this relaxed version of Emma. He followed her down a rock path zigzagging down to the beach. When she slipped, he shot out a hand and caught her arm. She smiled up gratefully at him. Her arm glided through his fingers. When her hand was about to break free of his, he laced them together, hoping she would allow him this small thing. She peeked at him shyly and grinned. The connection was like a warm glow flowing through him. When they reached the sand, she stopped to survey the area.

There were a few others at the beach. Some were tanning on outrageously colorful towels, others leaned back in short beach chairs reading books, children played tag, sand flying about like a storm, the plastic squeak of coolers opening only to drop with a plunk . . . it was carefree. Logan could use some carefree in his life.

Emma chose a spot under a large maple tree on the right where grass reached into an empty campsite. Logan set the basket down and pulled out a blanket for them to sit on. Once in place, Logan sat down and looked out at the lake. The water was all bouncing mirrors flashing up at him. It had been too long since he'd been here.

Pop and his mom had come on a day just like this to camp for the weekend when he was eight. Pop had showed him how to start a fire with sticks and how to set up his own tackle box for fishing. Things had been so simple before Joel's death. He had a family, friends he loved, and the whole world ahead of him. Now here he was again, a completely different person, with a completely different life than he thought he would have.

Emma glanced at him with a playful look on her face, threw down her hat, tugged her dress up over her head, and ran for it. She wore a black string bikini and his jaw dropped. "Last one in is a party pooper!"

She was in the water up to her thighs when he dove in, splashing her. She squealed and dove in after him. The water was cool against his hot skin. It gave him a zap of energy he hadn't had sitting in the heat. He broke the water's surface and looked for Emma. He didn't see her, and his heart stopped. "Emma!" He swam around, panic rising. He was twelve again. "Emma!"

When she popped up beside him with a splash to his face and a laugh, he cursed under his breath. Wiping the water from his face, Emma blinked wide eyes at him.

"Are you okay?"

"Yeah, sure. I'm fine."

"You don't look fine."

"Well, I am." He swam further out into the lake, needing to burn off the adrenaline Emma had spiked in him.

He swam hard and fast, like he did when he was a kid, not stopping until every ounce of energy was gone. Then he flipped to his back and floated, breathing hard. To his surprise, Emma, also floating on her back, bumped into him. "Fancy meeting you out here," she teased.

Logan felt like an ass but was impressed Emma had kept up with him and she hardly seemed out of breath. He didn't look at her, feeling like a fool. "You're a pretty good swimmer."

"Yeah, I know. I like water and it likes me too. A match made in heaven."

He chuckled at her. "You really do have jokes, don't you."

"If you can't laugh at life, what's the point of being here?" Her body sank into the water and she started to swim back. "I'll race you."

Logan sank, admiring Emma's stamina for a second and then started to swim hard for the beach.

By the time he reached the beach, Emma had her dress on and was pulling food from the basket. *How fast is she?*

Walking toward a little boy about the age of four, he was halted with a stop sign hand and frustrated blue eyes.

"Mister," came a small, hoarse voice from a towhead, "want to build a castle with me? It won't stay."

Logan peered around and wasn't entirely sure who this kid belonged to, in between what looked like could be two families. The boy's frustrated expression cut through him.

"How can I help?" Logan said, dropping to his knees, studying the scene before him.

"I put the sand in the castle bucket, flip it over and look, no castle."

Logan smiled. "You need water."

"What?"

"Water. The sand has to be wet for it to stick together."

"OHHHHH . . ." said the boy, his eyes getting large.

"Come on. I'll show you. But we have to get closer to the water."

The little boy jumped up and took Logan's hand, surprising him. The boy held the bucket up to him. Logan peered down at the little face so sure that Logan would teach him the ways of sandcastle building. The boy's little hand so tight in his. They walked down to the sand near the water and bent down.

He peered around once more to make sure he wasn't getting questioning looks from anyone. The only one who seemed to be interested was Emma. There was a dreamy look on her face that caused him to see the view from her eyes. A knot formed in his throat; he had always wanted a family, to do things like this. Life and work had gotten in the way of a dream. And after years, that dream dissolved in an endless caseload. He blew out a shaky breath.

"First, we have to fill the bucket with the wet sand."

The little boy's fingers dug deep, dropping the sand into the bucket. He paused, opening and closing his hands.

"What's wrong?" Logan asked.

"I'm too small."

Logan chuckled at the boy's pouting lip and placed the bucket on its side. "Shove it in this way." Logan helped. Once it was full, he stood the bucket up. "Now we have to pat the sand to get it nice and tight. And we flip it over."

When Logan pulled the bucket off it was a perfect sandcastle. The little boy gasped. "We did it! Thank you." The little boy high-fived Logan.

Logan stood. "Got it under control now?"

"Yes." He started to fill the bucket again.

Logan smiled and trotted over to Emma, who looked at him dreamy-eyed and this time it was him who smiled shyly.

"Oh my God, that was the most precious thing I've seen in a long time," Emma said, looking like she might cry. She held a soda can up to her heart with one hand and in the other she held a PB&J.

All he could do was sit down, feeling exposed and vulnerable. "How is the grand feast?" Logan asked, dropping back onto the blanket across from her. It took her a second, but she collected herself and tossed him a sandwich. "I am starving after that swim."

"No wonder. You're an Olympic swimmer."

"I had to be. My parents made sure I wouldn't drown."

Logan swallowed hard and was sure all color had drain from his face. He took a bite of his PB&J and was quiet, not letting thoughts about Joel and how he had drowned surface and drag him under.

Emma moaned next to him, eyes rolling back into her head to close. He stared; that was the sexiest sound known to man.

When her eyes opened, she took another bite, grinning shyly. "Food." She moaned again. Needing a distraction, he pulled out a soda pop and chugged it, next popping a few chips into his mouth.

"Sometimes I forget how nice it is out here," Emma said, leaning back lazily on an elbow, having devoured her sandwich.

"I know what you mean. I haven't been here since I was a kid."

She watched him, eyes gliding over his body. It caused him to flush and his body to harden.

"Why are you not married already?" She pointed to the little boy now on his fourth bucket castle. "Clearly you are a natural with kids."

He peered back at the boy playing all alone. Happy as could be. He shrugged. "Thought I was in love once. Even thought about asking her to marry me. But then I caught her having sex with our boss on his desk while I was still in the office working."

"No!"

"Yes. All I could do was walk out."

"Logan, I'm so sorry. That is terrible. You must have been crushed."

He picked at the blanket, unsure as to why he was really telling Emma this. It wasn't something he talked about to anyone. But Emma wasn't anyone. She was someone he was starting to care about. This was something she should know.

"How long had you been together?"

"Three years."

Emma was quiet for a long while. "I bet it makes wanting to get involved again difficult." Emma picked at her sandwich, dark clouds crossing behind her eyes. Logan didn't like the sound of her voice just then, so he ran a finger over her arm, needing to touch her, to reassure her everything was okay. She ran a finger over his and smiled.

"How about you. Why aren't you married?" he asked, needing to know.

"Oh, it's not dramatic or anything. There was a guy in undergrad. We dated my junior year and moved in together my senior year. When I got accepted into med school and had to move, he didn't want to come with me. Said I wouldn't have time for him. At the time I thought it was just because he didn't want to leave Cali. I was heartbroken. But he was right, I wouldn't have had time for him. I was always studying. I didn't have time for a guy and it didn't let up for almost nine years."

"I feel you. I didn't date when I was in law school or after for a few years. I met Honey at the firm I worked for. If she hadn't been in the office with me, working on some of the same cases, I don't think I would have bothered with the whole making time to date thing."

They both looked out over the lake in a comfortable silence Logan enjoyed. His eyes drifted back to the little boy and he grinned. He was up to about eight bucket castles and happy as could be. Talking to himself as if some grand scene was playing out around him.

Softly, Emma asked, pointing to the little boy, "Do you want kids?"

He sighed, letting the thought work around, opening up doors that had been closed for a very long time. "Yes. I was an only child. I hated it, but my mom struggled to have more. I would like a big family. The chaos of it all."

She tipped her head. "Really, an only child. Sounds like heaven. I have two older brothers and they are butts."

Logan chuckled. "How about you? Do you want kids?" He picked at some grass, not sure if he was being too nosey, but it was only fair to ask her, since she had asked him.

"Yes, I think three or four would do nicely."

"What about your practice?"

She grinned. "That was one of the reasons I came home and opened a practice in a small town, so I could have a family."

A smile took up his whole face. "So you came home hoping to find a husband."

She hit him in the shoulder. "NO . . . okay, maybe."

They both laughed and Logan stared at Emma, deciding it was the most lyrical sound he'd ever heard.

"Soooo . . . a defense attorney. What made you want to do that?"

"Oh, I don't know. I always hated the injustice of people being accused of things they didn't do."

"But aren't the people you help guilty?" Emma had a serious look on her face. Like she was suddenly all into the conversation. It was such a change for him. Sure,

Honey had been a defense attorney, but she never asked why he wanted to be one, or why he took on the clients he did. She had her own thing going and didn't bother to ask him about his.

"No, not all of them. I only took on cases that, after reviewing their files, I believed they were innocent. There were a few I had to take on that I knew they were guilty, but I just found the loopholes and got them off."

"Did you like it?"

"Sometimes I did, others I didn't."

"How long are you going to work for Mr. Miller?"

Guilt circled him with a razor wire. He needed to tell her that Mr. Miller was his father, not his employer, but he didn't know how. She would want to know why he'd lied and then he would have to explain the whole Verbeck feud and today he just wanted to enjoy Emma. So he stuck as close to the truth as he could.

"I'm not sure. There is so much to do on the ranch. The repairs on the house alone could keep me busy for three or four months."

She hit him with a beautiful smile. "So, you plan on being here for a while then?"

That was when he knew he was a goner. A smart, compassionate, humorous, beautiful, good-natured woman was worried if he would be sticking around. To get a woman like her to fall in love with him he would do about anything. Even risk running into Cole Verbeck.

Chapter Six

The sky was splashed with golds, pinks, and purples as she and Logan walked back to their vehicles. Emma didn't want to leave Logan but it was late and she had a full schedule at the clinic tomorrow, even though it was a Saturday.

It had been such a lovely date. The best. She felt so relaxed here away from town and her brothers' possible unhappy glances. She was able to be herself with Logan and it felt really good. It was hard getting out of doctor mode to go home and then strap on sister mode and babysit Cole and Peter. Well, that wasn't true; Peter wasn't home all that much, being the sheriff in town. He slept at the office a lot—or at least that is what he told her. She had other suspicions, and they involved Peter being the town rogue.

She had to keep more of an eye on Cole. When she'd come back home after her residency, Cole seemed more isolated than ever, and even grumpier than she remembered. He would come in off the ranch looking exhausted, covered in dust and smelling like cattle. The deep lines around his eyes and mouth made him look ten years older than he actually was. It had taken him a month to get used to her having food cooked and ready and the house clean and full of sunflowers. When she talked to him, she only ever got one-word answers. He would take a shower, come down from upstairs and eat, and then go to bed. He seemed so sad, so alone. She had made it her mission to go out and help him anytime she could after the office was set up. He never told her no. He would just point and tell her what he needed her to do. And a small sliver of gratitude would sparkle in their matching amber eyes. She worried about Cole.

"Can I see you again?" asked Logan, taking her hand, running a finger over the small peaks of her callused hands. His brows stitched together in a frown. "These don't look like doctor hands."

She snatched her hand back. She grinned weakly, ignoring the statement. They were getting rough moving hay and working on the fence line with Cole. She was so sick of barbed wire. When Cole had called her after work to see when she would be home to help, she had been secretly thrilled to tell him she had made plans tonight to hang out with a friend. He hadn't asked who and hung up the phone. She'd felt guilty for about two seconds and then shook it off, happy to have a break.

"I would love to see you again. I'm sad to say my schedule is pretty busy for the next couple weeks." Walking over to his truck, Logan opened the door and fumbled around in the dash. When he walked back over, he handed her a piece of paper with a phone number on it. "Here. This is my cell. Call me when you can squeeze me in." He flicked the end of his hat up, stepped closer and her back bumped into the tailgate of his truck. He placed a hand on each side of her, trapping her. She grinned at him, heat rocketing through her. His eyes glowed with desire and she tried not to squirm, trying very hard to keep her hands off him.

"Thanks." She held the paper up in between them. "If I get any cancellations, maybe we could do lunch one day."

He pressed his body against hers and she melted. A strong arm wrapped around her waist and she sighed, loving the feel of him against her.

"Thank you for such a nice time," she said. He leaned in and smelled her hair. His lips brushed her ear and a delicious shiver shot down her spine. Next, a hand ran through her curls. "You're so damn beautiful. I just want to take you home with me."

She laughed, flattered by his confession. If she didn't have her brothers to worry about, she might consider it. She didn't want to ruin this perfect afternoon with doing something she wasn't sure of. For now, she was happy to know Logan wasn't going anywhere anytime soon and that he wanted to see her again.

She ducked out of his hold and walked to her truck, waved his number and got in. Firing up the truck, she pulled out of her spot. Logan stood next to his truck, arms folded over his wide chest. His jaw was clenched but the corner of his perfect mouth was tipped up to the sexiest half smile she'd ever seen. She smiled all the way home.

❦

She'd managed to see Logan Wednesday of the next week for lunch at Burger Joe's. He had brought her sunflowers, held the door for her, and pulled out her chair; she melted with the sweet thoughtfulness of it all. It had been a long time since someone wanted her attention, and she was more than happy to give her attention to Logan. She wasn't sure how he felt about her. She knew he was attracted to her—hell, it was all static and heat whenever he got near her. But that was just attraction; that didn't mean he had feelings for her.

Their lunch had been the last time they'd seen each other, and it was going on two weeks. They had texted each other at least once a day, but Logan was just as busy as she was on the Miller ranch. She ached to see him again. She just didn't have any time with the clinic and helping Cole. She was exhausted, yet Logan found her every night in her dreams, playing in the sand with the little boy on the beach.

Chapter Seven

Two weeks had passed since Emma and Logan had gone to lunch and he was on edge. He had gone to town twice with Max and John for supplies, hoping to run into her. He'd seen her yellow truck at the clinic. He admired her dedication toward the care of others in her town. He didn't want to bother her at work, too afraid it would come across as needy. She had told him she was busy and he could respect that, remembering all his late nights working on a case.

With the amount of work waiting for him at the ranch, he couldn't keep coming to town . . . and he didn't want to leave his father alone for too long. Although Harold seemed to be regaining his strength with every day that passed, Logan worried about him all the same. He would have to give up the hope of running into her and simply wait for her to call him.

As busy as he was with his many duties, images of Emma continued to float around in his mind. He missed her laugh, and how she had perfect timing for one of her jokes. He dreamed of gathering her into his arms and losing himself in her. When he thought of her, he started to see a future—a future that he had placed on a shelf long ago and had collected dust.

He asked his father if he knew the doctor, but his father just ignored him, walking off and mumbling something about opening old wounds and that Logan would be sorry. Logan asked what the heck that meant, but his father had waved him off.

Finally, after a long day of making repairs to the roof of the barn and painting the stables, Logan found time to sit on the newly painted back patio. He admired it and the newly revitalized farmhouse. He'd gone with a soft yellow for the surface and a white trim. His mother would have loved it. He needed about three to six months more before the ranch would be idling like a well-broken-in diesel truck.

With a tall glass of sun tea in his hand, Logan tipped his chair back on two legs. He stretched out like a lazy dog. Emma was there in his mind again, her long, black ringlets framing her beautiful face, her eyes calling to him. His pulse raced. He wanted to talk to her, not just the short little texts she sent him every day. She made conversation easy, telling him about some of the crazy things she'd seen in her rotation of the ER.

He cursed and set the chair down on all four legs. It was getting harder to ignore the fact that he wanted to see her . . . that he missed her. Thinking it over for a time, he decided he'd go and find the doctor. Surely, he could come up with some excuse to see her at the clinic.

Twenty minutes later, Logan hopped into the white Ford pickup, feeling Zestfully clean and smelling like Downy fabric softener. Truly, he could win the affections of a particular doctor if he stayed within the "excellent hygiene" category of which most men in these parts seemed to fall short.

Off he went, excited as a teen in a titty bar. An odd kind of feeling rushed through him—a humming kind of energy in his blood that turned his gut into a hard knot. Would she be pleased to see him? Damn, he hoped so.

Otherwise, he would have to tuck tail and run.

As Logan drove into town, he thought about what lame excuse he was going to give to Emma. Maybe he could limp in and say his knee was hurt. No, he'd never had knee problems.

It came to him in a flash. A nerve pinched in his back from time to time. He knew what it was, but he could play dumb this once, just to be seen and touched by Emma.

Pleased with his strategy, he rumbled into a parking spot right in front of the small clinic. There was only one sign that read Havencrest Town Clinic. The windows and front door of the building were taped off due to it being repainted a neutral tan. Two other offices flanked it. There were a dozen pots overflowing with flowers. It made the office look friendly and tranquil. Hopping out of the truck, he drank in the scent of the wildflowers that reminded him of Emma.

He pulled open the office door and ran straight into a brick wall of a man. They locked eyes for what seemed like an eternity. Logan stepped back and clenched his fists.

Cole Verbeck.

The man was taller by two or three inches, with shoulders taking up the entire doorway. He had curly, black hair, amber eyes and hard, rough planes shaping his face. Logan looked around the waiting room. If there was to be a fight, he didn't want anyone hurt. Thankfully, it was empty.

"So . . . you finally decided to crawl out of that hole you've been hiding in for over twenty years!" Cole sneered.

"I haven't been hiding. I was sent away because of you. Half my life was stolen away because of you and your hate." Logan ground the words out, setting himself in his fighter's stance. His ten years of boxing were about to pay off.

"You get out of here and go back to where you came from," Cole laughed.

Logan didn't move. He wanted this to be over. Years of pain, guilt, and sorrow had made it impossible to truly live. From the corner of his eye, he saw Emma rush into the room with her mouth pressed tight and her brows stitched together in confusion.

"Emma, stay back. I don't want you to get hurt," Logan exclaimed.

She ignored him and grabbed Cole's shoulder. "Don't even think about it. You won't fight in my office. Besides, what has Mr. Johnson done to you?" she questioned, eyes cutting into Cole.

Cole laughed in Logan's face. "So, you're using your mother's maiden name? I suppose that's why I didn't know you were around until this past month." Cole turned to face Emma. "This is no Johnson. This is a Miller. It so happens that he's the Miller who got our brother Joel killed."

Emma's eyes went wide and her jaw dropped, only to be replaced by a frown and watery eyes. Logan's chest tightened. A vision of Joel flashed in his mind. The curly, black hair, the Verbeck signature light-amber eyes. Emma shared the same smile. How could he have not made the connection?

Before Logan had time to think, he was shoved out the front door of the clinic. He stumbled back but managed to remain upright. A fist flew at his face. He ducked and instinctively slammed a fist into Cole's ribs, twisting his hips just so to send all his strength into it. Cole tried to grab him, but he was too slow. Logan spun out of Cole's reach and shook his body loose, getting ready for the next blow.

"Stop it! Stop it!" Emma cried as she followed them

out into the parking lot.

"Get back inside so you don't get hurt!" Cole shouted.

"No. I'm not a child," Emma said. "If you don't stop this right now, I'm going to call Peter at the sheriff's office."

Cole laughed. "Go ahead. He'd probably want to help me kick Miller's ass."

Emma bit her bottom lip, seemingly unsure of what to do. As much as Logan wanted this feud to end, he wasn't going to beat Cole to a bloody pulp in front of her.

He stepped back. "I'm not going to fight with you, so get over it."

"What, you scared, Miller?"

Cole dove for Logan, grabbing him around the waist. They hit the ground hard, momentarily knocking the air out of Logan's lungs. Cole was on top of him and a large, meaty fist bashed into his side. Logan worked to push him off, landing a nice right hook to Cole's jaw, but not before Cole pounded him in the left eye. Logan saw stars.

"Get off of him," demanded Emma, pulling at her brother.

Afraid she could be hurt, Logan decided to end the fight. He grabbed Cole and rolled away from Emma. He was on top now, clutching Cole's shirt.

Heart pounding, adrenaline pouring through his veins, Logan almost didn't hear Emma's shriek.

With Cole's T-shirt in his fist, Logan pulled his right fist back as far as it could go and clocked Cole in the jaw. It was lights out for him.

Logan hopped up, his eye beginning to swell. Emma pushed past him and fell to her knees beside her brother.

"Was that necessary?" She tapped Cole on the cheek. "Cole, Cole, can you hear me?"

Logan backed up, giving her space. A metallic scent filled his nose. He ran a finger over his eyebrow where blood trickled down his face. He peered down the road toward town, but there was no one around. Emma continued to tap Cole and shake him. Guilt welled up inside Logan for disappointing Emma. This hadn't been what he was hoping for by coming to see her. He didn't feel guilty about clocking Cole, however. He'd wanted to do that since he was twelve and he had to leave Havencrest because of that big jackass on the ground.

"I'm sorry. I didn't know he was your brother," he said, wiping the blood trickling down his cheek.

Amber eyes glared at him. "I'm sorry too. Please leave before he wakes up." Tears glittered in her eyes, yet never fell.

Hesitantly, Logan sauntered back to his truck and climbed into the cab with a grunt. He looked over at Emma sitting on the ground, chest heaving, her body shaking. He had done that. He'd made her upset. A sick feeling inched up his spine. Things just became complicated in a hurry. He shook his head. Cole was lucky Emma was here because he would've taken a pound of flesh for every year Cole had taken from him. He clenched his jaw, hating himself. Emma was a Verbeck. Joel's little sister. He couldn't believe it. He hardly remembered her.

Starting the truck, Logan gave Emma one last gaze filled with longing and drove back to the ranch. By the time he reached home, the sun had set, and every lamp in the house was blazing. Logan let out a sigh and climbed out of the truck. For a split second, he thought about going into the back of the house to avoid his father. He wasn't in the mood to get criticized. But he wasn't a boy, and he would have to deal with his father sooner or later.

Chapter Eight

As the old pickup drove away to Main Street, a knot formed in Emma's throat, so big that she couldn't talk. Logan Miller. Joel's best friend before he drowned. Emma could hardly recall Logan. She'd been six when Joel died. The only thing she remembered about Logan and Joel is they were always together, and she wasn't allowed to go anywhere with them because she only ever got hurt. And they didn't have time for babysitting. It had always made her so mad she'd go crying to her mom. Some of that old hurt crept up and she smothered it down. Joel had been six years older than her; of course he and Logan wouldn't have wanted a baby tagging along.

Just her luck. She found a man deliciously attractive who talked to her as though she was her own person. He was kind, thoughtful, hardworking—and he was her brother's enemy. Salty tears burned her eyes. She tried to blink them away but the stubborn things kept hanging around. One thing she did remember clearly from when Joel died is how broken Cole had been. He had taken all his grief and targeted it toward Logan. The drowning had been an accident, but Cole had never seen it that way. At the funeral, Cole picked Logan up by the scruff of his shirt, his face an inch from Logan's. With the whole town there, he accused Logan of murder. Told everyone Logan had bullied Joel into swimming in the river the day he died, turning the entire town against him. She remembered that because when Cole threw him down and Mrs. Miller rushed over to make sure he was okay, Logan had stared at Cole with a look of shock and betrayal. Grief and pain for Logan welled up. It was because of Cole that Logan went away and Mr. Miller had almost worked himself to death.

Frustrated, she gave Cole a rough shake. Nothing. Unable to stifle her irritation with her brother's actions, she decided there was no time like the present and slapped him across the face. He groaned. A smirk tipped one corner of her mouth. She shoved him in the chest and stood up.

It took him a moment to get oriented.

"I hope he broke your jaw," she said.

Cole sat up and thumbed it. "Love you too, sis," he said, eyeing her critically.

She tried not to shrink under the weight of his stare, not wanting to be that shy little girl he always saw. Instead, she straightened her spine, lifted her chin, and then turned her back on him. Tossing her hair over her shoulder, she didn't say a word. She was good at ignoring her brothers, Cole in particular. She heard him grunt and the sound of his boots scuffing the ground. She hurried inside her office, not looking back.

"You got something you want to tell me?" she heard Cole say behind her.

"No, why? Do you?" she said in a huff.

"Don't act like that with me, young lady," Cole said. Their father had been dead for more than twelve years, and Cole had stepped right into his shoes all too well after his death. Peter didn't say much about it, but it pissed her off.

Slowly, she rounded on him, teeth clenched.

"You stay away from Miller. Hear me?" Cole said.

"Whatever is going on in that head of yours, keep it locked down. He's not for you. Understand me?" He raised a dark brow.

She bit her lip. She wanted to tell him to shove it and to go home. But when he sounded so much like her father, it was very difficult not to be that little girl again. So, she did the one thing that would get him off her back. She told him what he wanted to hear.

"Fine. He's not for me. Got it. Now go home and put some ice on your jaw. I have some calls to make. I'll be home late." Emma walked behind the front desk, not wanting to look at him.

"Fine."

She heard the hesitation in his voice, but after a few seconds, he stomped out. As he left her clinic, she heaved a sigh of relief. *What do I do now?* she asked herself. *Listen to Cole and be a good, obedient sister, or follow my heart?*

Trailing a hand across the wall as she went into her office, her fingers brushed over a picture frame. She paused and took it off the nail. She smiled weakly and ran a thumb over the glass. Cole, Peter, and Joel, all lined up on the porch stairs of their parents' home. Joel's hip was pitched to the side with a squirming little girl clinging to him. Sometimes she struggled to remember him. But she knew that for Cole and Peter, Joel's death had left them missing a piece of themselves. In a small way, she was glad she'd been little when the accident happened.

Hands shaking, she placed the frame back on the wall and sank into her desk chair. Logan had come to see her and found out she was a Verbeck. Would he still want to see her after today? She chewed her bottom lip. Could she be okay with not seeing Logan again?

Her heart ached in her chest. Her head fell back as she groaned. Why did caring about someone have to be so complicated? She stared at the ceiling. Then, suddenly, it came to her, because she let it. *She let Cole complicate everything.* In high school, she hadn't been allowed to date. She had been madly in love with Sam Blacken, and he'd wanted to go out with her, but she'd been a good girl and told him no. She'd wanted to go to San Diego State University because she had a full ride with an academic scholarship, but Cole had said she'd be a Boise State traitor if she went, and she was expected to be an alumnus. So she had enrolled into Boise State, ready to do what she was told. Then she'd gathered her strength and gone to SDSU without telling Peter and Cole. Cole hadn't talked to her for almost a year after that little stunt. She followed everything her brothers told her to do, all because she couldn't tell them no.

Sitting up, she slapped a hand on her desk. By God, she was saying no now. Her feelings for Logan were too strong to not give it a chance. What if he was her forever? It was her life, after all. She shot to her feet, then sank back down. But what would Cole do if he found out she'd disobeyed him?

Chapter Nine

Walking up the front steps to the house, Logan thought about the look on Emma's face when she'd asked him to leave. It was tearing him apart. He was so lost in thought that he hadn't noticed his father sitting in the rocking chair on the porch until he spoke.

"I see you've been fighting," said Harold, pointing at Logan's eye. "Let me guess, you ran into an old friend."

"I guess you could say that. I'm going to clean up and go to bed," Logan said, walking past his father. But his father caught him by the wrist.

"The hell you are. Sit your ass down. We're going to have a talk. You and me."

"Fine." Logan strolled over to the porch swing and flopped down miserably. Every part of him hurt. It had been years since he'd been in a fight, and he didn't want to make it a habit.

"You went to see Emma, did you now?"

Logan didn't say a word, only waited for his father to get the conversation moving so he could go to bed.

"You understand now what I was saying about opening old wounds?"

Logan leaned forward on his elbows. "Why didn't you tell me she was a Verbeck when I asked about her?"

"Would you have cared?" Harold one-eyed his son. "I saw that faraway look in your eyes when you were asking if I knew her. It would've been foolish to tell you to stay away from her. I'm old, but I'm not stupid."

"Well, it doesn't matter now. She isn't going to want to have anything to do with me knowing I'm the Miller who killed her brother. She'll never want to see me again." Just saying the words out loud stabbed a knife into his chest.

Harold shot from his seat in an explosion of movement, fists clenched at his sides. The vein on his forehead pulsed visibly. "You're no killer, and I won't have you saying that about yourself. It would break your mother's heart." Harold sat back down, weary.

Logan watched his father's body shake from head to toe with anger. "Pop, calm down. Okay, okay. I'm not a killer; but tell that to the Verbecks."

Harold peered at Logan, and he could see years of torment were eating at him from the inside. "I should have never sent you away to live with your uncle Clay—"

"Pop, come on, let's not talk about that."

"Shut your mouth, I'm trying to say something important. When I sent you away, your mother was heartbroken. She didn't agree with my decision. Didn't agree with how I was handling the situation with the Verbeck boys. But she stood by me. She let me take her son away so that he could have a better life somewhere else, unstained by the grief that circled that family. I thought I was doing the right thing. I thought I was saving you from a lifetime of torment from the Verbecks." He ran a hand down his face. "Your mother told me you needed to face Cole, to stand against what he was saying. To fight for your space in this town or you could never stay here." He sighed miserably. "But all I could see was that day at the funeral when Cole had you dangling by your shirt. The look of fear and grief on your face. All I could think about was keeping you safe from him. So many years lost, wasted. Your mother always knew there would be a day of reckoning because a wound that deep on both sides couldn't heal." He leaned forward, elbows on his knees. "Was today your day of reckoning? Are you ready to fight for your space to be in this town like your mother said?"

Logan slapped his hands on his legs. "Damn, what a mess. I come home and fall for the one girl in town I should've left alone."

"I'll ask you again. Is today your day to fight for what you want?"

His father's words were like a slow branding iron to his chest. He'd never heard his pop be more honest with him. A tumble of confused thoughts and feelings assailed him. He had been the obedient son, leaving his whole life behind because he was heartbroken for his best friend. Thought it was the price he had to pay for not being able to save Joel. The truth was, it wasn't a price he had to pay; not him, his father or his mother, but they had. The harder he tried to ignore the truth, the more it persisted. "Yes, I'm ready to fight." He stared hard at his pop. "Are you?"

"I've been fighting since I found out I was sick and you came back home. I've been fighting for you because you deserve the life I took from you. You deserve a life on your ranch with me. I don't know how much time I have, but I want it to be with you."

Logan's throat closed and tears burned the backs of his eyes. They would fight for what they wanted together. Logan was filled with such love for his father he could hardly contain it.

Harold leaned back in the rocking chair and Logan let the brokenness between them fill with love.

"That's the way it works most of the time," his father said after a few minutes.

"What, Pop?"

"Falling for the one girl you shouldn't."

The corner of Logan's mouth pulled into a smile, remembering Ian Smith's threat. "That reminds me. I met Ian Smith. He said you can't be dying yet. He still has to get even."

"Bah . . . that old fart? I'd like to see him try."

"Story around town is you stole Mom from him. Is that true?"

Harold cocked a peppered brow. "Yes, but you can't call it stealing if the woman wants to be stolen."

His laughter broke into the evening air, setting the cows to mooing and causing the crickets to stop singing for a second. The look on his father's face was priceless. Dead serious, it was. "So, you stole your friend's woman. The nerve."

"Ian didn't know how to treat a gem like your mother." Harold shrugged. "If you want to have a life here, there is only one person you have to concern yourself with, and here she comes."

In the distance, on the road leading to the ranch, a set of headlights was headed their way.

Chapter Ten

Emma fought the urge to put the truck in reverse and back out of the Millers' driveway, but she wanted this too badly to wimp out. It was a business call—that was what she told herself to calm down. She came to a stop and parked. Logan was sitting on the porch with Harold Miller. It took her a moment to unclench her fingers from the steering wheel. Tentatively, she opened the truck door and slid out. The evening breeze caressed her skin and set her dark curls dancing around her face. Her gaze fell on Mr. Miller, who was sitting on the porch. She wasn't sure how he was going to respond to her showing up unannounced, being a Verbeck and all. Mr. Miller had always been polite to her in passing, but now that may change because she was lusting after his son.

As she made her way to the house, she smelled the fresh paint and admired the sharp peak of the second story and the large, arched window above the front door. It gave the place a sense of charm and elegance. Stepping onto the wraparound front porch, she heard Mr. Miller mumble under his breath, "Always thought she was a cute-looking thing."

Then Mr. Miller stepped forward. "Good evenin', darlin'. Nice of you to come see an elderly dying man," he said, teasing her.

She relaxed a bit, a shadow of a smile forming on her

lips. "Good evening, Mr. Miller. Nice night, isn't it?" she said in a conversational tone, glancing at Logan.

Logan didn't say a word, only nodded. His face was hidden in the shadows.

"Nice enough." Mr. Miller raised his brows at her, and then turned to look at Logan. "Well, are you going to invite her in or just stare at her all night?" He waved them off and turned toward the house.

Emma stood there, unable to proceed, staring at the man who could change her world if he wanted to. And she prayed he wanted to.

Emma knew coming to see Logan was a terrible idea, but she'd lost all willpower to stay away, especially after seeing him this afternoon looking so miserable after the fight with Cole. Ignoring the fact that she was falling for Logan was utterly useless. Her heart had thrown her brain out on the curb and had driven off.

"I'm sorry to bother you both. I can leave," she said, fidgeting with her shirt and feeling way too exposed for her liking.

"No. Please stay," Logan blurted out, taking a step closer. "I could use a doctor."

Emma's heart galloped in her chest, pleased by Logan's reaction. Maybe he didn't hate her for being a Verbeck.

He gazed into her eyes, stripping her last remaining doubts away. Her cheeks heated, and he reached for her hand. As soon as their fingers touched, a sense of completeness overwhelmed her. It filled every part of her as though until this moment in her life, she'd been lost or waiting for him. It felt like coming home. Taking a shaky breath, she stepped up beside him and he led her into his house, followed by Mr. Miller.

"How are you feeling, Mr. Miller? Are the treatments going well?"

"They aren't working, but thanks for asking, darlin'.

You were always a good girl." Mr. Miller reached out and took her other hand and kissed it. Then he patted it softly. "Sure is nice seeing a woman around this old place. It has been too long. I'm going to bed," he said, and then he turned and walked down a narrow hall next to the stairs leading to the second story.

Sadness washed over her as she watched Mr. Miller disappear. The treatments had stopped working. Her heart ached for Logan. What must he be going through, and to add all this Cole business on top of it all. She felt terrible. His thumb rubbed the top of her hand gently, sending a pulse up her arm with every stroke. Her sadness eased.

"Come on. Let's go into the kitchen and I'll get the first aid kit."

She nodded. This was the first time she'd ever been in the Miller home. Joel had been here countless times when she was little, for sleepovers, and she had always been so envious as she watched Joel and Logan running through the pasture, to then climb over the fence and onto Miller land. All the way to this big house. For the briefest of moments, she connected with Joel and kept that connection close to her heart.

It was a simple house with clean, straight lines. Emma followed Logan as he navigated her through the house. It seemed sad, forgotten, with no knickknacks, flowers, or pictures on white walls. First, they passed a formal dining room, and back to a well-used kitchen that opened to a huge family room. It reminded her of her parents' house and how she and her brothers abused it as children. She was making up for that now, doing her best to clean it and love it while she saved to get her own place.

"I'll be right back. Don't go anywhere," Logan said. He disappeared around a corner leading to who knew where. As she surveyed the space, she considered it must be a utility room. She fidgeted with her blouse and then her hair. Logan reappeared, holding a small box.

He tossed the box onto the table in a nook at the far-right corner of the room and sat on the built-in bench seat, pushing the table back out of the way. His left eye was swollen and split along his brow following the curve of the bone. He must have hit it on one of the planters when he and Cole hit the ground.

"Logan," she said in a broken whisper.

He smiled at her. "Fix me up, Doc. I think I need it." He leaned back, tilting his head up for her to see him better.

She flipped open the box to examine its contents. There wasn't much—three butterfly Band-Aids, alcohol wipes, tape, a cold pack, extra-strength non-aspirin, and a few sterile gauze pads.

"Really? This is all you have for me to work with?" she criticized.

Logan shrugged dismissively. "And this." He pointed to himself. Emma almost chuckled. She dashed over to a shelf full of hand towels and retrieved a couple, running them under some warm water in the sink. Next thing she knew, she was in full doctor mode.

She stood between his legs, examining his face with a critical eye.

"This is going to hurt," she warned, and began carefully wiping the blood from his eye. Logan winced. "I'm sorry it hurts. If I were at my office, I could numb it for you. It may need stitches."

"I think I'll live," he said.

Emma felt his hands settle on her hamstrings. Her pulse raced. She didn't say a word but found herself leaning closer to him, wanting to be nearer.

The eye was purple, swollen, and painful looking. She couldn't believe her brother had done this to him. No matter what had happened in the past, Cole wasn't a scared, angry teenager anymore. He needed to grow up.

She bandaged his head as best she could with the supplies. His emerald-green eyes were captivating, magnetic, and they glittered in the lamplight of the kitchen. She could see the grief of the past, the courage to hang onto hope, and the desire to begin anew. She felt herself standing on the edge of a bluff. If she jumped from it, she took a chance at love. If she stood there watching, she knew she would always be watching. She wanted to jump.

Unable to resist touching him, she ran a hand through his thick, blond hair. He pulled her tightly between his legs and she bit her bottom lip, hiding her smile. She suppressed the tendrils of desire coiling through her veins, needing to talk about what had happened today.

"Logan, why did you say your last name was Johnson when we met?"

He sighed and tried to turn his head away. She didn't allow it.

"You can talk to me. I'm not Cole or Peter. I don't have it out for you."

"When we met, I'd been in town for a few months but I didn't leave the ranch. I always sent Max or John to get what we needed. I didn't want to take the chance of seeing your brothers. My pop told me Peter was the sheriff and that Cole was running the ranch. Staying home seemed the best choice.

"Max convinced me no one would know who I was if I went out because I had been gone for so long. It seemed a reasonable assumption, so I figured why not. I needed a break away from the Glade." He ran a hand down her back. "Then there you were, looking so shy and beautiful. I knew from the moment I saw you I would want to see you again. I just thought it was the best way to stay off the Verbeck radar."

She cupped his face in her hands. She completely

understood. Couldn't even be mad at him for it. If she had made the connection between him and Mr. Miller that day, she might not have gone to talk to him. She would have let Cole dictate her choice without even being there. It was frustrating how Cole affected so many lives.

"What are you going to do now that Cole knows for sure you are back in town?"

"Watch my back so I don't get shot."

She hit him in the arm. "My brother wouldn't shoot you."

Logan raised his good brow. "You sure about that?"

She bit her lip, thinking about how unhappy and lonely Cole had seemed when she moved back in. That Cole, he could shoot anyone for the simple act of stepping on his land. The Cole she worked with, saw smile from time to time when she would lay on some lame joke just to see him smile. She didn't think that Cole would shoot Logan because after today, he knew she cared about him. Cole wouldn't take away her chance at happiness, even if it was with Logan. Because if there was one thing she knew it was that Cole loved her, and having her home made him happy again. He wouldn't risk her wanting to leave.

"Things have been hard for Cole since Joel died."

Logan snorted, then winced with pain.

"You two have more in common than you think."

Logan folded his arms over his chest and leaned away from her. She had struck a nerve.

"Joel died and you both lost someone you loved. You left."

"I was sent away."

"You left your parents and started a new life. After a few months, my mother left. My father was crushed; he didn't hardly talk to us. All this pressure landed on Cole to keep the family together. It was like starting over, just like you had to do. Then my dad died, and few years later, your mom. Now your dad is sick. The both of you have known so much loss. It breaks my heart."

"You have too," Logan said, hands back on her legs. "All of those things Cole and Peter went through, so did you. *You're not crazy.* You don't want to punch me in the face."

The pad of her thumb caressed his chin. "I was little. I have lived longer in a life without Joel, without my mother, and almost without my father. Their mark on my life hasn't cut me as deeply. But if something happened to Cole or to Peter, I would never be the same. They helped shape me. Don't get me wrong, I too have been shaped by the past. But the people in my life now are the reminder that I have today and I share it with them. That is what I choose to focus on."

Logan took her hand from his chin and kissed her fingers. Suddenly he was far, far away, turning over what she'd said in his mind. It warmed her to know he valued her thoughts. She ran her other hand through his hair, not wanting him to drift so far away from her she couldn't get him back.

He pulled her close. Clinging to her. "Did anyone ever tell you, you were a keeper?"

She shook her head and he hit the light switch and they were cast in the glow of moonlight from a large window on the other side of the nook. There, in that moonlight, Emma jumped.

Chapter Eleven

Logan's breath skimmed the tops of her breasts. Her nipples hardened instantly, and desire deepened its claws. She was a woman—an intelligent, confident woman who knew what she wanted. From the moment she'd watched Logan playing on the beach with that little boy, she'd hoped for a future with this man.

She ran a hand over the sharp planes of his battered face. Blond stubble slowed her progress. She thumbed his chin, sandpaper against her skin. She liked it.

Logan slid his fingers down her right leg and gently pulled at the back of her knee. Her leg glided up over his hard thigh. She struggled to steady herself by placing an arm around his neck and pressing against him. Then he lifted her other leg and she sank into his lap. She glanced at his mouth and licked her lips, hungry for a kiss. She would wait. She wouldn't rush. This moment, no matter the outcome, would be a memory that would last a lifetime.

Logan cupped her bottom in his strong hands and secured her firmly against him. He didn't hide his desire from her, rocking his hips against her. She couldn't have been more pleased.

"I'm sorry about today," he said, lightly fingering a loose curl by her cheek. "For not knowing you are a Verbeck. The last time I saw you was at the funeral. All dressed in black, crying, holding your mother's hand."

She smiled faintly at the thought of him remembering her that way. "Would you have still asked me on a date if you had known I was a Verbeck?"

He tenderly traced the line of her cheekbone and jaw. "I would have wanted to see you no matter what your last name was. Do you know why?" He slipped his hand around the back of her neck and into her hair, leaning closer to her. Every nerve in her body seemed to misfire as if overloaded, but then her senses heightened to an awareness she'd never experienced before. Her body was on fire, desire feeding every cell in her body.

"Why?" she whispered breathlessly.

"Because it can be changed," he said, brushing his lips against hers.

Emma sobered in a snap and pulled back to look at him. "Changed?"

She didn't move. A wicked smile tipped the corner of Logan's mouth, and then he laughed a deep, rich sound. She frowned. Before she could respond, Logan claimed her lips. It was a slow, deliberate kiss. A kiss meant to set her on fire and it did just that. She returned it with her affection for him. He shifted his body beneath her and edged off the bench seat.

Afraid the moment would end, Emma wrapped her legs all the way around his waist, locking them at the ankles. She clung tighter to Logan, deepening the kiss, and her thoughts twirled happily out of control. Next thing she knew, she was pushed against a wall with Logan pressing between her thighs. A moan escaped her lips with the friction he created. Feather-soft, his lips trailed down her neck and onto her breasts. She arched her body into him, her arousal taking her higher. It was heaven, exquisite, and thrilling.

He unbuttoned her blouse, revealing her lacy, white

bra. He rubbed gently. His touch was more than she could handle and she moaned. She held her breath as he pulled the lace down from her breasts and dipped his head. She slipped her hands into his hair and over his shoulders, needing to feel him. Logan sucked one, and then the other, giving equal attention to both. She started to quake in his arms. She needed to feel him—all of him.

She tugged at Logan's shirt, forcing it over his head. He chuckled at her eagerness. She kissed his moonlit chest. He was tight and cut in all the right places. Gently, she ran a hand over the solid chest muscles. She peered up at him and their eyes locked. There, in that moment, she saw forever in his eyes. Her future unfolded like the best romance novel. She was powerless to resist the pull.

Logan struggled to control his desire for Emma. He wanted to rip off her clothes and bury himself deep inside her, to claim her as his one and only. With Herculean effort, he restrained himself. He wasn't going to rush. He wanted to enjoy her, savor her. She persuasively ran her fingers over his chest, inviting more. Her lashes fluttered closed and a sigh of contentment filled the space between them. It was a sound that wiped away any reservation he had. She was perfect for him. Everything he had seen for himself before college, before law school.

Gripping her round hips and pressing her tightly against him, he felt her legs tighten around him and she kicked off her shoes.

With one hand, he unfastened the top button of her jeans. She bit her bottom lip.

Arms around his neck, she lifted her body to allow him to shimmy her jeans off her hips and over her bottom. Slowly, he lowered her long, lean legs. Her jeans fell to the floor. He ran his fingers over her flat stomach. She released his neck and slipped off her blouse. She was the most beautiful creature he'd ever seen.

He heard a squeak from the wood floor behind him.

Emma froze and held her breath. Logan covered her with his body as he peered over his shoulder with his good eye.

The refrigerator light lit the room. "Don't mind me. Just an old man getting a drink and a snack," his father said as he grabbed a soda pop and a bag of salami.

"Pop, get the hell out of here, and don't let the door knock you on your ass on the way out," Logan growled.

"Don't be barkin' at me. I thought you went to bed. After all, the light is off. Give an old man a break."

"Pop, get out."

His father shuffled off.

As soon as he was gone, Emma dragged in a breath. "I have to go. I'm mortified," she said, trying to sneak out from behind his body.

"Why? He didn't see anything," Logan said. He kissed her lips and ran his fingers down her spine, pressing against her to try to soothe her embarrassment.

"He's Mr. Miller," she said, slapping his hand away from her breast and shaking her head. "I feel like a teenager who's just been caught making out."

"That is what we're doing." He brushed her hair to the side to kiss her neck. Her skin turned to goose flesh.

Seizing the moment of her indecision, Logan ran his fingers into her hair. He crushed his lips to hers, heart pounding.

⚜♥⚜

The taste of his lips was a delicious sensation Emma couldn't ignore. Her body was overcome with excitement, hope, desire—and love.

For a moment, the kiss left her weak and confused, but

only for a moment. She was heat and reckless abandon. A strong hand glided down her leg in a feathery caress and slightly tugged at the back of her knee. A question, it seemed.

What was she going to do? Her conscience told her to put her clothes back on and leave before Logan unraveled her completely. Yet her heart begged her to let him do as he pleased.

Gently, his fingers trailed back up her leg and dipped below the lace of her underwear, skimming the curls between her thighs. She hummed with life . . . and need.

His free hand skimmed her stomach, setting trails of fire within her. She wanted him to fill her. To claim her.

Her fingers found and caressed every muscle in his back. Logan slid her lace panties down her legs and cupped her bottom, lifted her, and pressed her to the wall once more. She sank her nails into his back, hissing with pleasure as he played with her. She hadn't felt anything so heavenly in a long time.

Logan was burning from the inside out. He was rock hard. Cursing, he fumbled with his jeans. Popping the last button, he tugged, pushed his jeans down his legs, and kicked off his shoes with his pants. Shaft freed, he gripped her hips and sank deeply into her tight core.

She was beautiful there in the moonlight, lips swollen from his kisses, flushed from desire. Dear God, he wanted her. Wanted to know everything about her. Needed her. He prayed she felt the same.

She arched into him, drawing him deeper. Both of his hands cupped her buttocks and together they created the tempo that bound their bodies together.

Heaven . . . that was where she was. Logan filled her totally. Her tight walls held him captive, and nothing could have satisfied her more. She loved the feel of his body against hers. She needed more. Sweat dotted her skin. She felt passion rising in her like a blazing, uncontrollable fire, searing the last thread of reason.

"Harder," she begged, surprising herself. Logan pressed her into the wall and a soft cry escaped her lips. Logan captured it as he pounded into her. A moan of ecstasy slipped through her lips. Her body began to throb. As Logan thrust one last time, the tight feeling that had been building inside her broke free. Pleasure, pure and explosive, rocked her to her core. Logan moaned and his head fell back. She felt him tumble over the edge as well.

ʕ˵•ᴥ•˵ʔ

He didn't want to let her go. He wanted to take her upstairs and make love to her again. His chest tightened.

Slowly, he released her legs so she could hold her weight. He brushed feather-light kisses over her neck. She moaned, and he smiled.

"Logan, I should go," she said, skimming her fingers over his bare chest.

"Why? How about I carry you upstairs and we make love again? This time on a bed, so I can see and experience all of you."

"If my brother finds out I'm here, he will come looking for me. And I don't want you to get hurt again," she said, cupping his cheek and peering at his injured eye.

"I understand," he said, clenching his jaw. Cole was once more affecting his life, and it would end today. He was done trying to keep Cole from the truth.

Reluctantly, he stepped away from Emma, not wanting to sever their connection. "There is a bathroom just down the hall over there. Why don't you clean up first before you go?"

He watched her gather her clothes, looking embarrassed. He didn't like it. There was nothing to be embarrassed about. Sex looked fantastic on her.

As she brushed past, he grabbed her arm and spun her around, pulling her flat against his chest. He kissed her with all the love he felt for her. She melted into him. *That's better, he thought.*

Breaking loose, she stepped back and looked at him dreamily. She gave him a bright smile, and when she turned away this time, he smacked her bottom. She jumped and laughed, throwing a hand over her mouth. "If your dad comes out here again and catches me like this," she whispered lifting a fist. "To the moon!" Then she rushed off to the bathroom.

She'd stolen his heart. He was hers forever. And by God, he liked it.

Chapter Twelve

Emma closed the bathroom door and leaned against it, all loose smiles. She flipped on the light switch and looked in the mirror. Her lips were pink and her skin flushed. She started to shake. Sadness, disbelief, excitement, and happiness filled her like a rising tide.

She thought about what she and Logan had done together. She ran a hand through her curls and sighed dreamily. She wanted to do it again, wanted to stay the night with him. But then there was Cole. The thought of her brother sent cold shivers down her spine. There was no way he would let her see Logan without some sort of fight.

Cole would position himself outside her office and drive her to and from work if he had to. She was sure of it.

After she dressed, she exited the bathroom and found Logan casually leaning against the wall in the kitchen. His jeans were low on his hips.

He half smiled and held out a hand. Lacing their fingers together, he walked her through the empty house and out to her truck. Stopping at the truck door, he pressed her back to it with his hard, sculpted body. She wrapped her arms around his neck.

"When can I see you again?" he asked, kissing her jaw.

"I'm not sure. Cole will try and stop us from being

together," she said, feeling frustrated.

"Like hell. He can't keep me away from you. I don't even want to let you go."

"Yes, he'll try. And no, I can't stay. I can try and talk to him, but I don't think it will make any difference. Right now. It will be too soon. Maybe in a few days." She looked into his eyes. Lines crested his brow and framed his beautiful lips. He was worried. She melted, falling a little more in love with him. He cared about her and wanted to keep her. It was a lovely feeling to be wanted.

"Let me take care of it. He and I have unfinished business. And, with my dad sick, I can't keep hiding from him. It makes my father worry too much. It's better to be done with it once and for all."

"What will you do?"

"Try and talk some sense into him." He pointed to himself. "Defense attorney. I can argue our case before the judge."

"I may have to see this," she said, running her fingers down his side.

He kissed her again, slowly, and for a moment, she forgot everything but him. Then he opened the truck door and she climbed in halfheartedly.

Waving goodbye, she headed down the drive and off Miller land. The evening ran through her head as she drove home.

She needed to think of a way she and Logan could spend time together without Cole catching wind of it.

♥

A few weeks later, Emma stared blankly at the computer screen in her exam room. What was she doing? She couldn't even remember. The last few weeks were like this foggy haze she just couldn't shake. It was weird.

"Honey, are you all right?" asked Mary Dawson, her

belly bulging with her fourth baby boy. She was lying down on the medical table.

"Yes . . . um . . . just blanked out for a second," Emma admitted.

Emma's fingers began pecking away at the keyboard. She could feel Mary's eyes on her, but she didn't turn around. Mary was a high school friend who had married Sam Blacken, Emma's high school crush. She didn't know why, but it was funny that Mary didn't like his last name and kept her maiden name, Dawson.

"Rumor has it that you and that fine-looking Miller boy are sneaking around trying to see each other."

Emma sucked in a sharp breath. *Rumors! Great!* Just what she needed to hear. Like she didn't have twenty other things to worry about right then, like being a week late for her period. A week. She couldn't think about it. She would start to panic. She hadn't taken a pregnancy test yet, but there were four of them in her purse. Never hurt to be thorough. She knew she could do it at the office, but she was waiting to go home and take them in the morning. It would be Sunday, her day off, and the clinic would be closed. She would have time to process.

"We are not sneaking around."

"Oh, so you two are an item then?" Mary leaned back on the table and fanned herself. "He came into the store yesterday, all dirty and sweaty, and I thought I would go into labor. My body wanted this baby out so Mom could have some fun."

Emma's jaw dropped.

"Don't look at me like that, Emma. It's only natural for a man who looks that good to get a woman wanting some action."

Emma laughed. "Mary, really."

"Honey, if you don't want him, I will take him, and you can have Sam."

"You keep him. He's a good daddy."

Mary looked wistful for a moment, then rubbed her enormous stomach and smiled, glowing a little.

Hot tears burned Emma's eyes. Mary looked beautiful just then bathed in her motherly glow. Emma had always wanted to be a mother but had put a career first. Now that being a mother seemed like it could be a real possibility, regardless of Logan, she couldn't help but wonder if she would be any good at it.

Her mother had loved on her and made time for her, letting her help cook. Emma swallowed hard. Yet she'd left, just up and gone one morning. No note, nothing left in her closets, nothing. She was seven then. Peter, Cole, and her father had all gone out looking for her for the entire day. She had been left home all alone. Emma had never understood how her mother could leave her family like that. She did think she could ever do that to her children, regardless of the situation. They were part of you. You could see it in their eyes, nose, fingers. Bits of you wanting to be loved.

"Speaking of action, when's this kid coming out? The last two were two weeks early."

Emma turned away from Mary, wiped her eyes briefly, and looked at the screen.

"I'm not your obstetrician, Mary. You came to see me because of your back, and you know I can't do much for you with the baby in there."

"I figured as much, but it is nice to have someone to complain to." Mary rolled off the table and stood up, bracing her back. "I can't wait to see you pregnant. Then you'll see how miserable it is bringing life into this world."

Emma's jaw dropped. "It can't be that bad?"

"You do it four times and get back to me about that," Mary laughed. She picked up her purse. "I'll see you around town," Mary said.

Emma waved goodbye, wondering if she really would be a miserable pregnant soon-to-be mother. She hoped not.

The next morning, Emma stood in her bathroom, gazing at all four pregnancy tests. They all had two lines. She was overflowing with joy, though fear crept in here and there about what Logan would think. She jumped up and down, spinning around like a giddy little girl. She was going to be a mama!

She did a little dance and stopped abruptly. She was going to be a mom. That meant morning sickness, squeezing a baby out of her body, never having a good night's sleep again, having to take time off work, and scariest of all, it meant having to tell her brothers. As if on cue, she bent over and threw up into the toilet. She sank to her knees and leaned against the wall.

How was she going to tell Logan? She couldn't hide from him forever. Since they'd made love, she'd been busy at the clinic and hadn't had a spare minute to sneak off and see him. She thought Cole was going to be the problem, not her schedule. When her period didn't show up, she'd ducked behind buildings and shelf racks, doing her damnedest to avoid Logan. She felt badly. She left instructions for her assistant to put Logan on hold until he hung up when he called, and she hadn't answered his texts. She just needed time.

Then, when he came to her office twice, she'd just watched him from across the street in the grocery store. On one occasion, he'd yanked on the locked office door, then was cursing and kicking rocks in the parking lot. Even though she had stepped behind the shelf to hide, she was happy to know he had come to see her.

She tugged at her hair. She had to tell Logan, but

how? Cole was going to kill her when he found out. She bit her lip, thinking of a way out of her dilemma.

She should stop worrying about Cole. For far too long she'd let her brothers rule her life. She put a hand on her belly. She had to do what was right for her and her baby. If she ever needed a push to stand up to Cole, this was it.

"Emma, you in there?"

She heard Cole's boots against the wood as he walked into her room. She jumped up, grabbed the pregnancy tests off the counter, rolled them in toilet paper, and then shoved them into the trash can under the sink. She smoothed her hair and opened the door. When she stepped out into her room, Cole was standing there, looking very displeased, his arms across his chest. The bruise on his square jaw was sick-looking shades of yellows and greens.

"What's up? Did you want me?" she asked, strolling past him to pick up her medical bag and place it on her small desk.

He pivoted on his heels and eyed her. She stiffened her spine, finding her resolve.

"Mary Dawson told me at the store that you and Miller are together. Is that true? Do you have feelings for him?"

"So what if I am seeing him?" she said, glaring at him.

"I told you to stay away from him. That he wasn't for you. After what he did to our family, I can't believe you would go behind my back."

"I haven't seen Logan in weeks," she said in a calm voice.

"Oh, well . . ." he said, unfolding his arms.

She walked up to him, her finger in his face. "I'm not a child, Cole. The sooner you realize that, the happier our family will be."

"What are you trying to say?" He leaned closer, not backing down, his amber eyes growing darker.

She was done. Her father had died when she was a senior in high school. Her mother had run off after Joel died, too broken-hearted to look at any of them. And her brother had hatred in his heart. She couldn't fix any of it, and she was done trying. All these years she'd sat quietly in the corner of what was her life, not wanting to make waves, not wanting to hurt anyone or remind them of the past. The thing was, she was hurting. She was sad and alone. She wanted love, and to not be seen as a child, but as a woman. The only way that was going to happen was to start acting like one.

"What I'm saying is, you can't run my life. I will see whomever I want, and there is nothing you can do about it."

His nostrils flared as he studied her with a sharp gaze. Her heart was hammering against her chest but a small smile tipped the corners of her lips when he blew out a breath. "You going to come finish helping with the fence in the west pasture? There are some heifers that get getting out."

She folded her arms over her chest. "Sure. As long as I don't hear one word about Logan."

He walked down the hall toward the screen door, where he held it open for her to follow. She smiled and grabbed her boots. Cole never said much, but she loved her time with him. He was so very much like their father. He would die working out on this ranch one day. She only hoped he could step outside himself and have a family of his own.

Hopping down the hall with one sock and boot on, she tugged on the other then she bustled out the front door and listened to the smack of the screen and Cole's boots crunching over dirt and rock. The sun was up and there was a soft summer breeze. She knew it wouldn't last long. Soon they would both be sweating and looking for cover.

She climbed into Cole's pickup and they drove over the land that was their home, happy to be together. She glanced over at him as they bounced along, pushing a curl behind an ear. Some of her fear about telling him she was pregnant withdrew as he grinned. He loved her. He would love her baby.

Chapter Thirteen

Weeks had passed, and Logan hadn't managed to see Emma once. Had Cole suspected that a relationship had formed between them? Was Cole the reason why he couldn't get a hold of Emma?

It was time for a showdown between him and Cole.

He missed her to distraction. His to-do list had come to a screeching halt and sleep became a commodity out of his reach.

"Get his legs," said Max, ready to pull the branding iron from the fire. "Rope them."

John's horse circled the calf while he positioned himself to release his rope. With a flick of John's wrist, the rope shot down and captured the hind legs of the calf. "Got him!" called John. "Drop him, Logan."

Logan blinked, confused for a moment, peering around the corral. He glanced at John, whose face was tight with irritation, his horse pulling back on the rope.

"Drop him, Logan," John growled.

Clarity finally sliced through his muddy thoughts. He ran up and yanked the calf down on his side, quickly tying the front legs. Max grabbed the branding iron while Logan and John held the calf in place. The calf bellowed for its mommy as the Miller family branding iron scorched his hide. After about ten seconds, Max stepped back, Logan and John released the calf, and the calf ran off, bucking.

"He's the last one for the day," Max said, throwing the iron back in the fire.

"Man, what's with you today?" complained Max as Logan turned and ran smack into his chest, staggering back a step or two.

Logan dragged a hand down his dirty face, frustrated with himself. Happy the day was at an end.

Max studied him. "It's a dame. I know that look; seen it in the mirror a dozen times." He slapped his knee and howled with laughter. "Hey, John, boss man over here's got WBR."

Logan rolled his eyes, not understanding, and turned to leave. Then John howled with laughter too. Logan shot a glance over his shoulder, his curiosity piqued. "What's WBR?" he asked.

"Woman brain rot," Max answered him, laughing heartily.

Great, Logan thought, throwing his hands in the air and giving up on his work for the day. He marched past his two ranch hands toward the house. Dust and sweat clung to him. Taking off his gloves, he slapped the dust from them. He needed a shower. The screen door slammed shut behind him and he saw Harold in the kitchen, banging around.

"Got any sun tea in that fridge, Pop? I could use a glass."

Suddenly, his father's eyes rolled back into his head and he collapsed to the floor. Logan rushed to his side.

"Pop, you okay?" Logan rolled him onto his back. No reply. Fear squeezed his chest. He lifted his father's wrist. There was a pulse, and he was breathing, but the pulse was weak and the breathing shallow. Gathering the man into his arms, Logan made for the truck.

"Max!" he bellowed. "Max, damn it, get out here!"

Max's shaved head popped out from around the barn

and he rushed over to him when he saw what was happening.

"Open the door."

Max hurriedly opened the truck door.

"Go inside, grab a blanket and pillow, and bring them to me."

"Sure, boss."

Logan gently placed his father in the truck and strapped him in. He could see a goose egg forming on his brow. "Great."

Where they lived, there weren't any ambulances that could go any faster than a person's own vehicle. He had to take him to McClain, which was about an hour's drive. It had a larger hospital, but not as big as in Boise.

Max reappeared with the items he had requested and handed them to Logan.

"Call Emma. Tell her to meet me at the highway so she can check him before I take off for the hospital."

"Sure, boss. How long?" Max asked.

"Ten minutes."

Logan wrapped the blanket around his father, then he raced to the other side of the truck. Jumping in, he put a pillow between the cab window and his father's head so it wouldn't bounce around. Once settled, he started the truck, which roared to life and sprang into motion.

❧♥❧

The phone rang in the kitchen. Emma sat up in bed, blinking sleep from her eyes. What time was it? She looked out the window. The sun was low but still bright. She eyed her alarm clock. It was six thirty. All she wanted to do was lie back down. Helping Cole had taken all her energy. She'd never felt this tired in her life. The phone rang again, insistently it seemed. She staggered out of bed, tugging her cut-off shorts on as she went, and headed down the hall in her bare feet. She answered on the fourth ring.

"Hello."

"Emma, is that you?" a low, gruff voice said. "Why aren't you answering your cell?"

It took her a moment to recognize it. "Max, is that you?"

"Yeah. You need to get in your truck and meet Logan by the main road out of town. Harold collapsed."

"When did he leave?" she asked, her panic rising as she looked at her watch.

"Just now. You'll have to take Cedar Road to get in front of him."

"Okay," she said, hanging up on Max.

She didn't think, only reacted. Doctor mode blocked out every thought of seeing Logan and telling him about the baby. She grabbed her keys off the hook near the front door and dashed for her truck, not even stopping to get shoes. She had a medical bag in her truck. It would have to be enough.

Cole came walking from around the side of the house. He looked at her, puzzled. "Where are you going?"

"Mr. Miller collapsed. I have to meet Logan by the main road."

Emma opened the truck door. As she climbed in, Cole caught her by the arm.

"No, you stay here. Let Logan deal with his father on his own."

She stared at Cole in horror. Who was this person? She didn't recognize him. Her Cole would not be so cruel. She yanked her arm free.

"I don't know who you are or what you have done to my brother, but get out of my way. I'm the only doctor this town has, and you'd do well to remember that. The next time you get hurt, maybe I won't help you."

Cole didn't say anything, only stared hard at her.

She started the truck and watched him grow smaller in her rearview mirror. For the first time in her life, she'd lost respect for her brother. Did he hate Logan so badly that he could be cruel enough to stop her from helping? It caused her heart to ache.

After a few minutes, she pushed all thoughts of Cole out of her mind and she went over all the things that could have caused Mr. Miller to collapse. None of them were good. She turned down Cedar Road and floored it.

❧♥❧

Kicking up a cloud of dust, the truck bounced down the road. Logan slammed his palm against the steering wheel. "Damn it." He stared at his father. He'd been so busy mooning over Emma that he hadn't paid any attention to his father since they'd started a new treatment. He couldn't fight off the cancer without some sort of fallout. A knot formed in his throat. "It'll be okay, Pop. Hang in there. Don't you leave me."

So many years lost to the past. He was just beginning to get to know his father on a different level. They were becoming friends. For just a second, he'd begun to see the ranch as home again. If his father died, he knew he wouldn't stay. He would have to leave.

Glancing up the road, he saw Emma pull to the side and park. He pulled over behind her. She rushed to the passenger door. Worry lines were present in her beautiful face. His chest tightened at seeing her so concerned.

"What happened?" she asked, opening the truck door carefully.

"He collapsed in the kitchen about ten minutes ago. I walked in, asking if he had tea, and he just went down. Hit his head hard on the floor. Already has a knot."

Emma pressed her lips together and went to work.

She checked his pupils with a small light, his lungs with a stethoscope, and his pulse. Then suddenly, her face scrunched up and she jumped back about a foot, eyes wide. "Mr. Miller?"

Confused, Logan glanced around the door and saw his father smiling at her.

He saw red. Fear morphed into anger. "What the hell are you doing, Pop? Are you trying to give me a heart attack?"

Harold's dark-brown eyes twinkled mischievously. "Someone's got to get you two together. You're driving me crazy acting like a bull that can't get to the cow in heat down the damn road."

Logan slammed a fist on the hood of the truck. He tugged at his hair, then swung his fists in the air.

Emma chuckled, realizing how outrageous his behavior must have appeared. But she paid him no mind. She must be used to outbursts like this, having two hot-tempered older brothers.

She cupped his father's tired face and kissed his cheek. She brushed his gray hair back and studied the bump on his forehead. "Thank you. It was extremely kind of you to scare your son half to death so we could see each other. But this was going a little too far," she said, running a finger over the bump on his forehead.

"I had to make it compelling now, didn't I? I'm a Miller, and we do things at a hundred percent. You're welcome, sweetie. I was getting tired of his sour face." Harold pointed to Logan. Emma shyly glanced over her shoulder. "He was starting to look worse than me."

Logan wanted to strangle his father. He couldn't believe the man had faked passing out. He could have seriously hurt himself. He leaned against the fender of the truck with his arms across his chest. He scowled at them both while trying to calm his temper.

ᘞ♥ᘗ

Logan looked very masculine resting against the fender, glaring at her and his father with the sun kissing his skin and the dust sticking to every part of him. His hair was slicked back, his green eyes studying her. Emma shivered with longing. She held herself back, fighting the urge to brush her body against his. Then, an unexpected thought pushed through the floor of her mind as she gazed at him. If she had a son, would he be as handsome as his father? She fidgeted with her shorts, shoving the thought away, not ready to think about an uncertain future. She didn't like to think about how Logan would react when she gave him the news of her pregnancy. Instinctively, she placed a hand over her flat stomach. Over a week late and four pee tests later, Emma knew she couldn't hide it forever.

But now didn't seem like the right time to talk about it. She could see the fire in Logan's eyes. After all, his father had played a cheap trick on him. If it had been her, she'd probably have burst into tears, overwhelmed with emotion, then laughed about it later. But from what she could tell, Logan wouldn't be laughing at any of this anytime soon.

She didn't know when she would get to see Logan again. Peeking out from under her lashes, she saw Mr. Miller studying her with his remarkably handsome face. There was a knowing in that face. She saw the same kindness in him that she saw in Logan, and her heart tightened.

Ever so gently, Mr. Miller reached out and took her hand away from her belly. A small smile pulled at his lips. He held her hand, squeezed it, and gave her a wink. There were tears in those eyes. He gathered her into a loving embrace. He kissed the top of her head and hot, salty tears burned her eyes. She couldn't believe Mr. Miller had accepted her without hesitation, despite their family feud.

"I'm fine, boy. Take me home," Mr. Miller said to Logan. Emma stepped back and closed the door to the truck.

Logan walked around to the driver's side and climbed in. He leaned forward, peering out at Emma.

"Follow me to the house. We need to talk."

All Emma could do was nod. She couldn't trust her voice after what had passed between her and Mr. Miller.

Logan turned the truck around and headed back to the Glade. Emma pulled in a breath, found some courage, and climbed back into her truck and bounced down the road after Logan.

Emma sat in the truck and Logan walked Mr. Miller into the house. She walked up to the porch and sat in the porch swing, trying to keep her heart rate from sending her heart right out of her chest. She pulled in a breath and then blew it out. After five minutes or so, Logan was pushing the screen door open and staring at her. He looked worn-out and defeated. Guilt reared its ugly little head at her.

"Did I do something wrong?" He sat next to her on the swing.

"No, nothing."

"Then why haven't you answered my calls or texts? I was starting to think Cole had you locked in a closet or something."

She picked at her shorts. "No. I've been busy." He reached out and took her hand in his, blowing out a breath.

"I thought you didn't want anything to do with me after the last time we were together." His voice broke, and so did Emma. She leaned over and took his miserable face in her hands.

"Oh, Logan. I'm sorry. I just needed some time to think about us, if there even was an us."

He searched her eyes. There was fear in them. It was too much. He brushed her lips against his, wanting him to know she was sorry. He pulled her deeper into the kiss as if she was his lifeline and she melted into him. Slowly the kiss softened and he pulled back, draping an arm over her shoulders, keeping her close. She rested her head against it and he played with her fingers, lacing them and then unlacing them.

"I wish I could pretend the last few weeks weren't hard, but they were. I was going crazy not hearing from you."

She looked at him.

"Emma, I don't think I could go through that again unless I knew we are committed to each other." He continued to play with her fingers. "I want to be with you, Emma. I want this. To see you at the end of the day, to talk and spend time together."

"I want that too. I want to be with only you, Logan."

"Then why . . . why didn't you want to talk to me?"

She pulled her fingers from him and sat up. I can do this. It will be fine. "I haven't answered your calls because I didn't know what to say or how to say it."

"Say what?" Worry lines creased his eyes and mouth. She reached up and rubbed them away. She closed her eyes and said a silent prayer.

"I'm pregnant. I wasn't sure until today. That is why I didn't come see you or talk to you before. I was afraid."

He sat forward and ran both hands through his hair. "Are you sure?"

"I took four tests. They all say yes."

He shot to his feet and pulled her up. Logan spun her around and around, causing her hair to sweep over her face. She giggled with joy at his reaction. He stopped and held her tight. "Oh, Emma." When he stepped away from her, he was a mask of indifference. She swallowed hard, not knowing what to think.

"Get in the truck," he said, stomping to the front door.

"Not until you tell me where we're going," she demanded.

Logan softened a bit and said, "Please. I would like it if you got into the truck."

She blinked at him.

"Get out here, old man. I know you're in there listening." Mr. Miller was out and onto the porch in seconds. She noticed Mr. Miller and Logan having some unspoken conversation with their eyes, and suddenly, she was filled with dread. What was Logan going to do?

All of them climbed into the truck. Mr. Miller and Logan looked as though they were heading off for a battle.

Logan started the truck and headed back down the dirt road. When the road forked about a mile down the road, he veered to the right toward her family's ranch. She gasped. Mr. Miller took her hand in his and squeezed it. She knew what was happening. Logan was going to confront her brother.

Chapter Fourteen

"Are you sure you need to do this? Maybe we could wait," she said, feeling sick to her stomach.

"Until when? When you're round enough to roll down the road?" Logan glanced at her, a smile tipping the corners of his mouth. Her heart raced.

Slowly, her home came into view. The large maple trees surrounding it were full of leaves, making it look welcoming and hiding the trouble within. The truck crunched over the gravel driveway and rolled to a stop.

She scanned the fields and the cattle pasture. She didn't see Cole anywhere, but that didn't mean he wasn't there. Before the truck stopped, she watched Cole push open the screen door and step onto the front porch with a shotgun pointed at them. Logan's eyes were locked on her brother.

"Why? Why now?" she pleaded.

"Because I'm going to marry you." Logan gave her a peck on the lips and climbed out, closing the door behind him.

"Don't let her out of the truck, Pop."

Mr. Miller nodded at his son.

Emma's mouth hung open for a second in disbelief. Logan wanted to marry her. It wasn't her idea of the perfect proposal, but damn it, she would take it.

"Why else would he fly off and possibly get himself

killed?" Mr. Miller said. "A woman is always to blame. I know that for a fact. I almost got myself killed by my best friend when I stole his girl and made her my wife. A woman can make a man do crazy things. If she's the right one."

Emma smiled so widely her face hurt. Logan wanted to marry her because . . . she couldn't say the words, couldn't even consider them without melting. Did he love her?

❦

"What are you doing with my sister?" Cole asked, shouldering the barrel of the gun.

Logan walked to the front of the old truck. "I'm here because I'm going to marry your sister. So, let's end this feud today."

"Like hell you are, Miller," Cole said, stepping off the porch.

Logan straightened, growing three inches in height.

"You won't touch my sister." Cole's powerful voice boomed out into the yard.

"I already have. She's carrying my child, and I will make her my wife."

Cole glared at Emma, and to Logan's surprise, she wasn't intimidated. She simply shrugged and smiled at her brother. In that moment, Logan was filled with so much admiration and love. Did she want to be with him as much as he wanted to be with her? He wouldn't force her to marry him. But, damn it, he would do everything to convince her that he was worthy.

"She won't want you when she hears the truth about Joel."

Logan didn't know what to say. Fear twisted in his gut. If she heard the story, she would never want him, but he was done running from the past. He had to have faith that she could see the accident for what it had been—an accident.

Cole stepped a little closer, his large body stiff, every muscle flexing. He began his story in a deep, clipped tone. "I saw them—Logan and Joel—on the sandbar. I'd just come from fishing on the other side of the river. I thought nothing of it. Joel and Logan were always together."

Logan took a deep breath, his chest lifted and his nostrils flared. He refused to allow the memory of that day to fill his mind. Too many nights as a boy he'd woken up in a cold sweat, screaming for his best friend.

"They were arguing," Cole continued. "I could tell Joel didn't want to go into the river. He said it had too much power and he was scared it would carry him away. So, he never went in."

Logan heard the creak of springs coming from his truck. Emma had moved over to the driver's side window. "Please stop," she pleaded to her brother. "You're only torturing yourself. It's done. It can't be changed. Blaming Logan all these years is just wasted energy."

Cole didn't move. His face was as blank as a sheet of paper.

"I watched Logan taunting Joel. I had a horrible feeling in my gut. I looked for a safe place to cross the river. Joel took off running beside Logan, but he was watching me—never took his eyes off me. I watched him dive into the water. I waited, holding my breath. Logan surfaced first, and I waited. No Joel. I knew something was wrong. I threw my fishing gear down and swam as hard as I could for them. When I made it to the other side, Logan was tugging a lifeless Joel from the water. Just like that, my little brother was dead." Cole lifted his chin, challenging Logan. "Joel dove into a rock and had snapped his neck and drowned."

Logan popped his jaw at the telling of the painful

memory. All those years in therapy brought him to this moment. "Yes, you were right. I did tease Joel about not wanting to go into the river. The thing you fail to realize, Cole, is that he dove in because he saw you watching. His big, strong brother." He took a step closer. "He wanted you to see he wasn't scared. If you knew Joel at all, you should have known that you couldn't make him do something he didn't want to do."

Cole and Logan were toe to toe, and Logan was ready for whatever Cole would do next when he placed the burden of truth on Cole's shoulders.

"No matter how much I teased Joel, he never cared about what I thought. But he cared about what you thought." Logan poked him in the chest. "When the police asked me what happened, I stuck to the simple truth. We ran and dove in. That was it."

Cole lifted a single brow.

"He wanted to show you he was brave. To make you proud of him for overcoming his fear."

Logan watched as the flames of hatred shrank within Cole's eyes, allowing something else to be seen for the first time. Logan had never told Cole the truth because keeping this secret was the last thing he could do for his best friend. He could carry the burden of truth and try and spare his brother from a burden no man should have to endure. He thought he was helping Cole by giving him someone to blame. But now, there was more at stake than just his happiness. He had Emma and the baby, and he was reclaiming the life he deserved to live.

He looked at Emma and his father, still in the truck. His father opened the door and climbed out. He walked up beside him and placed a hand on his shoulder. That was all the push he needed to get through this moment. He had to, not only for himself and his father, but for her. Logan knew this wound would need to be healed for him to have a life with Emma.

"I don't believe you," Cole said. "Why didn't you tell me?"

His father squeezed his shoulder, and his gaze never left Logan's. "Because he was a good boy, and he loved your brother like his own. If he could have changed that day, he would have. He has suffered for that moment for most of his life. You can change that," his father said, turning to stare at Cole. "You can give him his life back."

Logan became very still as he took in his father. He saw the man he remembered, a man not to be trifled with. It warmed his heart. He wished his father would get better.

Logan turned to Cole. "Joel was my best friend. You were his brother. That's why I never said anything. I tried to spare you as much pain as I could, but it obviously wasn't enough." His voice broke as he tried to stop a knot from forming in his throat.

Cole's face went ugly. Logan could tell that he was very close to tears, and that he was trying not to give in. "I called you a murderer. Made everyone believe you were. I shot your cattle, stole them. Your parents sent you to live with your uncle because they feared for your safety . . . because of me and what I might do. Why didn't you say something back then?"

"I've given as much as I can to Joel, but now I want to reclaim my life. I want to be here with my father on the ranch. I want to be with Emma. I want a family, and I want my children to grow up in this place. But I can't do that if I'm always looking over my shoulder for you, wondering when you'll strike to get your vengeance." Logan shook his head regretfully. "I don't expect things to change overnight, but I have to take the first step."

Logan walked over to his truck and opened the door for Emma. He took her hips in his hands and peered into her eyes. He saw love. His heart swelled, and for the first time in many years, he felt a woman's loving touch begin to mend his broken heart. Wrapping a hand around the back of her neck, he pulled her close. Chest pounding, Logan softly pressed his lips to hers. Their bodies molded together and time stood still. He'd found his soul mate.

After a moment, he released her lips and pressed his forehead to hers. He was free from the chains of the past.

"Emma Verbeck, will you be my wife? Not because you carry my child, but because I love you, and I need you in my life."

Tears collected in Emma's amber eyes. He rubbed the pad of his thumb over her cheekbone. He waited, heart pounding in his chest.

"Yes," she cried, and threw her arms around his neck, pulling him closer. She kissed him deeply. A throaty voice suddenly sounded beside them.

"Get a room. No brother ever wants to watch his little sister making out in public. It's disturbing."

Emma blushed and let go of Logan.

She then rushed over and hugged her brother tightly. "Thank you for not shooting him," she said teasingly.

"Oh, I would have shot to the side. You know, pepper his leg or something with the buckshot."

She slapped his chest playfully.

Logan watched the sibling teasing and felt an intense sadness. He missed that. He missed Joel. As he watched Cole and Emma, his heart lifted when he realized that he and Joel were bonded by blood now. He gazed at his soon-to-be wife and was filled with love and desire.

Cole walked over to him, brows stitched together, lips turned down in a frown. "Think you can handle a spoiled brat?" he asked Logan, half joking.

Emma glared at her brother.

Logan smiled at Emma. "I think I can handle her."

Then, out of nowhere, a fist connected with his mouth, causing him to stagger back, holding his face.

"What the hell was that for?" Logan complained, glaring at Cole.

"For knocking her up before you married her," Cole said.

Logan straightened. His father hadn't moved, only watched quietly with an amused look on his face.

Emma came back to him and rested her head against his chest.

"If I'd known Cole would be such a pushover, I would have made you do this weeks ago," she jested with him as she wrapped her arms around his waist and kissed him softly.

"Yeah, me too. Would have saved me the love tap from Cole," Logan said.

Cole was smiling like a madman, pleased with himself.

Emma pulled Logan's chin, turning his face toward her. He gazed into her eyes. "I love you, Logan Miller."

Epilogue

Emma made circles with her hand around her round belly as she swung on the porch swing. Cole sat next to her. She couldn't believe she was almost ready to pop. It seemed like yesterday that she'd given birth to baby Joel. Now here she was, three years later, having a girl.

Her mouth tipped up as Harold chased little Joel in the front yard. He had been in remission for two years. Joel squealed like a pig, trying to escape his grandpa. She was filled with a deep satisfaction that touched every part of her life. She looked at her brother and slapped his thigh.

"You need to find a wife and make a family," she said.

Logan stepped out from the house carrying a tray of sun tea.

"You know, you're not getting any younger," she continued, taking the tea Logan handed her.

"I don't have time for women," Cole said, shifting in his seat.

Logan chuckled and sat in the rocking chair across from her. "Stop right there, sweetie. Leave the poor guy alone. The last time someone said that to me, the next thing I knew I was falling in love, getting married, and then working on my second kid."

"And what the heck was wrong with that?" she asked, scowling at him.

Logan shrugged. "Oh, don't go getting all worked up.

The baby still has a week before you can force her out, so don't go getting mad about anything."

So mature. She stuck out her tongue at him and went back to watching Harold and Joel playing.

Logan quickly raised his glass to Cole in homage. "You're screwed." Then he took a swallow of tea.

Emma narrowed her eyes at Logan. "I just want him to be happy, like we are."

Logan stood up, walked over, and bent over her. He brushed her curls away from her face and then kissed her lips. She sighed. Then he kissed her belly. She had everything she'd ever dreamed of and more. The sound of a cork pop filled the air. Her eyes met Logan's.

"Um . . . Logan . . ."

A wide smile spread over Logan's face. "Batten down the hatches, gentlemen. It's go-time."

Cole looked at her, then at Logan. "What is she 'umming' about?"

"My water broke. The baby's coming

Delicate Dream

Chapter One

Bethany's hunk of junk—a faded, blue Datsun she called Dot—sputtered and died. The glowing, white lights from the glass double doors and the red of the Emergency Room sign were a beacon of hope.

"Don't break down on me now," she pleaded. "I promise to get you an oil change and new tires if you can make it to the front of the hospital."

The car rolled to a stop under a parking lot light more than a football field away in the large hospital parking lot. She groaned in frustration and tried to restart the engine. It clicked several times, but never roared to life. She clenched her fists. This was what she got for moving across the country for a new job at eight months pregnant. She had been offered a head chef position at Deveros, one of the most respected restaurants in Washington state. It was a once-in-a-lifetime opportunity, and she couldn't say no. Especially after telling them she was pregnant and due in a few months, and they still wanted her. But the baby was coming early and she didn't know why.

She picked up her phone, and it was dead. Dot's cigarette lighter outlet had burned out on the second day of her drive from Kentucky to Washington, so she couldn't charge her phone. Now here she was, alone in the hospital parking lot unable to call and have someone come out.

She glanced at the hospital doors longingly. She was

going to have to walk the rest of the way on her swollen feet with a baby trying to squeeze out. There was no time like the present to have a baby three weeks early in some unknown town in the middle of Idaho.

As she peered around the tiny car packed with her belongings, she regretted her choice to drive alone. Her friend Patrick had said he would drive with her and help her get settled into her new place and help when the baby came, since he was on summer break as a seventh-grade science teacher. But it was just her luck, he got a call two days before they were going to leave saying the school needed him to teach summer school.

She had taken a gamble and lost. There was no second-in-command if things went awry. And things were definitely awry.

She squeezed the door handle with both hands, praying the grumpy, old car would consent to her unlatching it. After two good tries and no success, she rested her forehead against the steering wheel and held her breath. The next contraction stole every ounce of her energy. Her abdominal muscles clamped down on her unborn baby girl, desperate to expel her. Bethany growled low, trying to get through the pain. She could feel her baby right between her legs. Deep breath in, deep breath out.

A few minutes later, her abdomen relaxed and again she squeezed the door handle, this time with more determination. "Let me out of here." If she didn't make it into the hospital fast, her daughter, whom she would name Olivia, would be born right here in the driver's seat.

"Come on, you pile of junk, let me out!" she said, teeth clenched, squeezing as hard as humanly possible on the handle.

Click.

Bethany sighed with relief and shouldered the door open. She climbed out onto wobbly legs, surveying the parking lot, holding the car door for balance. The hospital was set a mile off the highway cutting through town. It was surrounded by tall pine trees that shielded it from the world. It had been a wonder she'd found it in the dark. A variety of cars and trucks littered the parking lot, but no one was pulling in that could help her.

"I can make it, hopefully. Mama's got you, Olivia," she said.

The warm summer air wrapped around her, easing some of the tension from her body. Waddling slowly, she made her way toward the front of the car when a sharp pain forced her to double over. She protectively wrapped her belly in a firm embrace. Clipped breaths were all she could manage. Her stomach muscles tightened. Somehow, she lowered herself to the ground, ignoring the pebbles sticking to her legs. She wanted to scream for help, but the contraction was too intense. Focused on her baby, Bethany struggled to control her breathing.

An eternity passed as she waited for the contraction to stop, but it only grew more forceful. Something warm ran down her legs. She lifted her simple, cotton summer dress out of the way as an overwhelming fear laced around her heart. She touched her inner thigh to make sure it was amniotic fluid, but the dim light of the parking lot revealed a red, sticky substance on her fingers. Bethany choked on a sob. A metallic scent rode the air around her. Olivia must be in trouble . . . and if she was in trouble, then so was Bethany.

"Please . . . no," she whispered. Her heart hammered. Another sharp pain ripped through her. Her vision blurred and the parking lot light grew hazy, as if there was a ring around it. Thoughts of her mother drifted to the front of her mind and tears streaked her cheeks. As tough and as independent as Bethany was, she should have brought her mother with her. She tried to focus on the light, but the world went black and disappeared.

Chapter Two

A bouquet of flowers sat on the front seat of Cole Verbeck's truck, smelling up the space with a pungent aroma. He couldn't stop smiling, but damn, it felt good. He was excited to see his new niece. His sister had labored all day to bring another little person into the world.

He meandered down the narrow road of Highway 55, rising and falling with the Payette River. Crossing a concrete bridge, Cole leaned out his open window, breathing in the scent of pine and tall grass. He knew the land and all its twists and turns, having been born and raised in Idaho.

A few hours ago, he was lounging in his living room, his feet aching and hands blistered from a hard day's work of stacking hay in the barn. Then his phone started blowing up—typical of a Sunday night when Game of Thrones was on. He never understood why his younger siblings, Peter and Emma, and a few other friends included him in the group text despite him never having seen the show. Tonight, when the phone almost vibrated off the coffee table, he'd reached over and grabbed it to see what the fuss was all about. Sure enough, Emma had gone into labor. His brother-in-law, Logan, and Peter were already at the hospital. His two-year-old nephew, Joel Junior, had stayed behind with a babysitter.

And now Cole was on his way, making the hour-long

drive to McClain Hospital. Better late than never. When he finally pulled into the hospital parking lot, he drove past an old Datsun that was parked on the outermost part of the lot. He glanced into the rearview mirror and did a double take.

"What the . . .?"

He hit the brakes and put the truck in park, then turned around in his seat, his eyes squinting through his back window at the Datsun. A heavy feeling settled in his gut when he spotted a foot on the ground, poking out from the other side of the car. He quickly put his truck back into gear and spun around, then parked haphazardly next to the Datsun. He sprang from the truck and rushed toward the foot.

A woman with a round, pregnant belly was lying on the pavement.

"Oh my God!" Kneeling beside the woman, Cole brushed a few strands of her golden hair away from her mouth. He bent down and turned his ear to her mouth. Her breathing was shallow.

"Ma'am, can you hear me?" he asked, gently shaking her arm.

No response.

He scooped her small frame into his arms and gazed at the blood flowing down her legs. Dread filled him. The woman's body tightened in his arms. He could tell she was in labor.

Cradling her securely against his chest, he broke into a dead run toward the hospital. His cowboy boots tapped hard against the pavement. How long had she been there like that? Had someone left her, hurt her even? Why was she alone at a time like this?

The woman groaned weakly and reached a small hand up, gripping the collar of his shirt. "She's coming," she whispered.

Cole looked down, his eyes locking with her large, deep-brown eyes. The pain was alive in their depths. Sweat dotted her brow. There was no color in her lips or cheeks.

Cole pushed himself faster. The woman's weight was heavy and limp, her limbs swaying all over with each step he pounded into the pavement. His shoulders and back burned, his breathing strained. Finally, he reached the entrance and raced inside.

"Help . . . she needs help," he panted.

The woman behind the check-in desk stared at him dumbstruck.

"She's in labor. The baby's coming. Something's wrong. There's blood," Cole urged.

The woman sprang into action. "How long has she been in labor?" she asked as she picked up the phone on the desk and punched in a few numbers.

"I don't know."

The woman started rambling into the phone's receiver.

"I found her like this in the parking lot, alone," he said, unsure she heard him. He felt helpless. It was a familiar feeling he knew all too well—a slippery feeling, like something covered in slime. He wanted to grab it, but the feel of it made him cringe.

He peered down at the small creature in his arms. Somehow, she'd wrapped both arms around his neck and was resting her head against his shoulder now. She was breathing hard.

"She's . . . coming," the pregnant woman repeated with effort.

Fear and amazement rocked him. He'd stayed in the waiting room when his nephew was born two years ago, and his sister had screamed and cursed like a true Verbeck. But this woman was calm, despite the pain she was in.

He had done enough waiting. The woman needed to get to a bed. McClain Hospital was the closest and largest medical facility nearest to his hometown in Havencrest. Emma was the only doctor in town, so if she couldn't fix them up at the clinic, everyone went to McClain Hospital. Which meant he knew where most everything was. Fueled on adrenaline, he barged past the front desk and started looking for a room bed. This woman needed rest to prepare herself for the birth of her baby, right?

"Where are you going? Hold on!" a nurse yelled at him.

He stomped down the hallway, looking into the rooms despite the surprise of other patients. He found an empty room and quickly set the woman onto the bed.

"I'll tell them you're in here," he said, turning to leave. She caught his arm. Fingers dug into his bicep.

"Please don't go." Her voice was strained. "I'm scared."

He suddenly felt anxious, out of his element. He tugged free of her grasp. "I need to find a doctor," he said.

The woman's long hair outlined her pale cheeks. Her eyes were vivid with pain and pleading. He clenched his jaw as a wave of protectiveness washed over him. He didn't leave. He bellowed into the hall, "A doctor better get in here before I get pissed!"

The woman's heart-shaped face softened and she leaned back in the bed. "My name is Bethany Heart," she muttered before her eyes closed.

He studied her. "Cole Verbeck," he replied.

"Cole . . ." she repeated softly.

"I should go and see what's keeping them so long. Hang on." He stepped into the hallway. "Hello, can I get some damn help down here or what?"

A nurse hurried toward him, no lightweight.

"Okay, honey, you're going to have to lay back so I can check to see how dilated you are," the nurse stated, glancing at Bethany as she washed her hands and placed gloves on. "When did you start having contractions?"

"A few hours ago," Bethany said, closing her eyes.

The nurse started to lift her dress. Cole stiffened and turned his back to the women and walked to the doorway. He peered at the other rooms, wondering which room was Emma's.

Bethany let out a loud gasp from the pain.

"Should I get another nurse?" he asked, but no one responded. This was the largest hospital in the area, but a small hospital compared to those in Boise. The staff was small. He looked over his shoulder. Bethany was sitting up, and her hands and body were shaking. Being a cattleman, he'd helped with hundreds of births on the ranch. He could tell the baby was coming.

"The head is right here. I don't think the doctor will make it from the C-section surgery he is in." The nurse squeezed Bethany's shoulder. "It will be okay."

Bethany's face hardened with determination. It tugged at Cole. Her eyes held him captive for a moment. Her face was tight, and she appeared to be holding her breath.

The nurse was on the phone asking for help. "Shit," the nursed said, biting her lip. Worry crunched up her features. She rushed out of the room.

Cole stood beside the bed near Bethany's head, not wanting to see things he shouldn't. He didn't know how to comfort this woman, so he just stood there, hoping his presence was enough.

The nurse rushed back in pulling two pieces of equipment behind her and started attaching a belt of some sort around Bethany's belly, along with some other wires.

"What's happening?" he asked.

"You shouldn't be in here."

"He stays," Bethany ground out. She reached over and squeezed Cole's hand. Fear etched deeply into her face.

Tears gathered in her dark eyes and her chin quivered. "I can't do this alone," she sniffled.

The nurse was right. He shouldn't be there, and he did feel out of place. But again, he didn't leave. He stood in place because she'd asked him to stay. And he was a man of his word.

Bethany sucked in a sharp breath as one of the monitors started to go crazy. Cole held her slim fingers, surprised by their strength. Unable to suppress his male instincts to protect and comfort, Cole ran a hand down her cheek. The pad of his thumb brushed over her cheekbone. Her skin was soft and cool to the touch.

"Everything will be fine," he said.

The nurse looked at the monitor. "Try not to push with the contraction. We need time for the doctor to get here."

"No, no. I can't! She is coming out!" Bethany wailed.

"Don't push," said the nurse.

"I'm not!" Bethany screamed. "My body wants her out! I can't stop the contractions!"

With a gush of fluid onto the bed, the nurse announced, "The head is out."

With a groan from Bethany, the baby slid out and onto the bed. Tears ran down her cheeks and she blinked them away. Cole felt his heart thump and turn over like a sad, old hound submitting to its master at seeing such a feat of strength from this delicate woman.

Before the nurse could cut the umbilical cord or suction the baby's nose or mouth, blood pooled out onto the bed. The baby didn't make a sound; it wasn't breathing. Bethany's hand went slack and her head bobbed to the side. The nurse started yelling and all hell broke loose. Three nurses came running in. Seconds later, Bethany was being wheeled out of the room, pale and not moving while the others cared for the baby.

Cole stood stiffly in the hall as Bethany slipped away.

He started to follow her but forced himself to stop. He stood in the hallway staring out at nothing, emotions twisting him into knots.

Time slipped away as he prayed for the baby to cry out. If the baby didn't make it, Bethany would be devastated. And what life would that baby have if her mother didn't make it?

All of a sudden, the woman from the check-in desk materialized in front of him with a sour expression. He flinched in surprise and his brow stitched together.

She rapped him smartly with a clipboard and pointed down the hall to the waiting room. "Fill this out and hand it back to me when it's complete." Then, she sauntered off.

Cole looked at the paperwork; it was an admittance form. His jaw clenched. Who did she think he was, Bethany's husband? Clearly, she hadn't heard him when he'd said he found Bethany alone in the parking lot. It had been years since Cole had dated. And by years, try high school. The ranch required too much work with just him and his father to run it. Peter had never been interested in helping with the ranch for anything other than his daily chores. When Cole was twenty-seven, his father died of a heart attack out in the north pasture. Then the workload had doubled. There was zero time to entertain the thought of casual dating or being in a relationship.

He blinked at the paperwork again. He didn't even know what was happening or if Bethany was going to survive. The entire situation was overwhelming. He marched down the hall, slapping the clipboard onto the counter of the check-in desk as he walked past.

"Hey!" complained the woman.

"She's not my wife or my girlfriend. I found her lying in the parking lot. You take care of that."

Cole left the building.

Making his way over to his truck, Cole ripped open the door and snatched the flowers he'd brought for Emma from the front seat. He glanced at Bethany's rusted Datsun, the image of her motionless body lying on the ground imprinted in his thoughts. Why was she alone? Surely there was someone who cared for her, someone the hospital could call. Why had she asked him to stay? He was not a man to be easily swayed by the pleadings of a stranger. He kept to himself, not letting others into his life because being vulnerable was not on his to-do list. Yet he had been unable to tell her no. His life had been touched by such loss, and there was no room for more.

Breathing the evening air, he glanced up at the stars. They were all out to greet him. "Please, Lord, let Bethany and her daughter make it through this night safely."

Calmer, he marched back into the hospital and up to the front desk.

"I'm here to see my sister, Emma Miller. What room is she in?"

The check-in lady barely spared him a glance. "Room twenty-four, down the hall. Make a right turn. It's on the left side of the hall."

"Thanks."

Cole made his way down the hall and stopped in front of the doorway to room twenty-four. He cracked his neck and shook his arms, trying to shake off the extra energy helping Bethany had caused. He knocked softly, then opened the door to peer inside. Emma was sitting up in bed, gazing at Logan with such love. Logan was sitting next to her holding a bundle wrapped in pink blankets, making cooing sounds at their new daughter, Abbie. The need to back away and not intrude on the intimate moment prompted him to step back. Before he was able to fully retreat, Emma's dark eyes found him. She called out to him, her face all aglow.

"Cole."

Reaching out her hand, she gestured for him to come to her. He shook his discomfort off for intruding and strolled over to his sister's waiting embrace. He gave her a hug and a kiss on her cheek, then he placed the flowers in her lap. It was hard at times for Cole to see his sister as a wife, a mother, and a doctor. She'd grown up too quickly, and he felt like he had missed it somehow because he was always working.

Emma picked up the flowers and drank in their scent, as he knew she would. She loved wildflowers. Before marrying Logan, she lived at their family home, and there had been countless Mason jars full of wildflowers in every room.

"Thank you. They're beautiful. A little bit of home is always nice to have. Sit down and hold your niece. She's a perfect little Verbeck."

"She's a Miller, who just happens to look like her mama," Logan corrected. He walked over and held out the pink bundle to Cole.

Cole cradled the baby in his arms. He gazed down at Abbie. She had shiny, black hair, and her bottom lip poked out because her round cheeks were being squished by her small shoulders. There was no denying she was a Verbeck. The hair, the shape of her lips, and when he adjusted her in his arms, she scowled just like a Verbeck. A smile tipped the corners of his lips. She was perfect. His sister was lucky to have such a great family. He was happy for her. Perhaps he really was missing something from his own life. The more he looked at them, the more he started to believe it.

Chapter Three

Cole stared at himself in the mirror as he washed his hands in the hospital restroom. The lines around his mouth and eyes cut across his tanned, leathery skin, making him feel every one of the thirty-eight years that he was. He ran a callused hand over the stubbles of a beard, then through his shaggy mane of black hair. His amber eyes were tired. He pulled at the neck of his stained T-shirt that was dotted with holes along the collar. Man, what a sight.

When he got back to the room, Logan was sitting next to Emma on the bed and the little baby was sleeping in a nearby bassinet.

"I found a woman unconscious in the parking lot. Her name is Bethany. She was in labor," Cole blurted out. He didn't know why he told them, to be honest. Maybe it was because his niece was all healthy and pink—and alive.

Emma gasped. "Is she okay?"

"I don't know. They took her away and the baby wasn't breathing."

Emma looked over at her daughter. "What are you going to do?" she asked.

Cole peered at her, uncertain.

"What do you mean? The guy found her in the parking lot. He doesn't even know her. He pretty much did all he could do," Logan replied, coming to Cole's defense.

Cole stared at him, always surprised when Logan backed him up. Over the last few years since Logan married Emma, they had mended their friendship, but there were still cracks. When Cole was sixteen, he had been fishing at the river when he spotted Joel and Logan playing on the sandbar. They had been twelve, and insep-arable. Brothers by bond. Joel wasn't a great swimmer, and on that day, he'd dove into the water head-first into a rock, broke his neck, and drowned. Cole had tried to get across the river to save his brother, but it was too late. Logan had pulled Joel's lifeless body out of the river. For twenty-two years, Cole blamed Logan for his brother's death. Calling him a murderer, having seen Logan taunt-ing Joel to go in. He was so full of anger and heartbreak and guilt. He had accused Logan of murder the day of his brother's funeral. Everyone in town shunned and tortured Logan. The Miller family sent Logan away to live with his uncle.

Logan had forgiven Cole for accusing him of Joel's death. It humbled him beyond words that Logan could forgive, and that forgiveness had allowed him to break some of the painful chains that held him to the past and be a better man.

Emma rolled her eyes. "For God's sake, Cole, go find out what's going on."

"And if he doesn't?" Logan chimed in once more.

"Then I'll drag my butt out of bed and find out myself. That poor woman, found in a parking lot in labor, needs someone to be there for her." Emma tried to flip back her covers, but Logan quickly got up and pressed her shoul-ders back against the bed. A few hours after labor and Emma was already back in doctor mode.

"Relax," Logan said, staring meaningfully at Cole. "He's going. Right, Cole?"

The corners of his sister's mouth tipped up. She'd

received the reaction she wanted from her husband. Cole wouldn't let Logan suffer because of him.

"I'll go see if there is any new information."

Cole sat in the waiting room for two hours for any news about Bethany and her baby, but the nurses wouldn't tell him a thing. He knew he should just let it go and head home. But that would be pointless. He would lay there worrying about Bethany and her daughter. He had told her he would stay, so that was what he was doing. He was staying until he could see her and know she was okay.

Finally, a nurse waved him to the front desk. "Well, come here. I'm not going to yell the info for everyone to hear. Patient confidentiality apparently means little to you—or that visiting hours are over."

Cole looked around. He was the only person in the waiting room. He pushed to his feet all the same and hurried over to the desk.

"I am sorry to say that the doctor lost Miss Heart. She died." She paused. "But the doctor did manage to resuscitate her. She's stable. However, we haven't been able to locate any family members."

Cole gasped. He put his head down. He gripped the desk in front of him. So many emotions coursed through him in that moment. It was hard to process the information. When it finally sank in, all the life in him drained out. His head snapped back up.

Noting his reaction, she continued. "The baby is doing fine. It was a girl: six pounds, four ounces, and nineteen inches long. Miss Heart will be in the room across from Dr. Miller's. She will be under observation for a few days in case there are any further complications."

Cole nodded. He couldn't believe his reaction at the news that Bethany had died. It was like losing someone important, someone who mattered to him. He had only just met her, their interaction was brief, and it had been a scenario like nothing he'd experienced before. They were linked in that moment of need.

"Can I see her?" he asked.

"I suppose, though you'll have to wait a little while longer."

"Thank you."

To kill time, Cole wandered to the coffee vending machine and made a purchase. When he brought the questionable black tar to his lips to drink he hissed, burning his bottom lip. When he went back to the front desk, the nurse told him Bethany was in her room.

Cole leaned against the wall in Bethany's room relieved to see her, though he couldn't take his eyes off her. She was pale and motionless. He was afraid that if he looked away, she would stop taking the small pulls of air that managed to raise her chest an inch.

The nurse who had delivered Bethany's baby popped in. "Hi there. Long night?" she said, giving him a compassionate smile.

"Yes. I just wanted to make sure she was okay. I told her I would make sure she was okay before I took off."

"That is nice of you."

"What happens to her now?" he asked.

"She stays here until the doctor releases her, and then she goes back to wherever she came from." The nurse looked away and checked a few of the machines around the room.

"I see."

She rested her hand on Bethany's head as if to comfort her. Bethany didn't stir. "It's time for you to go," the nurse said. She gave him a look that reminded him of a mother chastising a child.

"I will as soon as she wakes up and knows that I

stayed like I told her I would."

"Umm-hmm. She wakes up. You talk. Then you go."

Cole held up three fingers in the Boy Scout promise and crossed his heart with the other.

The nurse smiled. "I'll be back."

Cole leaned against the wall once more. After a while, exhaustion nagged at him so he sank into the chair in the corner next to Bethany's bed and fell asleep.

Chapter Four

Bethany dreamed that strong, powerful arms cradled her, keeping her close like a priceless gem. She could see his glossy hair and wondered what it would be like to touch it. So she did. She caressed the raven-black locks one at a time. Eyes so amber it looked as though the sun was poured into them, touching her soul and filling her with warmth.

She felt so loved and so protected. What she wouldn't give to have a man who wanted to protect and keep her. It was a dream of the impossible.

What was that noise? A sound like snoring disrupted her dream. Bethany tried to open her heavy eyelids. A sliver of dim light seared her eyeballs and she closed them again. She tried to lift an arm, but it was too heavy.

She attempted to open her eyes again, struggling to get them opened to mere slits. She tipped her chin up and saw someone sitting in a chair next to her.

She forced her eyes to open wide and tried to take everything in, but it was all fuzzy. As her eyes slowly focused on the person beside her, Bethany felt her pulse racing. Cole. He stayed just liked he said he would. She felt lightheaded and her cheeks flushed. He continued to snore, hunched over in a chair with his legs stretched out in front of him. He looked big sitting there.

A baby cried from across the hall and reality slapped

her in the face. She looked at her belly . . . it was smaller than before. She lightly pressed on it. It was soft and sore. Panic rose so fast she could hardly find her voice.

"Cole." She tried to reach out to him, to shake him, but he was out of her reach. "Cole." Her voice was hoarse and her throat was dry, but she managed to speak a little louder. Where was her baby? Did something happen to Olivia? Was she okay? She vaguely remembered something not being right after she slid into the world.

The fear for her child had her struggling to pull her pillow out from behind her head, then she swung the pillow and smacked Cole with a resounding thump. Grateful that the pillow was stiff and firm, she whacked him again.

When the pillow smacked his face a second time, his eyes popped open. It took him a minute to wake up, and then he sat up. "Whoa, whoa now," he mumbled, blinking the sleep from his eyes.

"Cole, where is she? My baby, please tell me she's okay." Tears glided down her cheeks. She waited, watching his face. If he didn't say something fast, she was going to become hysterical. She could feel the panic twisting into knots in the pit of her stomach.

"Cole, please . . . where is my baby?" she pleaded, her voice hitching.

He reached out and took her hand, rubbing the pad of his thumb across her knuckles. "She's fine. She's in the nursery. I can have them bring her in now that you're awake."

"Oh, thank heavens. Yes. Please, I need to hold her."

Relief cascaded down her spine. The twisted knots inside her loosened. She pulled her hand away, afraid she was pushing her luck with this kind man. She had basically guilted him into staying with her because she was afraid to have Olivia on her own. But she was going it alone with this whole having-a-baby thing. She'd dated William, a coworker at the restaurant Southern Smokehouse where she was a sous chef. They dated for about three months when she'd gotten pregnant. Before she had plucked up the courage three months later to tell him, he was in a motorcycle accident and died. Her heart had broken, not for herself so much, but for her baby. Her daughter would never know her father and what a happy, upbeat guy he was.

Bethany had enjoyed her time with William, though she wasn't in love with him and he wasn't settling-down material. He was at the beginning of his career and was more ambitious than Bethany; he'd wanted his own restaurant one day.

At the funeral, she hadn't known exactly what to do about the baby. William was an orphan with no family to contact. So, she kept working as the sous chef at Southern Smokehouse feeling sadder and sadder with every day that passed with William gone and her belly growing bigger with his daughter. When Deveros called and offered her a head chef position, she knew this was her chance to start over.

Cole stood up and gingerly placed the pillow behind her head. He eyed her thoughtfully. "You know, most people usually don't wake others with a face full of pillow."

"Drastic measures had to be taken. I couldn't reach you with my hand. Sorry."

He smiled wide. "I'm sorry if my snoring woke you up." He gazed into her eyes. "Emma always said I could wake the dead."

His emanating confidence was like nothing she'd seen before. "It's okay. It was nice seeing you there. Thank you for staying," she whispered, feeling so guilty.

Cole leaned over and pressed the call button above her head. Heat rolled off his skin. He could be her personal sun, pulling her into his orbit. A nurse's voice sprouted out of the intercom, startling her out of her thoughts about the man who'd basically saved her.

"Yes, how can I help you?" asked the dry voice.

"Miss Heart is awake and would like to see her baby girl."

"Yes, right away," the nurse said.

Bethany shifted in her bed, unsure of what to do or say. It was all so awkward. There must be a reason for him to be in the hospital.

"Is there someone in the hospital that you came to see . . . before you found me?"

Cole scrubbed his face with his large hands. He had stubble on his chin and jaw. The room had no windows and the light was on low, casting a gray shadow over the room.

"My sister just had a baby girl too. My niece's name is Abbie." He shot a thumb toward the door. "She's across the hall."

"Abbie is a lovely name."

"Yes, it suits her. What are you going to name your daughter?"

Bethany shivered. "Olivia." She wrapped her arms around herself, finding it difficult to fight the cold.

Cole pulled his chair closer and fussed with the blankets at her feet. After a minute, he had her covered. His face was tight with concentration as he tucked the blankets in around her legs. He was meticulous and careful with her. It was endearing. She caught herself smiling at him. He paused, looking awkward, leaning over her legs. A weak smile pulled at his lips and he quickly sat back down.

"Thank you."

Cole opened his mouth to say something, but then the nurse barged into the room pushing a silent, pink bundle of blankets in a clear plastic bassinet on wheels.

Bethany's heart pounded as the nurse brought her Olivia. She reached out her hands to hold her and felt the weight of her child in her arms. Tears rushed down her cheeks. Her daughter . . . love and joy encompassed her entire being. She had brought life into the world. Olivia squirmed a little and Bethany tried to adjust her hold, but her arms felt tired and weak.

"She's been a little fussy. I think she is hungry. Are you going to bottle-feed or breastfeed her?" the nurse asked.

"I want to try breastfeeding and see what happens," Bethany said. Didn't every mother at least try to breast-feed? She wasn't going to be embarrassed; this was one of those things in life you had to deal with as a woman. She'd read *What to Except When Expecting* by Heidi Murkoff, and a few other books, and it all sounded like it was going to be a hot mess. She was willing to rise to the occasion.

"I'll send another nurse in to help you," the nurse said.

Suddenly, she felt self-conscious with Cole in the room. She stole a glance at him. He was facing the wall, picking at his nail. She saw color creeping up his neck. She wanted to chuckle, but she shook it off.

The nurse left them alone. Bethany undid Olivia's blankets to see all of her precious baby. She counted and touched all her fingers and toes.

Olivia had a perfectly round head covered in blonde hair. A squished face with round cheeks pushed both of her lips out, as if she was puckering for a kiss. The set of her eyes and those lips was no doubt William peeking through. But that round nose and face were a reflection of Bethany. Olivia was perfect.

Olivia directed her sleepy eyes at her. Their gaze met and at that moment, her heart filled with tenderness for this person she created. A connection formed between them. She was a mother now. She thought about her mother, Sabrina, and how amazing she was. Kind, adventurous, quirky, and optimistic. Her mom had a gypsy soul and had shown Bethany all the nooks and crannies of the US while her mother taught art, bouncing from university to university. Her mother wanted to show her how beauty waited quietly to be discovered.

Bethany learned that an artist saw the world in splashes of color and light. She hoped she could bring light and color to her daughter's life, even if it was through food. Yet the one thing she wanted most was for her daughter to have roots. And that was what she'd hoped to give her by going to Washington.

"Hello, sweetie. I'm your mama." She laughed softly as Olivia gave a big yawn and started to fuss. "It's not that bad, sweetie. I promise. I'm nice and loveable." Olivia paused upon hearing her voice and closed her eyes.

Bethany looked up at Cole. "Thank you for everything. You don't have to feel obligated to stay. We're okay."

Cole nodded. Did she notice disappointment flicker in his eyes? Maybe she was imagining it. She held out Olivia and said, "If you just put her in the bassinet and bring it to this side, I can reach her."

Cole did as she asked and placed Olivia into the bassinet. He then moved the bassinet closer to her.

There was an awkward silence, and Bethany didn't know what to think. All the adrenaline and energy she had when she first saw her baby flushed out of her and she was utterly exhausted.

"If it is not too forward, why were you out there alone . . ." Cole pointed in the direction of the parking lot. "Like that."

Bethany felt terrible. She had clearly traumatized this

poor man, and the previous guilt she felt grew. He deserved an explanation to ease his mind. No matter how tired she was. "I was traveling from Kentucky to a new job in Washington. My friend Patrick was supposed to come with me, since I was the size of a small house, but he got sucked into teaching summer school at the last minute. I had everything packed, so I went without him. I'm a big girl—or, I thought I was." She bit her lip and frowned. "Clearly, the jury is out on that last part. I don't think a smart adult would have risked almost giving birth in a car for a job." Her thoughts drifted away for a moment. "I just couldn't stay where I was. I had to leave. Start over."

Cole half smiled. "We all have moments where our ability to choose wisely is hindered. It has happened to me more times than I would like to admit."

It was sweet that he was trying to make her feel better.

"Well, I only wanted to keep my promise and stay like I said I would, to make sure you were okay. I should be getting home."

Cole gave her a nod goodbye, and just like that, the man who had saved her and her baby was gone. Bethany looked at the doorway, hoping Cole would come back and see her. She knew that was ridiculous, but it was a nice thought. He was a beautiful man. All tall, wide-shouldered, and rough-looking.

Olivia let out a wail, so Bethany gently lifted her back into her lap, pulled down her gown and then tried to breastfeed her. "Well, here we go."

Chapter Five

Two voices drifted in from the hall that morning. Bethany pushed herself up and listened.

"I heard Cole Verbeck was in last night. I wonder what brought him here?" came a mouse-like voice.

"His sister gave birth to her second child. But he found a pregnant woman in the parking lot and brought her in. He's handsome, all right, when you get past his grumpy expression. I think there's a gentle and honorable man beneath that gruff exterior. Any man who saves a woman in a parking lot and stays all hours of the night to make sure she's all right is a man worth taking a look at."

"Right? I hear his ranch is the most beautiful in all of northern Idaho. Not to mention, he produces high-grade beef."

"And how do you know that?" the woman exclaimed. Her voice sounded familiar.

"My grandpa used to buy prime beef from Mr. Verbeck's father. That's how."

"Huh. Well, that Cole Verbeck is some prime beef I wouldn't mind taking a bite of."

A booming laugh hung in the air. She could hear the women moving closer. Then a head popped into her room. It was Nurse Taylor, the nurse who'd brought Olivia into the world. She was a small, round thing who wore a frown. Bethany just loved her.

"How are you doing?" She walked over and handed Bethany a bag. "Here are some clothes, a phone, and a charger I got out of your car for you."

"You're the best. I need a shower and to call my mom. She's going to flip when I tell her Olivia got here early."

"Girl, you know you could have used the hospital phone for that. My mom would reach through the phone and strangle me if I waited a day to call her."

"I know. I have been too tired to deal with her."

Nurse Taylor's frown deepened. "Not too tired to talk to Cole Verbeck." She wagged her brows up and down, and Bethany couldn't do anything but laugh at her.

"What woman doesn't make time for a handsome man like that after he swept in and helped me and my daughter?"

Nurse Taylor's round face went sour and then she sighed. "You got me there. To be honest, I would probably do the same thing." She shoved the other nurse forward. "Okay then. It is time for me to go home. I'll be back tomorrow night," she said, sounding weary. "This is Bridget. She will be your nurse for the rest of the day."

Bridget waved. Bethany nodded, and the two women left. She leaned back and gazed at Olivia. So Cole Verbeck had a reputation for being a grump. Bethany liked grumpy people. It was a kind of challenge to get them to like her. She found they were fiercely loyal friends because they didn't have many. Your value to them was much higher than most.

She remembered the scowl on his face when she asked him to stay in the room with her while she was in labor. She had been afraid at that time. It was ridiculous and crazy, yet there was something about him that made her feel safe and protected when she had looked into his eyes. They were eyes like her father's, deep and knowing below the surface. It was as though her father had been protecting her from above and had sent Cole. It felt like he was letting her know he was there. It was more than she needed to find the strength to have her baby. She smiled wide in thought.

She pulled out her charger from the bag and plugged in her phone. She pulled in a deep breath, readying herself to talk to her mother. She dialed. The phone rang but there was no answer. She blew out a breath. Was it bad she felt relieved?

Bethany left a message. "Hi, Mom, just checking in to let you know I'm good. Give me a call when you have a chance." She was so not leaving a message about Olivia on her mom's phone. She would never hear the end of that. It would only freak her mother out and make her worry. As much as her mother was a free spirit, since her father died, her mother had become a bit of a worrier. In that respect, the two of them couldn't be more different. Bethany went with the flow, managing what she could and didn't sweat the small stuff. That was why she was such a good chef. She never raged at anyone.

Pulling in another breath, she called the apartment manager about her apartment. "Hi, I was calling to let the manager know I will be a few days late to sign paperwork for the apartment and do the walk-through."

"Who is this?" a dry, female voice said.

"Miss Heart."

"Hold please."

Next, a male voice was on the line. "I'm sorry you missed the walk-through, Ms. Heart. In the paperwork I emailed you last month it stated that if you missed your appointment, it fell to the next person on the waiting list. The demand for a downtown apartment is high. There is no room for mishaps. The apartment has been let to someone else who actually showed up."

The line went dead. Bethany's jaw dropped and she

held the phone away from her head and peered at it in disbelief. What the hell just happened? Did that jerk really give away her apartment? He didn't even give her a chance to explain. Bethany bit her lip. *Shit.* Now she had to find another apartment. She would have to stay in a hotel for a few days. It wasn't the end of the world, but seriously.

Feeling her nerves start to vibrate, she dialed Deveros next, knowing she was supposed to be there now filling out paperwork, getting to know the staff, and learning the menu and seeing where she could add her touches here and there.

"Deveros, how can I help you?" came a chipper voice.

"I need to speak with Mark."

"One moment please."

Bethany wrapped her finger around the phone charger, praying the owner, Mark, would understand why she wasn't there."

"Hello, Mark speaking."

"Hi, Mark, this is Bethany Heart, your new head chef."

"You were supposed to be here three hours ago."

"I know, and I'm so sorry about that. I ran into a bit of a problem getting there."

"And why is that?"

"Hmm, I went into labor early and had my baby sooner than expected. I know we talked about me taking a week or so off after she was born—"

Mark let out a frustrated growl. "Listen, Ms. Heart, you were supposed to be here today. I had the entire staff come in to meet you and you're not here. That makes you—and me—look bad. When can you get here?"

"A few days. I haven't been released from the hospital yet."

"I'm sorry. I can't wait. We will have to go with our

second choice, Erik Gregory."

Bethany bolted up. "Erik Gregory? You can't." Bethany had trained Erik three years ago. He had stolen five of her recipes that she kept in a notepad she always carried. She had been working on one and was called to do something and set it down. Then Erik snapped a few pictures, and the next thing she knew he was working down the road featuring her recipes.

"Yes, I can, and I will. He has been checking in with us to make sure you were what we wanted. We just can't wait for you. I'm sorry. I can check back in to see if you are interested if Erik doesn't pan out."

"I don't understand. You knew I was pregnant. You know I would only have about four weeks of work under my belt before I had to take time off. I'm just asking for that time now is all."

"Have a good day." Again, the line went dead. *What a bunch of assholes.* "Have a good day my ass!" Bethany yelled into the phone. Olivia wiggled and she slapped a hand over her mouth. "Shit. What am I going to do? My apartment and job both in one day, kaput." She blew out all the air in her lungs and dragged her hands over her face, trying not to cry. That was it. She needed a shower. She hit the nurse button.

"Yes, Bethany."

"Can you take Olivia to the nursery? I need a shower."

"Sure thing. Be there in a minute."

When the nurse came in, Bethany kissed Olivia's fat cheek and headed to the shower with her clothes and overnight bag. Thank God. She needed to brush her damn teeth. She rubbed her sore boobs. Her milk was coming in, and no book had prepared her for how much that hurt.

Bethany awkwardly made her way to the bathroom, not yet adjusted to the emptiness of her body. Dreading what she would see in the mirror, she pushed the bathroom door open with her eyes closed tight. She took a deep breath and slowly opened her eyes. Her reflection came into focus. She groaned. She looked as terrible as she felt. Pale, crazy hair, and her belly felt squishy when she poked it. She hoped she would take after her mother's naturally slim frame and trim down in a few weeks.

Putting her clothes on the back of the toilet along with a few bobby pins, she stripped off the robe the nurse had given her and then her hospital gown. Her body ached everywhere. She turned on the water and pressed close to the wall until the water heated up. She leaned her swollen breasts into the water and moaned blissfully.

The warmth eased some of the ache, and she relaxed. The box where she'd kept her emotions locked away since William died toppled over. Hot tears blurred her vision. "She is beautiful, has your lips and the set of your eyes. I wish you were here to see her."

Tears mixed with the water from the shower. "I'm off to an excellent start as a mother. You would totally be laughing at me. Lost my apartment and job in one fine stroke. What makes it worse is that dumbass Erik managed to steal from me again. Out of all the places to work he applied for the same job." Bethany wasn't sure she was talking to William anymore or just to herself. She wiped her tears. No, she wasn't going to cry. She had too many things to be thankful for.

Bethany reached for the small soap that sat on the shelf in the shower and began to soap her body carefully. Her strength seemed to leave her, and Bethany placed her hands on the wall to keep from falling. Her beautiful baby girl almost didn't get a chance to live. She couldn't stop the tears this time and let them flow. She sank to her knees on the hard tile, allowing the water to wash over her. The thought of never holding her daughter rocked her world. Seconds turned to minutes. Bethany contained one emotion at a time until she was herself again.

When there was nothing left, not a single emotion, she stood up and massaged the shampoo into her hair. When she rinsed the last of the conditioner from her hair, Bethany turned off the water and stepped out of the shower. She dried off and ran her fingers through her hair the best she could. Then she pulled her hair back into a bun, anchoring it to her head with the bobby pins. She slipped on her undergarments, trying not to wince when her bra felt much tighter. Carefully, she pulled a clean, light-blue cotton dress over her head and smoothed it over her body. She studied her reflection in the mirror. Her skin didn't have its natural golden glow, but she had improved her appearance well enough.

Gathering her belongings, Bethany strolled out into her room and froze.

Cole was there, and she was delightfully surprised. "What are you—"

"I came to see my sister and wanted to check on you and see how you were feeling. I hope today was a good day?"

Bethany walked over to the bed and sat down. She touched a button on her bed and the room brightened. He was wearing a denim shirt and jeans, and was holding a brown cowboy hat. She gave him her best smile and ran her fingers over her clean, blonde hair. It was nice to have company after receiving her crappy news.

"How is your sister doing with the new baby?" she asked.

Cole glanced around the room, fidgeting with the brim of his hat. *Is he nervous?*

"Not sure yet. I came to see you first."

"Oh." Heat ran up Bethany's cheeks and set them on fire. He sat down in the chair next to the bed and placed his hat on his knee. "How is Olivia? Has she been ornery?" he asked, peering around for her.

"She is in the nursery right now. I had to get cleaned up. I'm so thankful the hospital has a nursery for the new-borns, since it is just me. I wasn't too sure I would ever get a shower. But yes, she's been a sweetie."

He gazed at her, and those big eyes warmed her up.

"When do you think the hospital will release you?"

"I get to leave in a day or two."

"My sister might get to leave tomorrow as well."

The thought of not seeing him again made her feel a little blue. "That's good for her." She picked at the blanket next to her. "I guess I won't be seeing you after this. So, I want to say thank you once again for finding and helping me. Words can't express how thankful I am. You saved my life, you know." Some invisible force was strangling her chest.

"No thanks required. Anyone would have done the same."

"I'm sure you're right." Bethany went very still and stared fixedly at the blanket. She was feeling out of her element, which was unusual. Bethany was easygoing and talked to everyone. She always knew what to say to make others comfortable around her. Yet this man made her all tongue-tied.

"Are you from around here?" he asked.

"No. I was born in Chicago and moved around a lot. My mother is an artist and teaches everywhere she can for a year or so, then we find a new adventure. My father adored my mother. He was a history professor, so adventures were his favorite. He died of a brain aneurysm a day before I graduated high school. One minute he was there and the next, a memory."

She went quiet for a moment, remembering her father's round, scruffy face and how his handlebar mustache always tickled her skin when he kissed her. His warm embrace folded in around her and she knew he was there with her. She let out a sigh.

"As much as I liked watching my mother paint and my father do research, I found myself falling in love with food. It was my one constant when we moved here and there. Didn't matter where we were; I had food there waiting to be made and discovered. I guess you could say I'm from everywhere in the US."

Cole leaned forward, intrigued. "I've never been any farther than Boise," he chuckled. "What brought you here to McClain?"

Slowly, the awkwardness was replaced with quiet appreciation of his interest in her. She smiled. "Just passing through. I was supposed to be in Washington today to start a new job."

"Is it a chef job?" he asked, brows raising.

"Yes, a head chef position. I have been a sous chef for the past few years at different restaurants. I try to stay in the general area of my mother, wherever that may be. For now it has been Kentucky; before that it was Maine, then Illinois, and Colorado before that I think. It starts to blend together. But after Olivia's father died, I thought it was time to make a change of my own because I wanted to."

"I'm sorry for your loss. What happened, if you don't mind me asking?"

"It's okay, we hadn't been together that long. Only dated for a few months. He died in an accident. He was on a motorcycle and got run off the road. The car didn't see him."

He cleared his throat. "So, this is *your* adventure then?" he said, moving back on to happier things.

She tipped her head, not really seeing it like that until now. "Yes, my adventure."

"When they release you, you'll be back on the road to Washington then?"

She leaned back on the bed, slipping her legs under the blanket. "No. Since I didn't make it to Washington, I lost my apartment and my job. It is back to the drawing board."

Cole popped his jaw and looked like he was deep in thought.

"Everything okay, Cole?" she asked, wanting very much to reach out and touch his arm. She held herself back, so she decided on teasing him. "You wouldn't happen to know anyone around here who wants a personal chef or a restaurant that needs an amazing chef, would you? It would save me a trip back to Kentucky to live with my mother." She laughed. "And let's not forget Dot, my car. I have to get her to a shop and see what the heck is wrong with her before I go anywhere."

Cole studied her with a lopsided grin on his face. She didn't know what amused him, but it was a great look for him, handsome and dopey.

"Dot," he grinned. "Looks to be on her last leg."

"Don't pick on her. I have had her since I started driving. The car was my father's when he was my age. I just can't let her go."

He stood. "Maybe don't get rid of her, just retire her for safety purposes." He put on his hat and Bethany went all gooey. "I don't want to take up too much of your time. I'm sure you're tired. I should leave."

Bethany almost pouted, but she held back. She had done all the talking and wanted to know more about him.

"Good afternoon." He gave her a nod and walked out.

She was so going to dream about him tonight and she was going to like it. "It was nice while it lasted."

Chapter Six

Cole sat at the kitchen table staring into the blackest cup of coffee he'd ever made. The sun colored the sky beyond the mountain ridge that hugged his family's property. The morning light illuminated the room. He should be out working the field, turning the hay. He peered out the large glass windows. Dew clung to the grass in the fields. The hay would have to wait until later.

Dragging a hand through his hair, Cole scrubbed his rough, bristly face. The image of Bethany lying on the ground in the hospital parking lot preyed on his mind. He scowled at his reflection in the glass window.

Bethany lost a job she hadn't started and an apartment she hadn't moved into. It was bizarre to him how something like that was even possible. He didn't know why that bothered him so much, but it did more than he wanted to admit. Her golden-blonde hair and those dark-chocolate eyes stroked something inside him.

Cole took a sip of his coffee and groaned. Who was he kidding? *I'm screwed. I want to help her. It's the right thing to do. I want to do what is right.* Maybe a few years ago, he could have walked away and turned his back on Bethany and her daughter. Filled with hate and the pain of his brother's death. His mother wasn't able to deal with the death of her son, so she'd run off, and his father's broken heart slowly killed him. After Logan and his dad,

Harold Miller, forgave him, he'd remembered the man he wanted to be and sought to change. Now, he couldn't bring himself to ignore Bethany's situation.

A loud sigh escaped his lips and he glanced around the kitchen. Rusted pans were piled up in the sink and there were grease marks on the stove. It wasn't that Cole didn't clean—though he always procrastinated and let dishes pile up in the sink—but his younger brother, Peter, was a stinking slob. When Peter came home from work, it was like a confetti blast going off. His items landed everywhere. Luckily, Peter wasn't home too often, being the sheriff and all, but when he was, watch out.

The house could use a woman's touch and cooking. Cole liked to barbeque, and he could make a mean potato salad, but the truth was, he just didn't have time. His life had consisted of two eggs and toast in the morning, nothing for lunch, and two PB&Js at dinner.

It had been a few years since a woman lived in his family home and cooked for him. Emma moved out after getting married to Logan, and Cole didn't make time for dating. The idea of taking a woman to dinner in the hopes that she would like him was time he couldn't waste. He knew he was a handsome guy and that many of the ladies in town would like a chance to go out with him. He was a grumpy sort, and as soon as a woman saw that, he knew they would hightail it out of here. His time was valuable. He watched how he spent it.

Peter kept his women away from the house; didn't want them getting ideas for anything long term. Peter wasn't one to commit to a relationship, so they never came floating around. Cole was lonely. He would never tell Emma or Peter that, but he was. The more he saw the life Emma and Logan were building together, the more he wanted that very thing.

He couldn't stop thinking about Bethany; couldn't get

her face out of his mind. She was upbeat and friendly; it was refreshing, and so opposite to him. He enjoyed her company. He had been enthralled in her story yesterday about how she had grown up. She had been so open and willing to share her history. He had a dozen questions for her, but he kept them to himself.

He slapped the table and his empty plate bounced. He was going to offer her a job. She did say she was open to being a personal chef. He never splurged, and had put all his money in the bank. *Why the hell not?* It would be good for him to have someone to talk to at the end of the day. *But am I losing my mind? Is she going to think I'm crazy?* Bethany had a newborn, and he didn't know the first thing about taking care of a baby. Peter would have a cow if he showed up with Bethany and Olivia. It was one thing to have a beautiful woman around, but a baby was another.

He took a large mouthful of the bitter coffee and choked it down. He felt resolved in his decision. It was his choice. Peter would have to deal with it, since he didn't help with anything on the ranch.

Cole marched out of the house, the screen door slapping shut behind him. He was off to feed the cattle and see how his pregnant beef cows and heifers were doing so close to calving season.

The day passed in a checklist of tasks. By the time he was showered and heading to the hospital, Cole was a ball of nerves as he made his way down the hall to Emma's and Bethany's rooms. Holding two clutches of wildflowers, one in each hand, he froze as laughter bounded toward him. Emma. She laughed again, and Cole followed it. He took two tentative steps closer. What was Emma doing in Bethany's room? He stiffened before entering.

"Oh my, that's so funny. You should have seen him," Emma said, then she looked surprised he materialized in the doorway.

A thoughtful smiled curved Bethany's mouth and Cole couldn't stop staring at her. He wondered if she was unaware of how captivating she was when she smiled. Her eyes shone, and her skin had a glow. Her hair cascaded over her shoulders as she cradled Olivia in her arms. He was pleased to see her looking healthier.

He strolled over to Bethany and presented her with the flowers.

"For me? They're beautiful. Thank you," she said. She lifted the flowers to her nose and inhaled deeply. A soft moan passed her lips. Cole couldn't take his eyes off her. "Sweet peas. I haven't smelled them in years."

A throaty sound came from Emma, who was sitting at the edge of the bed cradling a pink bundle in her arms. Cole handed her the other bouquet.

"Thank you, you're the best," Emma said as she smelled the flowers. She turned to Bethany. "Did you know he has brought me flowers twice? My husband hasn't brought me flowers . . . and to think I gave birth to this perfect angel for him."

Cole smirked. Emma was the perfect balance of being a smart-ass and showing kindness and strength.

"I'm sure your husband will do something wonderful for you," Bethany said cheerfully.

On the drive over, he had worried over his decision to offer Bethany a job in his home. He tried to convince himself that this had nothing to do with how attractive she was, but he couldn't deny something shifted inside him every time he laid eyes on her.

Logan's blond head popped in from the hall. "Are we having a party in here?" he teased, standing in the doorway.

"No," said Cole, sounding slightly irritated. This is stupid, he chastised himself. *What am I thinking, asking*

a woman I hardly know to move in with me and cook?
Feeling out of place, Cole tried to retreat. As he started to
leave, Logan blocked him.

"No need to leave. We can go," Logan said. He took
Abbie from Emma. Emma was still a little slow moving
around, but she got up on her own. She gave Cole a kiss
on the cheek.

"Be nice, or I'll have to hurt you," she said.

After his family left the room, Cole stood waiting; for
what, he wasn't sure.

Bethany laughed. She was leaning back in the bed,
looking pleased about something. "I didn't think I would
see you again." She let out a sigh. "I'm glad you came.
Your sister is funny. I haven't had a laugh that good in a
while."

"I'm sure it was at my expense," Cole said, frowning.
"May I?" he asked as he held out his arms. Bethany didn't
hesitate and handed him the pink, squirmy bundle. Olivia
made a little noise and stared at him with wide eyes. She
was so little.

Bethany watched him, amused. She placed her flowers
on the nightstand and smiled. His chest puffed up with
pride. She liked his gift.

"Thank you for taking her. Olivia has been up most
of the morning," said Bethany, adjusting her blanket and
lowering the lights.

Cole pulled the chair close to the bed and sat down. He
peered at the bundle in his arms. Two squinty little eyes
blinked at him. He gently pulled the blanket away from
her round face so he could see her better. He wondered
what she thought of him. He laughed at himself. It was a
ridiculous thought. One of Olivia's tiny hands stretched
open and gripped his finger tightly. She yawned and
closed her eyes without releasing him. He was trapped.
How could such a small thing render him helpless? He

scowled at the pink bundle intensely. There was a pulling in his chest.

The idea of having someone to talk to at the end of the day and seeing this little treasure could fill a part of Cole he had forgotten he wanted. He mustered his courage and the words fell out of his mouth. "I want you to come cook for me and stay in my home." He sounded more demanding than he intended. Silence hung in the air, the weight pressing down on him. He was afraid to look up, but when he did, Bethany's eyes were wide. A small grin made her eyes sparkle.

Cole plowed ahead. "I have a large home. You can stay with me until you find something better."

"Are you offering me a job as your personal chef?"

"Yes."

"Olivia and I get to live in your home, on your ranch, where you raise beef cows?" she said in disbelief. Her legs bounced in what looked like excitement. Cole was skeptical to think she would say yes at first. This had to be promising.

"Wow, I'm speechless—and that is hard to do."

Cole gazed at Olivia, who was fast asleep, sucking her bottom lip. She was still holding his finger tight.

"I spend sunup to sundown working my ranch in Havencrest. My brother, Peter, and I own it together, but Peter is the town sheriff, so he seldom helps. He isn't home much. After Emma married and moved out, the house has become very quiet." He paused for a moment, wondering if he sounded like a blabbering idiot. His eyes met Bethany's. "It would be nice to have someone to talk to."

Cole hoped this piece of truth would sway Bethany to come stay with him. Yes, he was attracted to her, but he genuinely cared. When he'd held her in his arms with her life in the balance, something happened . . . a connection that tethered himself to this woman, and her wellbeing made him steadfast in his decision to get to know her.

When Bethany was seven years old, she and her parents had taken a trip to Florida to visit her grandparents. She only remembered three things from that trip: the alligators, the sweltering heat, and the way she felt when she jumped into the deep end of the pool.

She couldn't swim—had never learned—but that day they'd gone to the community pool because it was 113 degrees and too hot to do anything but sit in air-conditioning. The pool wasn't too crowded, though there were a few families lingering about, and about ten or so kids.

"Go have fun, cool off," her mother had said. She was wearing a polka-dot one-piece bathing suit.

Bethany headed toward the shallow end when her father grabbed her hand and said, "Let's be daring and go in the deep end." He pointed to the diving board where some kid just dive-bombed into the water, making a big splash. Bethany was afraid, and her father sensed that. "It's okay, I'll be with you. You never know until you try, right?"

And try she did. She made many attempts at jumping into the deep end, even though she was afraid. Things always seemed to work out the way they were meant to. Her father had been a big believer that when one door closed, another would open. She always tried to look at the world in that way because it was like taking a piece of him with her. It had helped keep her from becoming the worrier that her mother was.

As she stared at Cole, her mother's voice echoed in her head: *You don't even know this man! You just had a baby!* But then her father's voice seemed to win out: *You can't let any adventure pass you by.*

What a sweet confession, Bethany thought, flattered. What were her options? All she had was her broken-down car, a tank of gas, a few thousand dollars in savings, and everything that was inside Dot. She would have to get her car fixed before she could go anywhere. And how long would that take, a day, a week? She could ask her mother to come get her and Olivia, but the thought of leaving Dot behind made her tear up. She didn't want to bother her mother. This had been her shot to go on her own adventure, and it could still be that with Cole's offer. Something new and fresh.

Working for Cole would give her time to get settled into being a mom, and she could finally work on new recipes. She knew Cole couldn't afford her salary, but not having to pay for rent and food was a bonus, and more than likely a wash. It was an opportunity she didn't think she could pass up. She could cook whatever she wanted. She wasn't stuck following someone else's menu.

She looked deep into Cole's eyes and tried to read his thoughts, but his face was a mask. She needed to take care of Olivia, and that was her priority. She made her decision right then and there. "I accept," Bethany said, clapping her hands together.

"Really?"

"Yes. This could be just what I need."

Cole didn't say anything. A smiled pulled so tight at his lips she thought they would bleed. Anticipation raced through her. He glanced at Olivia with such affection that a lump formed in Bethany's throat. He rubbed the pad of his thumb over her daughter's little fingers.

"I didn't think you would say yes," he said, and he placed a hand on Bethany's.

His hand was rough against her skin, causing it to tingle. Her pulse quickened. He gave her a firm shake, yet he didn't release her hand. His eyes gleamed. She wished she knew what he was thinking. Finally, Cole leisurely let go of her hand. Heat moved into her cheeks.

The deal was made. A home on a ranch where she could cook anything she wanted. A roof over her head for her and her daughter.

She beamed at Cole. "Thank you . . . for this chance."

Cole nodded. "Will you be discharged tomorrow?"

"Looks that way."

"I'll be here tomorrow to pick you up." He handed Olivia over to her, and then he handed her a slip of paper with a phone number on it. He strode to the door. "See you tomorrow."

"Okay," Bethany said. She watched his backside as he left, admiring his maleness. Then he was gone. This felt right.

"Okay, Dad, I hear you loud and clear. A new door has opened, and I am stepping through it. The adventure continues."

Chapter Seven

Cole stared at half a dozen baby carriers. For the first time in his life, making the wrong choice terrified him.

"Do you need any help?" a cheerful voice came from behind. Cole turned and saw girl, no more than eighteen, standing there smiling at him. How could a girl her age know anything about car seats?

"No thanks, I got it," he said, annoyed by the interruption.

"There are so many things to consider when purchasing for an infant these days," she said, unaffected by his no-thank-you. There are travel systems, infant car seats, convertible car seats . . ."

Cole walked past the girl, ignoring her. He bent down, reading the descriptions on the box. The girl followed him.

"Let's not forget car seat bases and accessories: head supports, buntings, foot muffs, sunshades, and mirrors. The list goes on and on."

Cole's irritation grew into anger. He just wanted to be left alone. Logan was right: Cole wasn't much of a people person. He was an introvert, and he liked his alone time. That was why he loved the work he did—so many hours of being alone with his thoughts, and it was necessary for his wellbeing. That was all going to change.

Yesterday, Cole had asked Bethany to come work for him and live with him and Peter. Quite frankly he was somewhat confused about the whole thing, but he knew he was doing the right thing. He and Logan decided to grab some lunch, and Cole insisted on driving. Boy, did he regret that. He'd suddenly felt a panic attack coming on. He'd rolled down the window for some fresh air, worried he was going to drive off the road.

"Are you all right?" Logan had asked from the passenger seat. "You look a little pale."

"I don't have a lot of time to prepare," Cole had said.

"Prepare for what?"

"I've asked Bethany to stay at the ranch with her baby."

Logan looked surprised. "Why would you want to do that?"

Cole's nostrils flared. "I have the room and she's a chef. I'm tired of PB&Js."

"And it has nothing to do with Bethany's blonde hair and big, brown, doe eyes?"

"No, it doesn't." Cole was feeling a little better so he sped up, taking the turns a bit harsher than he intended.

"Slow down, man," Logan said. "I'm just a little surprised, that's all. I mean, you're not much of a people person . . . you like having your space. Having a new roommate is one thing, but a baby that cries and poops is another thing. Are you sure?"

Cole had sighed. He knew Logan would be the voice of reason. It was part of his personality. Logan was a former defense attorney, so he had a logical way of looking at things. Emma and Peter would both be ecstatic over the fact that Cole had invited a woman to live with him, not taking into account whether it would actually be the right choice. They made decisions based on emotions. Cole operated in the middle—usually he was rational, but this decision seemed more emotional.

"I'm sure . . . I think," Cole had responded. "Honestly, I went with my gut on this one."

Logan smiled. "I think everything will work out. If anything, Emma will be happy to have a new friend."

He couldn't fully wrap his head around the magnitude of his decision: allowing a woman to live in his home. Having a woman around the house would change things, and change was never something to take lightly. But he knew deep down that he was doing the right thing.

Now, Cole was standing in a store that sold lots of baby things that he knew nothing about. He picked up a box with a smiling baby in a car seat on the front, hoping for some revelation.

"Listen, sir, I am here to help. Please let me help, as I can see you're struggling."

Cole turned abruptly. "I said I didn't need help five minutes ago," he snapped.

The girl leaned away from him and took a step back. She folded her arms across her chest. "I have two older brothers, so that look"—she pointed to his face—"doesn't work on me. You can keep trying to intimidate me and waste both of our time, or you can listen to my suggestions. I can help you make a selection."

A warm heat flooded his face. Was he really trying to intimidate this young girl? He shamefully shook his head. "Sorry. This place is kind of overwhelming."

"It is for first-timers." The girl pointed to a box. "That one is the best-selling item. It has a five-point harness, comes with additional head and neck support, and the frame is solid steel. There is memory foam for extra comfort, and it comes with a base. The color is neutral, for either a boy or a girl, but you can get it in purple or blue if you prefer. Also, if you want to get a stroller later, there's a model that goes along with it."

Cole was quite impressed. He felt bad for dismissing her so quickly. It was obvious she knew her stuff. "Thanks," he mumbled.

"Sure," the girl said in her cheery voice, and bounced off.

Cole picked up the box the girl had recommended, examining the picture on the front. The car seat was gray, not girly in any way. He cursed under his breath. Would Bethany prefer gray or purple? The unfamiliar territory was pushing his anxiety level to the limit. It was ridiculous. He heaved the box onto his wide shoulder and headed for the checkout counter. As he walked past the diapers, he spotted the word "newborns" and grabbed two packs. He also snatched a pack of butt wipes. The meager items would have to do until he could get Bethany to the store because he honestly didn't know what a newborn baby would need.

Chapter Eight

After three days of being in the hospital, Bethany was being discharged, and in a few hours, she would be leaving with Cole. It all felt surreal, like an out-of-body experience. She called her mother.

"Hello, my love. How is my granddaughter doing? You must send me more pictures of her."

"She's doing great—just got done eating, burping, and pooping. You never told me the first few poops are like tar. I thought there was something wrong with Olivia."

"Sorry, dear. I'm sure I blocked that out because it was unpleasant. Will you be heading to Washington for the new job? You did call and let them know what was going on, right?"

"Yeah, about that. Yes, I called—"

"And . . . what did the owner say?"

"They couldn't wait for me to get there and get situated with Olivia. Get this, they got Erik Gregory to take my position. I didn't even know he was a candidate."

"No."

"Yes, the snake."

"I'm sure that man is a fruit fly you can't kill. So what are you going to do? You already signed a lease agreement up there. Are you going to find something else there?"

Bethany rubbed her temple, preparing herself for her

mother's outrage. "So, they gave my apartment to some-one else."

"Oh for the love of God, Bethany. You are on the other side of the country with a new baby. Just get on a plane and come live with me until you figure it out."

"I don't have to come back and live with you. Something popped up here."

"Really, is there a restaurant needing a chef out there?"

Bethany wrinkled her nose and stared at the ceiling. Should she tell her mother the whole truth or just part of it so she wouldn't worry?

"Yes, I found a job and a place to live."

"Well, that is very resourceful of you. I knew I would rub off on you after all these years."

Bethany cleared her throat and decided on the whole truth. It was safer that way to know everything. "You know the gentleman that found me in the parking lot I told you about?"

"Yes." There was a hint of suspicion in her mother's voice.

"Cole Verbeck, he runs a ranch. He asked me to be his personal chef and to stay at his home."

Her mother sighed. "So let me get this straight: the handsome man who found you in the parking lot wants you to live with him and cook for him?"

"Yes."

"Sounds like a marriage. Are you not telling me something?"

"Oh, Mom. It's a job. And it's a roof over my head. I won't have to try to find an apartment, and then figure out how to furnish it, while also job hunting and taking care of Olivia. This way, you don't have to rearrange your life because of me."

"Are you sure you're not going to be on some missing person flier?"

"Mom!" Bethany snapped.

"Hey, things like that happen."

"I have met his sister, Emma. She's a doctor, and her husband used to be a lawyer . . . Mom, I get to live on a ranch. It feels like a dream. Dad would love it."

Her mother went quiet for a minute. "Yes, he would. You better keep my granddaughter safe."

"I will."

"You get settled and I will fly out to see you. Call me every day so I know everything is fine or I will worry and not sleep."

"I will. Love you."

"Love you too. Give Olivia a kiss for me."

Bethany blinked at the phone when her mother hung up. That went way better than anticipated. It eased some of the tension from her body to know her mother wasn't going to reach through the phone and strangle her. With that out of the way, Bethany took a nap before showering. When she walked out of the bathroom toweling off her hair, she smiled when she saw Cole there. His eyes met hers, and his gaze felt like a caress. She stifled a shiver of heat.

She offered him a smile. He tried to step toward her, but his feet seemed rooted to the floor. He managed a small nod of greeting. Bethany walked past him, brushing his arm. Struck with a blast of awareness, she sucked in a breath and quickly placed her towel in a bin in the corner of the room. When she turned around, Cole was holding a baby car seat with a bow on it.

Her hands went to her mouth. Her heart drummed against her ribs. Oh my . . . a car seat for her Olivia. It was the sweetest thing she'd ever seen.

Cole set the car seat at her feet. "This is Olivia's ride to the ranch."

She didn't quite know how to respond and threw

her arms around his neck for a hug. "Thank you. Your kindness is appreciated. I hadn't gotten any of that stuff because of the move. I knew I wouldn't have room in Dot, and I didn't want to rent a U-Haul and run everyone off the road with it. Not to mention the little bugger came early. So I thought I had more time to shop." She let go of him and gave him a smile that she hoped would convey her gratitude.

"I knew she would need one because Emma told me. Can I get your keys to Dot so I can load her onto the trailer while I wait for your release?" That made it sound like he was waiting for her to get out of jail. She gave him the keys.

"Is there somewhere we can take her to get fixed?"

He gave her a wink. "Yes. To my house."

"Cole, you don't have to fix Dot."

"I'm sure it wouldn't take long to fix, so please don't worry about it."

She sighed. "Thank you again. You're amazing."

His cheeks colored. It was the sexiest thing she'd seen. This strong, handsome guy was blushing because of her. She liked it.

The next hour was spent waiting for discharge paperwork. Yet she didn't wait in her room. She snatched Olivia and they walked to the waiting room where she watched Cole load Dot onto his car trailer. He was something to watch, to be sure. All muscle flexing in the sunlight. Two other nurses had stopped to admire him as well. When Nurse Tayler tapped her on the shoulder, Bethany jumped.

"All done. You are free to go."

"Really? Just in time." Cole was walking back into the hospital. "Just have to grab my stuff and put Olivia in the car seat."

He spotted her and strolled over. Finally, it was time

to leave, and Bethany was grateful for it.

He opened the door as he held the car seat with Olivia in it. Then climbed in and placed Olivia in the center of the bench seat and pulled out the seat belt. Olivia was wide awake and looking at Cole. Bethany couldn't help but smile at her curious face. She was alert for only being a few days old. Cole pulled the lap belt over the car seat and slipped the belt under two plastic pieces as indicated. After he fastened the belt and pushed on the seat, locking Olivia in place, he peered over his shoulder. She stared at him. When he climbed out of the truck, Bethany cleared her throat and her gaze roamed the area. Cole reached his hand out to assist her and she didn't hesitate. Bethany pressed her lips together as she took his hand. *Just breathe.*

Cole helped her onto the bench seat of the truck next to Olivia. He closed the door as gently as he could; he didn't want to startle Olivia. Then Cole placed Bethany's bag behind the driver's seat and climbed into the truck. As they were pulling away, Bethany watched the hospital grow smaller in the side mirror, and then they turned a corner and the hospital disappeared.

Chapter Nine

Cole lounged casually against the seat, his arm resting in the frame of the rolled-down window. Bethany stole a glimpse at him. The heat of the day swept in and wrestled free some of her hair from her bun. She closed her eyes and allowed the warm air, the scent of summer, and her hopes for the future to fill her completely. Bethany opened her eyes and peered down at her sleeping bundle of joy. A new adventure. *Their* adventure. Tenderly, she caressed Olivia's round cheek.

"How long are your days on the ranch?" Bethany asked, wanting to break the silence. Truth be told, she was truly interested.

Cole focused his gorgeous, amber eyes on her and she shuddered, looking away. "I'm drinking my coffee by four thirty in the morning. I'm out working by five," he said in a curious tone.

"Oh God, four thirty. That will be rough," she responded.

"What do you mean by that?"

"Well, I wanted to get up and make you breakfast before five o'clock."

"I didn't ask you to do that." Cole's brows pinched together.

"You wanted a personal chef, so let me chef it up." Cole didn't say a word, so she continued. "When do you call it a day and head back to the house?"

Cole's eyes narrowed. "When I'm done."

Bethany couldn't understand why he was being elusive. He wanted a cook, so she was going to cook.

"Well then, if you don't have a set time, I'll try and have dinner on the table by five. If I eat later than that, I feel sick to my stomach." She studied him. "Does that work for you?"

He shrugged. "Whatever you want."

"Do you work through lunch, or do you come to the house?"

This time, he didn't look at her; he sighed as he stared out the window. She watched as the wind played through his hair. Okay, it was clear now. He didn't like being pegged down. She let it go.

She fixed her eyes on the countryside as they headed to Havencrest. She hoped the townspeople were kind. The curvy roads and the high mountains were beautiful. As they drove, the road stretched out before them like a snake slithering through the rocks. After an hour, the land became flat and broad fields of tall grass bobbed and swayed with the wind.

"What do you like to eat?" she asked, breaking another silence.

"Food."

Bethany wanted to tease Cole. Having met Logan and Emma, she had a feeling they were the only source of humor this man had in his life. She was in too good a mood to let him sit there. Not today.

"Then sushi it is. I hope you like raw fish."

"The only way you're going to get your hands on some raw fish around here is to go fish for it yourself."

She smirked. He took the bait. She laughed, a smile taking over her face. "That's fine. I like to fish. Need to get a license for it."

Cole glanced at her. The beginning of a smile tugged at his lips. He did have a sense of humor after all.

"I eat anything. Peter and I take turns cooking, and Peter is definitely no cook."

"Will he be at the ranch when we get there?"

"No. He doesn't get off until later."

"Does he know about our arrangement?"

Cole straightened and stared out the window again. He didn't say anything. *Great, just great.*

Olivia slept the entire drive, and Bethany was paying the price. Her breasts were achingly full of milk. If she didn't wake up her bundle of joy soon and feed her, she was afraid she would leak through the breast pads the nurses had given her. Bethany shifted impatiently, anxious for the trip to come to an end. She was so getting on her phone to order a breast pump and other items as soon as she got the address to her new home.

Another half hour passed before Cole broke the silence. "Well, here we are, Havencrest." He slowed to make a right onto a dirt road.

Bethany didn't see much of a town before he turned. She spied a gas station and a sign that advertised camping. She was fine with that. There would be plenty of time to see the town. Right now, her breasts were asking to be unloaded, throbbing like they had a life of their own. They needed to hurry up and be there already.

The old truck bounced down the dirt road, making for a painful ride. Pine trees eclipsed the sun for what felt like miles until the rows of trees ended and she could see the horizon. Deep-green fields sprawled across the land like a patchwork quilt. Cattle roamed beyond the fields. Bethany forgot about the pain in her breasts as she took in what was going to be her new home. She couldn't have asked for more. A lovely steeple house that was painted in a light yellow came into view. What a delightful-looking home.

As they drove closer to the soft-yellow house, she noticed a dark-haired boy riding his bike in the driveway. A tall, blond man had his back to the road, but as Cole approached, the man turned and started walking to the end of the driveway. It was Emma's husband, Logan.

They finally parked. Cole sat stiffly in his seat.

"Hey, there. Headed home?" Logan asked.

Cole gave a nod. "How's Emma doing? I bet she's happy to be home."

"Sure is. Being a doctor, she sure makes a poor patient."

Cole chuckled. The sound made Bethany smile.

"She never liked being poked at, even as a kid." Cole glanced over at Bethany and gave her a half smile. Her cheeks heated under his stare.

Logan popped his head into the window. "How are you doing? How's motherhood treating you?" he asked.

"It's going, I guess. I've got nothing to compare it to, however. Olivia hasn't been complaining much."

Logan and Cole chuckled in unison.

"You're doing great."

Just then, Olivia began to stir in her car seat. Her little feet started to kick and her tiny lip poked out. She let out a wail, finally awake and demanding attention. Bethany still had to get used to her daughter's zero-to-sixty temper. It didn't take more than thirty seconds of Olivia's crying before the sensation of her milk glands clenching down responded to her cry. The next thing she knew, round, wet circles appeared through her dress.

"Oh my . . . oh my . . . I'm, uh . . . not good." She felt so embarrassed.

"We better get moving," Cole said.

"See you in an hour in the northeast field. We have to finish haying." Logan sent them off with a wave.

"How much further do we have to go?" Bethany asked, doing her best not to sound impatient, but she was becoming overwhelmed. Olivia's fussy cry had turned into a full-blown cry of distress.

"Just down the road . . . about five minutes."

Bethany bit her lip. "I'm sorry. I have to feed her. I hope you don't mind pulling over."

Without saying a word, he pulled off the side of the road and turned off the engine. Bethany took his silence as her permission to go for it.

As fast as she could, she had Olivia out of her car seat. She tossed a small blanket over her shoulder, freed one of her engorged breasts, and offered it to Olivia. Thankfully, Olivia had no problem latching on. Everything felt awkward, with Cole sitting there and staring out the window. Next thing she knew, Olivia was choking. Bethany pulled her away, and to her horror, milk sprayed Olivia in the face.

I'm drowning her. Olivia wailed once more. For the love of God, this should be easier after three days.

"I'm sorry," she said. Olivia's cries grew louder, so Bethany did the only thing she could think of. Hormones, lack of sleep, and wanting things to go well today all mounted on Bethany's shoulders. A tear ran down her face and she clenched her jaw. She wasn't a crier. She wiped the tears away quickly, hoping Cole wouldn't see them. She pressed on her breast and forced some of the milk out, relieving the pressure. Then she reattached Olivia and finally, the crying stopped. She adjusted the blanket to hide her exposed breast.

After ten minutes of feeding, Bethany readjusted and offered Olivia her other breast. She studied Cole from the corner of her eye, wondering what he was thinking. He didn't seem bothered by the delay. He stared out at the land, giving them some privacy. There was a calm steadiness to him, and she hoped some of that steeliness would rub off on her.

"Is the land out there yours?" she asked.

He nodded and pointed out the window. "From the tree line, just before the flat land that bleeds into the pastures to the mountain's ridge over there. It touches Logan's on the west side, just there. You can see a bit of fencing."

Bethany's eyes widened. That was a lot of land.

"It's beautiful," she said. She peeked under the blanket at Olivia, who was finally asleep. *Thank you.* Carefully, she wiped Olivia's mouth, pulled her bra up, and put Olivia on her shoulder. She patted her daughter's back and two small burps escaped her lips. Olivia appeared to be in a milk coma. She placed Olivia back into the car seat and strapped her in. Then Bethany readjusted herself and focused on her breathing.

"Thank you," she said.

Cole started the truck and pulled smoothly onto the dirt road.

After a short drive a tidy, white, two-story ranch house loomed on the horizon. A mix of colorful flowers framed the house, giving it a pleasant and homey feel.

"I'll give you a quick tour so you can get settled in, then I must get back to work," Cole said.

"Okay," she agreed, feeling uncertain but excited at the same time.

They parked next to a large wraparound porch. Plant pots hung every ten or so feet with an array of colorful petunias. There was a porch swing and a rocking chair next to the front door. Two large glass windows were set on either side of the front door. It reminded her of what she'd dreamt Anne Shirley's home would look like at Green Gables.

Cole unfastened the seat belt holding Olivia's car seat

and then slipped out of the truck. Bethany lifted the car seat out and did her best to cover her milk-stained dress behind Olivia's seat and blanket before climbing out of the truck to follow Cole.

"You'll stay in Emma's old room. It's on the first floor. It has a restroom, but no shower or bath. You'll have to go down the hall."

She climbed five stairs to reach the large porch. Cole held the front door open for her as she went inside.

The walls were a light tan with white trim, and the hardwood floors were polished to a high shine. There were pictures of old barns hanging on the walls. To her right was a room with a stiff-looking sofa and a shiny, oak coffee table. She didn't get a good look because Cole was already moving, leading her past the formal dining room on her left. A good-sized crystal chandelier hung above a dark, sturdy table. Eight chairs were lined up perfectly around it.

Bethany was awestruck at the elegance of it all and the comfort it brought. She didn't realize just how lucky she was until now.

Next, they moved down a narrow hall to emerge into a room painted in a soft, sky blue. The room was larger than she'd expected. She could easily fit a crib and changing table. She was going to have to order all her baby stuff she'd been holding out on until after the move. But for now, Olivia could sleep with her in the queen-size bed that was close to the outer wall near a window. She could see for miles. It was a breathtaking view. There were dark-blue nightstands on each side of the bed and a large matching dresser with a mirror on the adjacent wall. Next to the bathroom was a large, walk-in closet.

"You can do what you want with the room. We could paint it, some type of mural for Olivia. We can change anything you want."

"Really? That's sweet of you. But it looks lovely as it is."

Cole's eyes were bright with approval. She liked that look on him.

Cole made his way back down the hall, past the formal dining room, and through a swinging door. Bethany tried to keep up with his long-legged strides.

They emerged into the kitchen. An old, worn-out table was set off to the right. Counter lined the two walls forming an L, and a large island with the sink dominated the room. Polished oak cabinets were everywhere. This was some kitchen. There was plenty of counter space for pots and pans, cutting boards, and other kitchen items. A zing of anticipation caused her smile to widen in approval.

Cole pointed to two doors at the back of the kitchen. "The door on the right is the laundry and pantry room, and the door to the left takes you out back. Upstairs is only mine and Peter's rooms and another bathroom. I hope it is okay, but I have to go finish up some work. Please feel free to look around. I won't be back until around five or six. I have a lot of catching up to do."

Suddenly, all pleasure left her. She knew he was behind on his work because of her, though he didn't say it. She would make it up to him with a dinner that would knock his socks off.

"I'll unload the car from the trailer tomorrow if that works for you and have a look at it. I'll grab your bags and boxes out of it and set them on your bed."

"Thanks."

Cole walked out, leaving her alone. She inspected the space.

Once the bags and boxes were on the bed, Cole spun on his heels and hightailed it out of the house. He didn't look back, not from the porch, not from the barn, not from the east field. He didn't look back until he was safely mounted on his tractor and back in his element.

He ran a hand through his hair. Bethany's tears in the truck rocketed him to the past. He thought of his mother and her tear-stained cheeks after Joel's death. He remembered her trying to comfort him, Peter, and a small crying Emma. It opened an old wound best forgotten. He tried to harden himself against the pain and leave the past where it belonged. But there was something about Bethany that made him feel things, as if they were somehow connected.

His mood grew dark. He began to rethink his job offer. He didn't want to deal with old emotions. He had faced many of the old pains when Logan and he reconciled, but it was still hard to leave the past in the past from time to time.

Cole stretched, trying to unknot the tension that was building in his chest and shake off the feelings. He couldn't withdraw his offer, even if it caused him to struggle. A job offer was as good as a promise. And he was a man who kept his promises.

Just as he was about to fire up his tractor and get to work, Logan came driving toward him and pulled up alongside the tractor.

"You okay?" Logan asked.

"Why wouldn't I be?" Cole replied in his usual grumpy voice, not liking how Logan was staring at him. "I have work to do. And if I recall, aren't you supposed to be herding the cattle out of the west fields to take them toward the slope of the north ridge?"

"Max is saddling the horses. Emma wanted me to come check on you, is all. She heard Olivia crying when you drove off."

I'm not home ten minutes and Emma is sending out spies. It chafed his pride. He would show his little sister that he could be tolerant to change. He didn't have to be a hermit. He could adapt.

"Tell Emma that I'm a big boy, and I have my big-boy pants on. Everything is fine."

A smile split Logan's face and he laughed. "It would be more fun if you told her that yourself."

"I have work to do, and so do you."

"I'm going, I'm going. Emma and I will swing by tomorrow to see how Bethany is settling in."

"Do that," Cole said, wanting Logan out of his hair so he could get his work done. He wanted to forget the regretful expression on Bethany's face when she'd cried in front of him. He should have comforted her; should have told her everything was going to be okay. But he didn't, and he hated himself for it.

Logan waved as his truck crept away from his tractor. Cole revved up the tractor and let the noise of the engine drown out every other sound around him. The smell of diesel saturated the air. He breathed in the familiar scent and put the tractor into gear. Pushing his concerns for the future aside, he got to work. Things needed to get done.

Chapter Ten

Bethany stood near the kitchen window holding Olivia, swaying back and forth, rocking her daughter to sleep. Cole had been gone about two hours, and she'd spent that time feeding her fussy baby and putting away some of her items into the closet and dresser. Now that Olivia was almost asleep, Bethany was able to take a few deep breaths and get a sense of her surroundings. It was all so surreal and exhilarating.

She recalled her outburst during their drive home. Her cheeks flamed with the memory. "Poor Cole." She could laugh about it now that she'd managed to pull herself together. But she had to admit she was a bit of a mess.

Looking out the window, she could see the hay fields, some fat cattle grazing, and the sunlight shining on the lush, beautiful land. It seemed like the house was at a perfect vantage point. Like a sentinel watching over the vast, open spaces. She wondered if Cole's family built the house.

Olivia let out a cry, forcing Bethany to turn her attention back to her daughter. Was she still hungry? Bethany winced at the thought of breastfeeding Olivia again. She sighed and sat at the kitchen table to nurse her. Olivia greedily latched onto her, feeding to her heart's delight. Bethany wasn't so sure about this breastfeeding business. After having her fill, Olivia dozed off again.

In the distance, she saw Cole on a tractor far out in the field. He looked all-American, sitting on his metal steed. She giggled but sobered up when the doubts washed over her. *Lord, please let everything work out.* She raked her eyes around the large kitchen, wondering where to start.

The kitchen was simple, clean, but held a feeling of loneliness. She could fill it with good-smelling and tasty food.

Bethany tried not to panic when she pulled the garlic bread out of the oven and spotted a black rim around it. Her first day on the job and she was going to get herself fired. She cursed under her breath as she placed the tray onto the hot pad. Why did every oven have to be moody? It was six thirty. Thank the stars, Cole wasn't home yet.

She rushed over to the large window and opened it, fanning the smoky air out of the kitchen with her towel. After a few minutes, she rummaged for a knife and cut away the burnt area, then sliced the bread. She threw the ruined parts away. On the table, Olivia slept in her car seat, oblivious to the goings-on around her.

Bethany straightened and rubbed a hand in the small of her back and massaged her neck. She was tired, but she pushed on, setting the table with plates, utensils, and glasses. She laid the dish of spaghetti, the not-so-pretty garlic bread, and the impromptu salad she'd put together onto the table. Then she went to the fridge and retrieved the pitcher of sun tea she had made earlier. It wasn't a gourmet meal. She'd worked with what she found on the fly.

The front screen door squeaked open and slammed shut.

She smoothed her clean, pink dress and brushed the back of her hand over her hair. Cole's frame appeared in the kitchen doorway, covered in dust and pieces of hay.

He hesitated.

"I hope you don't mind eating at the kitchen table. I didn't know if it was okay to use the formal dining room," Bethany said with a warm smile.

Cole glanced at the table. "It's fine. I didn't expect you to cook tonight. I thought you would be resting."

It was sweet of him to be concerned for her. Her smile widened.

"We both have to eat, right?" She walked over to the head of the table and pulled out a chair for him. "Please have a seat while everything is still hot."

Cole's lips pressed together. "I'll go clean up."

"Great," she said.

੭♥ਏ

Cole was amazed and shaken at the sight that met him when he came home. Bethany had cooked dinner. Determination shone in her face with a steadfast glow. However, beneath the glow, he could see the weariness in her smile. But she had stuck to their agreement. He didn't know what to say to her.

He walked into the bathroom and flicked the light on. He turned on the faucet to wash his hands. The water turned brown the moment his hands touched it. When he caught his reflection in the mirror, he scowled with dismay. His face was a mask of dirt. He washed his face and neck, then looked at himself a second time. It wasn't pretty, but that was as good as it was going to get.

As Cole toweled his face and hands, his jaw clenched at the realization that Bethany was pushing herself because of him. The thought made him uncomfortable. When he went back into the kitchen, Bethany was sitting in the chair next to his. She spooned spaghetti onto his plate. He strolled over and took the spoon from her. She would not put food on his plate as if he were a child.

"Thank you, but I can fix my plate."

Bethany's cheeks colored and her gaze left him. She nodded her head. The silence lengthened between them, making him grow even more uncomfortable. He studied her out of the corner of his eye. She poked at her food for a minute and finally decided to take a bite.

Cole examined the table. There was a nice-looking salad, garlic bread, and delicious-smelling spaghetti. His mouth watered. He couldn't remember the last time he had sat down at this table and actually had a complete meal.

"Everything looks delicious and smells wonderful."

Bethany's eyes glowed. "Thank you. It's the best I could do with what you had."

Cole pressed his lips. "Make a list of groceries you'd like to have in the house and I'll get them for you tomorrow."

"No, you have work. I can do it. If I can use your truck?"

"The keys are always by the front door. Take them anytime." Cole twisted his fork into a mound of noodles, then placed the noodles onto a piece of garlic bread and took a bite. There was a blast of flavor.

"Mmm . . . this is good. What did you do?"

"There are chunks of sausages and a little of this and that." Bethany took another bite of her food. She relaxed a little. Cole liked her when she was relaxed and smiling.

"How was work?" she asked, glancing at Olivia in the corner.

It felt odd to have someone to talk to at the end of the day. Peter normally didn't get home until after Cole was in bed. Cole was a solitary man. He worked his ranch. It made him happy. But to be here like this with her, it showed what he was missing.

"There are not enough hours in the day. I have a lot of

work to do tomorrow."

"Like what?" Bethany asked. "Is there anything I can help with?"

Cole smiled. He found her endearing. "No. If you can make the house presentable and keep my belly full, I couldn't ask for more than that."

Bethany's gaze found him, and he tried to memorize all of her.

"I think I can handle that," Bethany replied with sparkling eyes.

Cole shifted in his seat and went back to enjoying his dinner.

Chapter Eleven

The bed was soft and comfortable. Bethany lay on her back and stared at the ceiling. Olivia stirred and Bethany wanted to cry. She was exhausted, and Olivia waking would mean having to feed her and rock her back to sleep, only to do it all over again in another hour or two.

Just then, she heard footsteps down the hallway, and then the door flew open. Bethany froze. A man marched over to the side of the bed, mumbling about the light being on and went to turn the light on the nightstand off. The man had a sharp, smooth jawline and cropped, black hair, with shoulders just as wide as Cole's. He jumped back in alarm when she moved on the bed, having just noticed her. *This must be Peter.* Olivia broke into a cry.

"Whoa," he said. "Who the hell are you?"

"I'm Bethany . . . and this is my daughter, Olivia. C-Cole said—"

"No kidding. Why are you in my house? Is my brother living a double life I don't know about?" Baffled, he stomped out of the room and down the hall.

It was clear Cole hadn't told him about her and Cole's working arrangement. Why hadn't he told him?

Peter's voice carried down the hall. "Why is there a woman and a crying baby in our house?"

Bethany got out of bed. She picked up Olivia and held her close, rocking her back and forth. She pressed her breast into the babe's mouth and it was silent once again.

A few moments later, Peter's muffled voice carried down the hall: "Who is she?"

Bethany walked over to the door and listened to the conversation.

"Her name is Bethany Heart. She's going to be staying here with her daughter. I hired her to be a cook."

"Wait, did you just say cook, and you didn't bother to run it by me?"

She patted Olivia softly on the back as she stole glances down the hall. Cole stood before Peter, bare-chested, wearing bright-yellow Sponge Bob pajama bottoms. She couldn't believe it. She stifled her giggles. It was hilarious seeing a tough, strong man like Cole in Sponge Bob pajamas. Cole was an onion, and she was only too eager to peel back his layers.

In the dark, the two men resembled one another. Cole, however, had slightly wider shoulders, no doubt due to all the physical labor.

"I have to get some sleep. I can't believe you didn't bother to tell me. I am a sheriff, for Christ's sake," Peter snapped. "I thought she was an intruder!"

"I don't know what you're complaining about. You come rolling into the house at random hours of the night . . . that is, if you come home at all. How can I run it by you when you're never home?" Cole glared at his brother.

"Well, that's why Edison invented the phone, so you could call me. I don't have to be here physically."

Cole growled. "I didn't plan this a month in advance. Now you know. I figured it wouldn't be a big deal to you. She's going to be running this house. So get used to the idea of a woman floating around—and a baby. I'm going to bed. Some people have real work in the morning. If you want to talk, tomorrow is soon enough."

A woman floating around? What the heck did that

mean? Was that really how Cole saw her, too delicate to be of real use? Olivia burped in Bethany's ear. She stepped out of view and laid Olivia onto the bed. Bethany scowled at her daughter, but it was meant for Cole. Tomorrow she would show him what she could do . . . and Peter too.

Chapter Twelve

The alarm rang in his ear. Morning was here too soon after a long, sleepless night. Every time Cole closed his eyes, golden-blonde hair and dark-chocolate eyes surfaced, taunting him. Those eyes produced a steady pulling in his chest. Unable to resist the urge a second longer, Cole dressed and made his way down the stairs. In no time, he stood before Bethany's bedroom door. Seeing that it was open a crack, he knocked softly and entered.

The room was gray with the morning sun. Bethany's golden hair was spread around her as she curled around Olivia protectively. They were both sleeping. Bethany seemed like a delicate dream—a dream he wanted. He wanted to see her smile at him as she had done at dinner the night before. It caused a stirring within him that he never experienced before. Duty drove him, and his focus had always been the farm and his family. But a new need seemed to divert his focus. This need to please her, to make sure she was happy, choked him. Cole frowned to himself. *I want more from myself and for myself. I want something better.*

Cole leaned against the doorframe with his hands in his pockets. There had to be something he could do to show her that her happiness mattered to him. But what? Then, it came to him. A crib for Olivia. Sure, he could buy her one, but he wanted it to be more than a crib he hastily picked out at the store. He wanted it to be a symbol of something more.

ᕙᕗ♥ᕗᕙ

Morning light filled Bethany's room. She blinked her eyes slowly as the crow of a rooster filled the air. She had always wanted to live on a farm or a ranch. She felt blissfully at peace. She couldn't have asked for a more beautiful sight to wake up to as she peered out her window.

Olivia had slept the rest of the evening, and for that Bethany was thankful. It was only four hours of sleep, but it was a start. Quietly, she roused Olivia for a feeding and a diaper change. She was getting the hang of anticipating her daughter's needs, and it was reassuring she wasn't going to screw it all up.

Changed and with a full belly, Olivia just went right back to sleep. Bethany placed her in the car seat and hurried into the kitchen to make Cole and Peter some breakfast, but to her surprise, coffee was made, and bags of groceries covered the table.

Bethany set Olivia in the corner of the room and walked over to the table. She peered into one of the bags and saw bananas, grapes, and green apples. The thought of apple pie popped into her mind. She could almost smell it. She closed the bag and hurried over to the back window. Cole was already out in the field, sitting high on his tractor. She sighed dreamily. He was something. She spun around and wondered if Peter was still here. Slowly she crept up the stairs and listened to what was behind one of the two doors in the hallway. She could hear snoring coming from inside. This must be Peter's room.

Bethany would win Peter over with her food. She carefully made her way down the stairs and back into the kitchen. As fast as she could, she put the groceries away, which proved to be somewhat of a challenge. She didn't know where everything went, so she started her own system of organization. It was her kitchen now anyway. Bethany worked it out and had all the items in their place. She fired up the stove, mixing together an egg, cheese, diced tomatoes, and chunks of ham for an omelet. She paired it with fluffy pancakes. This would be tasty, she thought, with strawberries. It would fill the house with a delicious smell that was sure to rouse Peter. His curiosity would lead him right to her. She hoped that perhaps they could be properly introduced over some delicious food. She made fresh coffee. Nothing was better than the smell of freshly brewed coffee in the morning.

Twenty minutes later, Bethany caught a set of honey-golden eyes staring curiously at her. She pulled in a breath and smiled softly.

"Good morning. I hope you're hungry."

Peter stepped into the kitchen in his uniform. He held a striking resemblance to Cole. His head tipped to the side as he studied her.

"Please have a seat. I'll fix your plate."

He didn't move.

Suddenly, there was a hot ball in the pit of her stomach. She held her smile and prayed that he would soon come to a conclusion about her so the awkwardness filling the room would stop choking her.

His eyes brightened. "So what's on the menu? I could smell breakfast from my room," Peter said, strolling over to the stove.

"Pancakes and an omelet," she answered.

Peter wrinkled his nose, and Bethany's heart thumped hard in her ears.

"I'll take the omelet but will pass on the pancakes."

Bethany's smile fell. "What's wrong with pancakes?" she asked. "Do they look funny? Are they not brown enough?"

"Nothing is wrong with the pancakes. It's what you got on top of them."

"The strawberries?"

"Yes, ma'am. I'm allergic to them." Peter went to the table. As he pulled out a chair, there was a loud grating noise. Olivia began to fuss.

Before Bethany could get to her daughter, Peter blocked her path. He walked over to the car seat and crouched down. "Hey there, sweetie, why so fussy? You must be the stinker I heard last night," Peter said. He looked at Bethany. "Can I hold her?"

Bethany eyed him. It wasn't like she could tell him no. He did have a niece and a nephew. Maybe he was good with kids. "Sure," she said.

Peter held Olivia up, examined her, and then placed her near his shoulder, walking with her back to his seat.

Bethany wiped her hands on the dish towel she'd tied around her waist to cover her cutoff shorts. Olivia stopped fussing and was now googling at the man who had disturbed her sleep.

"What's her name?"

"Olivia." Bethany scooped up the omelet and placed it on the plate next to the stove. She hurried over and set the plate in front of Peter.

"I can take her so you can eat. Would you like me to make you some fresh pancakes minus the strawberries?"

"She's fine. I'm comfortable with kids. Don't worry about the pancakes. I'm fine with the omelet," Peter said with a wink. Bethany took that as a good sign.

A knock came from the front door followed by the smacking sound of the screen against the wall. Bethany heard quick feet. Next, a dark-haired boy skipped into the kitchen.

"Look, there's a little brat now," Peter said playfully.

He scooted his chair out and gathered the little boy up in his other arm for a one-armed hug. "How's my most favorite nephew?"

"Good."

"Joel, you get your butt back over here," a familiar voice said. Then Emma walked into the room. Her raven hair was in a loose bun and she wore a light-green dress. "We let ourselves in, as is our custom. Hope that's okay? Oh my, I smell pancakes," she said. A look of pure delight crossed her face as her eyes caught sight of the stack of pancakes.

Happiness bubbled through Bethany. She so enjoyed Emma's company.

Emma carted in a pink car seat and placed her sleeping bundle of joy next to Olivia's.

"Oh yum, can I have some pancakes? I'm starving. I fed Joel but was too tired to feed myself."

"Please do," Bethany said, handing Emma the plate she'd fixed for Peter. "Peter just informed me of his strawberry allergy."

"Yeah, he's allergic to almost everything." Emma took a seat at the table.

Bethany inwardly cursed. How was she going to win him over if she killed him? She rubbed the stress out of her neck and pulled at her white T-shirt. She quickly strolled over to get some coffee cups and poured coffee for everyone. Then she took a seat at the table.

Bethany surveyed the scene before her. Peter whispered in his nephew's ear in between bites of egg while cradling Olivia. Emma sipped her coffee and moaned in delight over her pancakes. Bethany's heart felt light. She'd always wondered what it would be like to be part of a big family. Being an only child has its pros and its cons. Loneliness was definitely a con. Being alone made her hungry for the affection only a big family could give.

She soaked up the moment.

"How are you feeling? I'm exhausted. How did you have the energy to get up and fix breakfast?" Emma pointed at Peter. "For him of all people?"

"I'm tired, but Olivia only woke up once. It seems she likes sleep better than food."

Emma's eyes widened and her jaw dropped. "Olivia only woke up once? I'm so jealous of you right now. Abbie wakes up screaming every two hours. I haven't gotten any sleep in days."

Bethany felt sorry for her, but she smiled at Emma's theatrics. "As for the cooking, it is what I do. Although, I'm going to have to get up earlier if I want to cook for Cole in the morning. He was already out in the fields by the time I got up."

"And that's my brother," Peter said, taking the last bite of egg. "All work. He wouldn't know a good time if it fell in his lap."

Emma lifted a single brow. "And the good times never seem to leave yours."

Peter leaned back, patting Olivia's back softly, who was falling asleep once again. Bethany couldn't believe how natural it seemed to him.

"Listen, Emma, you can't fault a man for wanting more from life than just breaking his back."

"Ha. Breaking your back. You haven't helped Logan and Cole for months. You remember that you own part of this ranch? If you want out, you need to talk to Cole. Be honest."

Bethany felt tension spring into the room. She took a sip of her coffee and then glanced at Peter, who was glaring at his sister. Emma didn't seem to be intimidated. Bethany admired her strength.

"Emma, it's not like I'm not doing anything. I'm a sheriff, and the job requires a great deal of my time. I help when I can. I don't want to get into this now."

Bethany stood and leaned over the table with her hands outstretched toward Peter. "I'll take her. She needs to eat. Thank you for holding her."

Peter turned his hard stare away from his sister. When his gaze found Bethany's, his features softened and he half smiled. He handed the baby to her. "So how did you get Cole to hire you? He never asks for help."

Bethany felt uncomfortable. "I met Cole under unusual circumstances. I was on my way to Washington for a new job, but Olivia showed up earlier than planned. My almost-new employer found someone else because I was delayed in getting there. Cole asked me to stay here with him and cook. I have been wanting to put together new recipes and try them out. With Olivia, this is the perfect arrangement. Cole has been a sweetheart, my knight in shining armor."

Peter chuckled while Emma said nothing. However, there was a look of hopefulness in her expression that Bethany didn't understand.

"Are we talking about Cole or someone else?" Peter asked.

Emma punched Peter in the shoulder. "Cole can be nice . . . sometimes."

Peter laughed even harder. He messed up his nephew's dark hair and lifted him off his knee. "Sorry, little man, but I have to go to work."

"I want a ride!" cried Joel.

"Not today."

Joel stuck out his lip, tipped his head to the side, and batted long, dark lashes at his uncle. "Please? I want to talk on the speaker and do the siren."

Peter rolled his eyes and then took Joel's hand. "Only down the road and back, okay?"

"Yay!" Joel took off for the door.

Bethany smiled. Before Peter walked away from the table, he held out a hand. "Peter Verbeck. Pleased to meet—"

Bethany took his hand. "Bethany Heart."

Peter smiled. "It's a real pleasure, Bethany. Thank you for the unexpected and tasty breakfast," he said, and he walked out.

Emma held up her fork; a piece of pancake clung to the end, syrup dripping off it. "Don't listen to him. Cole can be very sweet when he wants to be. He just never has a reason to be to Peter. Peter irritates him to death."

"Do you mind if I go and feed Olivia? It will only be fifteen minutes or so."

"Don't mind me. Is it okay if I fix another pancake for myself?"

"Please do. It's your brother's food. The batter will only go to waste."

Chapter Thirteen

After Cole finished turning the hay, he parked the tractor and walked into his woodshop that was attached to the barn that housed all his heavy equipment. He inhaled the thick scent of pine. He ran his hand over the pile of wood he'd brought from town this morning after getting groceries for Bethany. He hoped the groceries had everything she would need. He knew he should have let her go and do it, or at least waited until she made a list, but he wanted to get the wood for the crib.

Cole dusted off a notepad from his workbench and reached for a pencil. Pulling a piece of paper from his back pocket, he looked at the dimensions he wrote down earlier for a toddler mattress. He transferred the dimensions into the notebook and began to sketch simple, classic lines. It had been a while since he'd built anything, and he wanted this to have a hint of something special.

The hours passed and the sky grew dark. It wasn't until he had to squint to see his pencil marks on the wood that he turned his gaze to the wide-open door. He had done it again. His watch said it was eight thirty. He had been late for dinner two nights in a row.

Cole wanted to put his tools away before heading to the house, but the thought of Bethany waiting for him made him put it off until tomorrow. He was caught between habit and guilt. He didn't like leaving things unfinished. This was new, having to answer to someone else.

As he ambled into the kitchen, Cole was met with silence. He swept his eyes around, hoping to see Bethany, but she wasn't there. His gaze landed on the table and the nicely wrapped plate of food. He felt like such a jerk.

He went to the sink and washed his hands. When he sat down at the table and surveyed his meal, he felt even more like a jerk. There was a nicely cooked steak, mashed potatoes with gravy drizzled over it, and peas and carrots. Beside it was a smaller plate with a buttered biscuit. His mouth watered. Cole pulled off the plastic wrap. He was about to get up to grab some silverware when he noticed a set tucked into the napkin next to the plate.

So this was what it felt like to have someone take care of you. A strange feeling crept up Cole's spine, causing him to stiffen. He could vaguely recall his mother tending to him when he was about seven, though not much past that. Being the oldest, he was usually the one looking after his siblings when his mother worked on the ranch. He was his father's helper in most things. Work was where Cole found his value—and his joy. A hard day's work made him feel good in a way Peter didn't understand. He tried to relax and enjoy this meal from Bethany. Bethany was an indulgence that he didn't feel guilty about. He thought he would; guilt tried to settle on him, but he easily brushed it away.

Cole cut a piece of the steak, examining it. He sniffed the meat and took a bite. It melted in his mouth. He cut another piece and dipped it into the gravy. The gravy was so creamy and the potatoes so soft. He hadn't had food this tasty in forever. On a good night, he would cook hamburgers occasionally, or bratwurst, and add some canned beans or chips. Peter would cook now and then, but most of the time it wasn't eatable because it was usually burnt.

Cole chewed his food slowly, in ecstasy. Dear God, Bethany could really cook.

As he savored his dinner, he looked around the kitchen. It was spotless, and on the center of the table sat one of his mother's crystal bowls resting on a lace doily. How could he have missed that? He noticed picture frames hanging on the walls and he exploded to his feet, knocking over the chair. Fork in hand, he marched over to the wall. The pictures were from his youth. A photo of Cole, Peter, and Joel with their arms draped over each other's shoulders, and Emma sitting in Joel's lap. A photo of his parents on their wedding day, and another of his mother holding Cole on her hip when he was a baby.

He lifted his fist to knock them away. He couldn't look at his mother. She'd left them. Left Emma when she was only six, when Peter was fourteen, when Cole was sixteen. It was a time in his life when he should have been playing sports and enjoying high school and girls. But instead he had to raise Emma, the only girl of the bunch, who really needed her mother. It wasn't enough that they'd all lost their brother, but to also lose a mother seemed cruel and unfair.

His father had taken every picture of his mother down after she'd run off because she was too depressed over Joel's death to stay and care for the rest of her family. Rage strangled his every thought. His pulse hammered and his breathing labored. Memories that were safely locked away came rushing back and he was powerless to stop them. He lowered his fist and dropped the fork, then leaned against the wall for support. Anger masked the grief and sorrow that assaulted him. His life was filled with emotional pain. Building a wall against it had been his only saving grace.

Bethany heard a noise coming from the kitchen. Olivia was sleeping, so she quietly went to see if Cole had arrived. She tiptoed down the hall, her hand skimming the wall. She moved past the formal dining room to the kitchen. To her surprise, Cole had his hands on the wall. He was gazing at the pictures Emma had found in the attic earlier in the day. Emma had cried when she found them. Bethany sensed there was a story there, but she didn't think it was the right time to ask. She walked closer, wanting to be near him.

"Cole, are you okay?" she asked.

At his silence, she continued. "Do you like the photos? Emma found them in the attic. She didn't want them hidden away."

"They should have stayed where they were," Cole replied sharply. His eyes were as cold as ice. Bethany shuddered from the chill. She took a step back. There was definitely a story there.

"I'm sorry, Emma said it would be good for you to remember the good times." The words were acid in her mouth and she instantly regretted saying them.

"If I wanted to see these pictures, I would have made a place for them already," Cole snapped.

Bethany's heart sank. Clearly, she had gotten caught in between something she didn't understand. "I'm sorry, Cole. I can take them down. Emma insisted they go up."

His anger dissolved with the seconds that passed between them. He pushed away from the wall and moved past her. He gently placed his plate into the sink.

Bethany couldn't take her eyes off him. He turned his back on her and her throat closed. He was hurting, and she was hurting for him.

Cole stopped before leaving the room. "The food was excellent. I think that was the best steak I ever had. Thank you for leaving out the plate for me. I'll try harder to be on time for supper tomorrow."

Bethany's mouth fell open. "It's okay. I don't mind waiting up for you. You said you wanted someone to talk to, some company."

Cole nodded and left the room. She could do nothing more but watch him go.

Chapter Fourteen

Bethany didn't know why Olivia was so upset. She wouldn't stop crying. She paced the bedroom, trying to calm her fussy daughter. She had been changed, fed, but still refused to sleep. She glanced at the alarm clock beside the bed and rolled her eyes. It was two in the morning, and she was pretty sure Olivia had woken everyone up. Maybe some fresh air would help. She hustled out to the front porch with Olivia kicking and screaming.

The cool morning air touched Bethany's cheeks in a soft caress. She walked the porch, bouncing Olivia in her arms. The air seemed to calm her, but she was still unhappy. Olivia's bottom lip pushed out as her face scrunched up.

"I know, I know. I'm doing it wrong. I wish you were big enough to tell me what the problem is. Please don't cry."

Bethany started to cry, feeling like a failure. She thought about calling her mom, but she didn't want to worry her at this hour.

"It's okay," she cooed, but Olivia continued to cry with her. What kind of mother was she if she couldn't get her daughter to calm down? *Seriously, I get a big, fat F.* She'd always wanted to be a mother, and when she found out that she was pregnant, she walked around with a smile on her face for an entire week. That was until she had to figure out how to tell William. She wondered if he would have grinned like the fool he was and been excited or if he would have frowned and cursed her. She would never know, and it hurt a little that he wasn't here to see his daughter. Maybe he wouldn't have even wanted Olivia. She sighed and wiped a tear away.

The front door creaked opened. Cole's dark eyebrows slanted in a frown at her.

"Everything okay?" he asked, stepping onto the porch. His chest was bare, and his pajama pants had the Tasmanian Devil on them.

A smile pulled at the corners of her mouth and her heart hammered. "I can't get her to stop fussing. I'm sorry she woke you up."

Cole closed the distance between them in two strides. He gazed down at Bethany's fussing bundle. "Don't worry about it. I couldn't sleep anyway. Can I take her?" he asked in a soft voice.

"Yes." Bethany held the irritable little person out to him, glad for some help and a little breather.

Cole gingerly cradled Olivia in his arms. He walked over to the porch swing with Bethany following close behind. He sat down and placed Olivia in his lap. Bethany stood off to the side, silently watching.

"Sit," he said.

With the moon shining off Cole's smooth skin and tight muscles, Bethany felt wrapped in invisible warmth. He was a definite turn-on. There was something about his hilarious pajamas that made her want to sit in his lap. Instead, she sat down beside him on the swing.

Cole took Olivia's little feet and worked them like she was pedaling a bike. Olivia's face scrunched up, as if she was in great pain. Bethany reached out to take Olivia from him, but he blocked her.

"Watch. Give it a minute. I'm not pushing hard," he

said.

"She doesn't look comfortable."

"Would you be comfortable if your stomach was full of gas?"

As if on cue, Olivia farted. Cole continued to work her little legs. She let out another fart, and her face finally relaxed.

Bethany let out a laugh. "Poor thing. That was a lot of air."

Cole chuckled. She could hear the smile in his tone. It affected her more than she'd like to admit.

"I think she'll be okay now," he said.

"How did you know to do that?" she asked. There was so much she didn't know, and she felt lost.

He looked at her and smirked. "Honestly, I watched Emma do it the other day and Abbie let out a huge fart." They both laughed. "I'm winging it."

Cole placed Olivia on his shoulder, holding her in place with one hand. He pushed the swing back and forth with his long legs. Bethany leaned back and soaked up the heat that radiated off him. This was the closest she'd been to him in days, and she totally wanted to scoot closer.

They sat in the rays of the moonlight cloaked in silence. A sigh of contentment escaped her. She couldn't remember a time she had felt more at peace. She closed her eyes, dreaming of what it would be like to be held by Cole. It was a naughty thought, but she had it all the same and was okay with it. He was such an interesting man. Kind, thoughtful, hardworking, and so much more.

"I want to apologize for earlier. I shouldn't have left you like that," Cole said, interrupting her fantasy.

She wasn't expecting an apology. Wanting to reassure him, Bethany gently placed her hand on his forearm. The muscles beneath her fingers flexed. She softly squeezed them.

"You don't have to apologize. They're just pictures. I will take them down."

"They are more than pictures. My past isn't something I like to talk about. It is dark and painful. Those are a reminder of the pain."

The sharp planes of his face, those eyes, and that body . . . he was a striking man. There was strength in him.

"I understand. We all have a past. We all have pain. I hope one day you will trust me to understand your story."

He slowly pulled Olivia off his shoulder and placed her in Bethany's arms. She smiled at him, thankful for his help. "You're good with Olivia, whether you admit it or not." After her hummingbird heartbeat slowed, she pulled her gaze from Cole and looked at her daughter. She was finally asleep. Bethany saw this as her cue . . . it was time for bed. She started to get up, but Cole's strong fingers wrapped around her arm, keeping her in place. Her body ached for his touch, so she rested her hand on top of his. Pulling in a breath, she closed her eyes while caressing his fingers. It wasn't enough. Tenderly, she took his hand and placed it on her warm cheek. When she looked up, she saw that his eyes were glowing with a savage inner fire.

She held her breath. His fingers cupped her cheek. She kept her eyes locked on his, wanting this moment to last for as long as it could. Cole's hard body inched closer and pressed against her side. The pad of his thumb caressed her skin, and her desire strangled her senses. Every caress from his fingers was a message of something more. The sound of his deep breathing made her core tighten. His scent of hay and soap caused something to flare in her chest, burning hot and hungry.

Cole was a breath away. Was he going to kiss her? She nuzzled his hand encouragingly. His thumb ran over her bottom lip thoughtfully. She couldn't wait any longer.

She leaned forward and pressed her lips to his. The instant their lips met, Bethany was overwhelmed with desire. Cole hesitated for a second. He cupped her face with his large hands and kissed her deeply. His tongue glided over hers in a seductive dance. The kiss sent the pit of her stomach into a wild swirl. *Oh yes.*

His hands gently circled her waist, pulling her closer to him. He was careful not to disturb Olivia. Her core burned. She ran a hand up his chest, around his neck, and into his hair. He moaned against her lips. Did he want her as much as she wanted him? Her hunger grew. Her lips moved over his, tasting him . . . wanting more. Bethany's emotions were a raging storm. She was losing control. She pulled him closer but couldn't. Cole gently pulled away. She blinked at him in the moonlight as the fog of desire cleared from her mind. *Oh shit.*

"We should slow down some," Cole said in a hoarse voice.

She didn't want to stop. She leaned forward for another kiss, but Cole got up and walked to the front door.

"I'll see you in the morning."

Heat rushed to Bethany's cheeks, and not in a good way. "Yes, in the morning," she said, embarrassed. *Damnit.*

She watched Cole disappear inside the house. Bethany's hand went up to her flaming cheeks and her fingers touched her lips. What was she thinking? Kissing her boss? A sexy, beautiful boss that she wanted to lick every inch of. Shit, she was losing her mind. She would blame it on the hormone imbalance and being sleep-deprived. That had to be it. *Yeah, right!* It was because he was sexy as hell and so damn sweet in his grumpy way. She could wait a lifetime and never find another Cole Verbeck. She just hoped she didn't freak him out too much with the touching and the kissing.

Bethany got up and made her way back toward her room. All she wanted to do was hide. She was the mother of a daughter who was almost two weeks old. Shame washed over her as she closed the bedroom door and climbed into bed with the sleeping Olivia. *I'm an idiot.*

Cole stood at the top of the stairs, hidden in the shadows. His blood was rushing through his veins hard and fast. His body was rigid with need. He patiently waited for Bethany to emerge. When the door opened and she entered the house, he studied her closely. She glowed. He breathed a sigh of relief. He had been on the edge, almost forgetting about Olivia sleeping between them. He ran a hand through his hair. What was he doing getting involved with Bethany on such an intimate level? She had kissed him, right? But those lips, the way they moved over his . . . dear God Almighty, he wanted to feel them again.

After he heard the door to Bethany's room close he headed straight for the shower, even though he knew it wouldn't tame his desire. Maybe if he had more experience in this area, he wouldn't feel so clumsy.

The next morning, Cole was pleasantly surprised to find Bethany in the kitchen. There were biscuits and gravy waiting on a plate for him. She beamed at him and continued to buzz around the room. He searched for Olivia, expecting to find her in a corner, but she wasn't around.

"Where's Olivia?"

"She's still sleeping. I wanted to make sure you got fed before you started working. Breakfast is the most important meal of the day."

She rose on her tippy-toes as she tried to place the

flour onto the shelf in the cupboard. He stepped up behind her, wanting to be near her if only for a moment. He pushed the flour further back on the shelf. She froze when his fingers touched hers. She leaned into him. Relief flooded into him, relaxing his tense muscles.

"Thank you," she said, turning around, her body rubbing against his. His groin hardened as her hips grazed it. His eyes found hers. He watched as flickers of emotion played across them. He felt a shiver ripple through her. She wanted him as much as he wanted her. All the desire that was stirred up in their last encounter came rushing back.

"Thank you for making me breakfast. I know you're tired." He didn't move as they spoke, not allowing her to get away. Color flooded her cheeks. He took her chin gently.

"It's why I'm here . . . to take care of you." Bethany wet her lips with her tongue.

"I thought that's what I was trying to do?" he said, his voice betraying his need.

Without thinking, Cole pressed his lips against hers, gently covering her mouth. He needed to taste her again before he left her for the day. He gathered her into his arms and held her snugly against him. She placed her hands on his chest. He waited for her to push him away, but she didn't. As he deepened the kiss, he was becoming lost in her scent, in her taste, and in the feel of her soft body in his arms. Bethany was giving him more to think about than just work and the ranch. He didn't know how he felt about that, but damnit if he was going to stop kissing her this time.

"Breakfast is getting cold," she stammered in between kisses.

He knew he should stop, but he couldn't.

"I can warm it up," he said, trailing kisses down her

jaw and down her neck.

She squirmed against his lips, giggling. Oh, the things he wanted to do to her. He pulled back, wanting to see the smile that came with that giggle. Bethany's chocolate eyes shone bright, a smile lighting up her beautiful face to reveal her straight, white teeth. Desire brought a glow to her skin and her freshly kissed lips. It was just too much to resist. Cole's heart thudded in his chest and he wondered if this was what it felt like to want someone more than anything else.

She gently pushed him back. He allowed her to squeeze past him. He stood still, willing his pulse to slow down. When he was under control, he walked over to the table and sat down to eat his breakfast. Bethany went to his side and handed him a hot cup of coffee. The smell warmed his insides.

"Thank you. This is a nice way to start the day," he said.

Bethany sat down in the chair next to him with a cup of coffee for herself. She sipped quietly, her cheeks still blushed red. He grinned at her and took a bite of the biscuit loaded with gravy and chunks of sausage. The sweet saltiness of the gravy and sausage along with a soft, chewy biscuit had him moaning low.

"Umm," he said, swallowing a bite. "If you keep making food like this all the time, I may have to make our arrangement permanent."

Bethany's eye brightened as she peered at him from over the edge of her coffee cup. She smiled, pleased at his remark. "That would be something, wouldn't it?" She glanced at the pictures on the wall. "Would you like me to take them down now and take them back to the attic?"

Cole shifted in his seat and took another bite of his food.

"Is the baby in the picture Emma?"

She had said last night that she hoped he could trust her enough with his story. Did he trust her? If he cared for her like he thought, he did trust her. His story was part of him, and she should know it.

"Yes. I think she was about a year old, maybe two. I don't remember a lot from back then."

Bethany studied him.

If he cared for Bethany, she had a right to know who he was and what his life was about.

He pointed to the picture with Emma. "That boy hugging my mother was my brother Joel. When he was twelve, he drowned in the river not far from here. Not long after that, my mother ran off and left us. She couldn't look at us. She only saw Joel, and the pain was too much for her. A few years after she left, my father died. Worked himself to death, some say, but I think he died of a broken heart. Being the oldest, I was left to take over the ranch and the family."

Bethany's eyes were wide. "No wonder you didn't like looking at the pictures. It must have been a rough time for you."

She got up and started to take the pictures down. Cole went to her, took the pictures from her hands, and put them back on the wall.

Tears were pooling in her eyes. "I'm sorry," she said.

"No. It's time I put this all behind me. Emma was right. There were good times. I just wasn't ready to see that. I need this. I need these to remind me that there was a time when we were a happy family. That there are things worth remembering." His gaze fell to her lips, wanting to kiss away her sadness, but he held back. He took her hand and kissed it tenderly. "I have to get to work. I have a project to finish."

"Okay," she said in a small voice. "What would you like for dinner?"

"If you're cooking it, anything you make will be just fine with me."

He gave her chin a little brush of his finger and he walked out the back door, fighting the urge to taste her lips one more time.

Chapter Fifteen

The day passed by swiftly. With Emma coming by to have lunch, Bethany was worried dinner wouldn't be ready for Cole on time. But by some miracle, Olivia stayed asleep long enough for her to slap together an excellent meal. Breaded pork chops, fried asparagus, and the corn bread would all be ready in a couple of minutes.

As she placed the plates on the formal dining room table, Peter walked through the front door looking grim. She smiled, her eyes following him as he lazily moved toward her.

"I was only just setting the table. Cole said we could eat in here. I hope you don't mind."

Peter stopped at the far side of the table and placed his hands on the nearest chair. He pulled in a deep breath. "So, what are we having for dinner? Smells so good in here."

"Pork chops," she said as she placed the white plate onto the table. She hoped Peter liked her. He had a suspicious nature. It was no wonder he was the sheriff.

Peter straightened. "I can't remember the last time I had them. They smell great."

"Please have a seat."

"Don't mind if I do." Peter plopped down into the chair where Bethany had just placed the plate.

She scurried into the kitchen, grabbed a plate of food,

and headed back out to set it on the table. Peter was lounging back in the chair. He scrutinized her as if he were a lion examining his prey. Bethany tried to ignore him. She went back to the kitchen, peering at the clock. Cole would be showing up soon. He said he would be on time for dinner today, and she was excited to see him.

She recalled Cole's handsome face cloaked in rapture as he ate her food. She wanted to see that look on his face again. A bonus would be to see Peter enjoy her food just as much.

Appearing once more in the dining room, this time with a plate of corn bread and a pitcher of sun tea, she set the food in front of Peter. She hoped the smell of the food would lighten his mood.

She dashed into the kitchen. A second later she emerged with napkins and eating utensils.

Peter snatched a chunk of corn bread and bit into it. Bethany watched the hard lines on his face disappear as he chewed.

"Oh, man." He swallowed and moaned. "That's good stuff."

"Thank you. I know it is," Bethany said, fussing with the arrangement of food. But a little blush stained her cheeks at the praise.

"You're not a modest chef at all."

"Why would I be? I have been cooking for years. I have trained all over the US."

Peter leaned back into the seat, giving her his avid attention. "All over, you say? Do you know any Cajun recipes?"

Bethany sat down next to Peter. "Maybe I do. Maybe I was just working on a dish for my recipe book I'm working on."

"Excellent. I vote for Cajun food tomorrow." He leaned forward. "I can put in a request even though I'm not Mr. Grumpy Pants?"

"Yes, requests are appreciated." She chuckled.

Peter took her hand and held it lightly. Bethany was surprised.

"I shall never go hungry again. And I will be coming home at least four nights a week. Fridays, Saturdays, and Sundays, I will be staying at friends'," Peter said, wagging his dark brows up and down.

So, Peter was a playboy type. She wasn't that surprised; after all, he looked just as good as his brother. Yet Cole felt more like a family man.

Peter patted her hand. "The question is, do I wait to eat with Cole, or do I pig out and say I'm too full to help with ranch work?" Peter chuckled. "Only kidding. I'll go see if Cole needs help."

Bethany slapped Peter's hands away. "Smart man!"

He chuckled hard. The sound was deep, like Cole's. Peter raised a brow. "Smarter than my family thinks. But let's keep that between us."

Bethany sighed with relief after Peter left. It felt like she'd made some progress with him. Peter did make her smile. She slapped her hands together; so, he likes spicy. He was coming around. Then she rushed back into the kitchen to get the surprise apple pie she'd made for dessert.

❧♥❧

Cole stood next to the crib admiring his work. A sense of accomplishment washed over him. He ran his fingers over the smooth, white paint and the pink and purple daisies he had painted on the legs of the crib. The last time he had painted flowers was when Emma was seven. She'd asked him to make her room happy after their mother left, so he and Emma had painted daisies on two of her walls. Before Emma had gone to college, she painted over all of the flowers—and that was when he knew she didn't need him anymore.

The paint was dry, and everything looked good. How was he going to get the crib into the house without Bethany seeing it? He feared that the task would be a bit challenging. He scrubbed a hand over his rough jaw and looked to the back door that led into the kitchen. Then he thought about the large window in Emma's room. It was big enough to accommodate the crib in one piece if he could manhandle it just right. But he needed that window to be open.

Cole decided to spy on Bethany and see what she was doing. Stealthily, he moved onto the back patio and glanced into the kitchen window undetected. And there she was, puttering around in the kitchen, as he figured she would be. Bethany was in front of the oven one second and then in the pantry the next. He enjoyed watching her work. It didn't seem like it had been that long since she came to his home, but she ran around as if she had been here for years. He liked it, maybe even loved it. His feeling grew stronger every time he gazed at her.

Cole's chest heaved. Now wasn't the time to ponder such things. He had a mission. The day was warm and the air light. The odds that Bethany had the window open were good. Tearing himself away, he crept around to the other side of the house. Cole slapped his knee in satisfaction. The window was open about three inches, just enough for a breeze to enter the room.

Cole swung around and headed back to his workshop. As quickly as he could, he lifted the crib after placing the mattress on it. He waddled with the crib to the other side of the house, careful not to let Bethany see him through any of the windows. Cole couldn't stop grinning. This was the most fun he'd had since . . . he couldn't remember. Just thinking about the joy on her face added a spring to his step.

Opening the window as high as he could, he peered around the room and spotted Olivia asleep on the bed. He would have to take extra care to be quiet. If he woke Olivia, she would give him away and spoil the surprise.

He shimmied through the window and leaned out to grab the side of the crib. He lifted it, tilting it at an angle to allow two of the legs to reach into the room. Cole grunted softly with the effort. He finally managed to bring the crib inside without waking the baby. Before finishing his task, Cole went down the hall that led to the formal dining room. He glanced around and listened for Bethany. Pots banged in the kitchen. Satisfied, Cole returned to her room.

He placed the crib against the wall closest to Bethany's bed. As he pushed it up against the wall, one of the legs let out a terrible, high-pitched raking sound. He cursed, glanced at the door, and sank to the floor. This was not how he planned the surprise. But he heard Bethany talking to Peter. When did Peter show up?

They hadn't heard the noise. But to Cole's dismay, he heard the bedsheets rustle. He rose up to his knees and peered at Olivia, whose hands and feet were jerking around. He hoped she would settle back down, but the baby started to fuss. He reached over and rubbed her belly. She fussed more. What the heck was he going to do? When Emma was small, he used to sing to her to calm her down.

Eyeing Olivia, he bent down next to her.

"Twinkle, twinkle little star . . ."

Olivia kicked her feet harder and her face scrunched up. Cole couldn't blame the poor kid. He wasn't a singer. He glanced at the window and then at the door. He had to make a choice: calm her or jump out the window and let Bethany come. He sighed with some resignation. He would give it a few minutes more.

Cole laid his head next to Olivia's and tried a different song. In the smoothest, softest voice he could muster, he recalled the song his mother used to sing to him when he was upset.

"You are my sunshine, my only sunshine . . ."

Olivia blinked at him with heavy eyes. Cole continued, feeling his affection grow.

"You'll never know, dear, how much I love you. Please don't take my sunshine away."

He couldn't do anything more but smile at the little fart. Right before her eyes drifted closed, she wrapped her hand around one of the fingers rubbing her belly. She trapped him neatly and completely. Cole knew this little person was somehow changing his life. He would do anything to keep her safe and happy. He kissed Olivia on the forehead and slowly pried her fingers off his, then he climbed out of the window. Bethany would surely be surprised when she saw the crib. He wished he could witness the look on her face.

꙳♥꙳

Bethany's mind filled with thoughts of new recipes as she sat waiting for Peter to check on Cole and see if he was coming for dinner. She wondered about Deveros and if Erik, the little traitor, was managing to mess everything up yet. Erik was a good sous chef, but he didn't know how to lead a large staff. She gave Deveros about a month before they called her begging for her to come fill the position once again.

But what if Mark the owner did call her back? Was she going to leave Cole's? What did she really think was happening here? She wasn't sure. Was she willing to pass up an opportunity like Deveros to find out? Running her own kitchen had always been the goal.

Bethany chewed her thumbnail as she walked down the hall to check on Olivia. Worried thoughts raced through her mind. It made her stomach roll just imagining the possibilities of leaving, which was silly because she'd only been here going on two weeks.

When she stepped into the room, her jaw dropped and it took a moment to register what she was seeing. There was a white crib with painted flowers running along the railing and legs. She couldn't believe it. She strolled over and ran her hand over the wood. The flowers were purple and pink. She gave it a shake. It was too sturdy to be store-bought. Not to mention, she'd never seen any other like it. Had Cole made it just for Olivia? Maybe it used to be Emma's from when she was a child. No, it looked new. It didn't matter. She pulled out her phone, snapped a picture, and sent it to her mother. She was going to love it. Bethany was relieved that she hadn't hit the purchase button that morning on her Amazon cart with a crib in it.

How did he get the crib into the room without her knowing? Bethany leaned out the window and scanned the area, but Cole was nowhere to be seen. She picked up Olivia from the bed, who was still fast asleep, and gently laid her on the crib mattress. Tears trickled down her cheeks. Cole had done this for her. Bethany gently touched her daughter's round cheeks. She looked perfect in the crib, like she could be in a magazine.

She wiped her tears away. *God, Cole is turning me into a crier.* She fussed with her hair and returned to the dining room. Cole was there with Peter, sitting at the table. His eyes were bright with emotion.

She walked over to Cole, ignoring Peter and interrupting their conversation. She took Cole's hand in hers. At his mere touch, heat shot through her body and collected in her core. Her knees weakened. She studied his handsome face as if to memorize it.

"Thank you for the crib. It's the most beautiful thing I've ever seen."

She kissed his palm. His rough hand on her lips gave her the shivers. Cole's face softened. A smile pulled at his mouth. His thumb caressed her skin.

"What did he do?" asked Peter, marching down the hall into Bethany's room.

Cole quickly kissed her forehead and took her hand in his, pulling her along as he trailed after his brother.

Peter stopped just inside her room and stared at the gift Cole had made for her.

"Way to put the moves on her. A crib?" said Peter, shrugging. "Sweet baby Jesus, can we eat now? I am starving, and the smell of Bethany's food is only making it worse."

"Go for it." Cole gestured to the dining room. Peter scooted by and vanished down the hall and into the dining room.

Cole's arms wrapped around Bethany in a gentle embrace. His eyes drank her up. He backed her against the wall and took her lips in his. There was a dreamy intimacy to their kiss. Every day, her affection for this man deepened and intensified. She was coming undone. She knew she would fall in love with him if she stayed here for long—or perhaps she already was in love. It happened on the day they met, when she pleaded for him to stay with her so she didn't have to have Olivia alone. She had given him her heart.

She didn't hold back. She returned his kiss with all the heat and passion she felt for him. Rising to her toes, she wrapped her arms around his neck, pressing her body closer to his. She wanted all of him.

Cole's lips devoured her, one hand trailing roughly down her tank top and cutoff shorts. His fingers skimmed the hem, teasing her. Fireworks were going off beneath the surface of her skin. Cole cupped her bottom and squeezed. She giggled against his lips. She liked to see him hungry for her. Her hands dropped from his neck and quickly explored the skin underneath his nicely fitted blue T-shirt. Her hands slithered along his flat stomach and caressed his back. Every muscle in his body quivered at her touch. Cole responded by pulling her hips closer to his, his hands digging into the flesh of her butt. He released her lips, leaving her mouth aching. He trailed feathery kisses down her jaw to her neck, inhaling her scent. Breathe. *Just breathe.*

Cole lifted his head, unable to contain his smile. Bethany's dark eyes sparkled, and he knew she held him in the palm of her hand.

Never before had he wanted a woman like he wanted her. He wanted to take care of her, and it surprised him that her happiness meant so much to him. He would not allow the pain and anger from his past to destroy what they had. He had to forgive himself to move on and allow good things into his life.

"You like my gift?" he asked, lowering his head to kiss her softly once again.

"Yes, I love it. It's very thoughtful of you. Did you make it yourself?"

He brushed his lips over her forehead and kissed her again. "Yes. I made it." He rested his cheek on the top of her head and held her tight in his embrace. He whispered, "For you, I think I would do anything."

Cole pushed away from the warmth of her body. He stared at her lips hungrily. But knowing Peter was waiting, he took her hand, and with their fingers laced together, they walked into the dining room. Peter, true to his word, couldn't wait any longer. He was well into his plate, his mouth busily chewing his food.

Peter raised an eyebrow at their interlocked fingers, shrugged, and continued to eat.

Cole pulled out a chair for Bethany. He was confident that she had feelings for him, but were they enough for her to want to stay beyond their working arrangement?

Chapter Sixteen

Two months passed on the Verbeck ranch, and life couldn't have been more wonderful for Bethany and Olivia. Bethany had enough time to outline her recipe book and write down countless recipes. She couldn't believe it. She and Olivia had a routine well in place, and Olivia seemed to flourish in her environment. Almost three months old, she had quite the personality.

It was a beautiful day. Cole held Olivia in his lap as he sat beside Bethany on the front porch swing. Cole stuck out his tongue at Olivia, and she stuck her tongue out at him in return. Bethany laughed lovingly at their playful interaction.

"How long do you think she can keep it up before she loses interest?" Cole asked, stealing a glance at Bethany, his eyes bright with merriment.

Bethany's heart sang with delight at seeing Cole's affection for her daughter. "I'm not sure, but it looks as though you're wearing her out." Olivia's eyelids were starting to close.

"Well, that was easy." Cole kissed Olivia's cheek and carefully stood up. He walked over to set her into a baby swing. He was a different man with Olivia. It softened him. The usually stiff and grumpy Cole was nowhere in sight.

The sun was sinking. The warm summer air was giving

way to cooler autumn nights. Bethany pushed her foot out to start the swing moving. She closed her eyes and savored the scent of wildflowers and the earthy smell of the ranch. It was an odd mix of scents she had to get used to, but the smell meant something to her now. It meant home.

Cole strolled back to the swing, his expression sober. She stopped the swing so Cole could reclaim his seat.

He casually leaned back and draped his arm along the back of the swing. He rested his hand on her shoulder and pulled her closer. Bethany eagerly obeyed, molding her body against his side. She set her head against his shoulder and looked out into the nicely mowed yard. The day couldn't get better than this. She pulled her legs up and tucked them to the side. Cole's arm wrapped around her. His warmth seeped into her, and her body hummed. Oh, the things this man was doing to her heart.

"There's something I want to talk to you about."

There was a faint tremor in his voice, as though some emotion was choking him. Bethany's pulse beat faster. What could make him look so serious? She moved to sit up straight and make herself less vulnerable, but Cole stopped her.

"How do you feel about making our arrangement—"

Her phone rang. She pulled her phone out and blinked at the number.

"It's Deveros," she said.

Cole sat up and pulled his arm back, frowning.

She answered the phone. "Hello, Mark. It's good to hear from you. How are things going at the restaurant?"

"Terrible. I have had two sous chefs quit because Erik is yelling at everyone."

Bethany wanted to smile, but didn't. "Why is he yelling at everyone?"

"Dinner service has been backed up for the last few

weeks. I am losing customers right and left. Not to mention servers. Please come save my restaurant. I'm sorry I wasn't more flexible to your situation."

Bethany leaned back. "You want me to save your restaurant?" She knew Mark would regret his choice, but now she didn't know what to say. Working in a restaurant like Deveros had been the dream since she started cooking. "I will have to think about it. Things didn't work out before for a reason, and you were the reason. I'm not going to put myself in a situation like that again."

"I will double your pay and secure an apartment for you before you get here."

"Really." She blinked again. "You want me that bad."

"Yes."

"I'll get back to you in a day or so. Have a good day." She hung up.

Cole stood and leaned against the porch railing. He looked nervous. "They want you to go there, don't they?" He folded his arms across his chest.

"Yes. Erik is wreaking havoc. Mark, the owner, said he will double my pay and get me an apartment. He sounds really desperate."

"Well, I've had your cooking for almost three months and I've gained five pounds. It is the best." He smiled, but it didn't reach his eyes, and Bethany didn't know why but her chest started to ache.

"What are you going to do?" His voice was even; too even.

"I'm not sure."

He shoved his hands into the pockets of his dirty jeans. "I have to get back to work." And just like that, he walked off. "Don't count on me for dinner tonight. I'm going with Logan to bring the cattle around to his property. We may camp for the night."

"What were you saying before the call?"

"It isn't important."

"Are you sure?"

"Yeah."

He walked off without looking back or giving her a kiss. She frowned. Cole could be so hard to read at times. Bethany didn't know what to think. She knew he cared about her and Olivia. How much, she didn't know. They never talked about a relationship. It was an unspoken affection. Would he let her leave? Did she want to leave? She had jumped at the opportunity to work at Deveros once. Did she want to give it a go again? Leave Cole and the ranch behind to start something new? Something that was just hers and Olivia's? She thought about William, and what he might want for them if he were here. She didn't know. She was going to need time to figure out what was best for her and Olivia. She sighed. A cow in the pasture a few yards away mooed at her. "Well, tell me how you feel then."

She had a lot to think about and where she was willing to place her bets. Judging by Cole's reaction to the phone call, she was betting he cared more about her than he showed. She cared about him . . . hell, she loved that he was a pain in the butt. But was she willing to bet on a future she'd been working toward for years for love that may not be there?

Cole sat on a wood crate in his woodshop scowling at the floor. Had he almost asked Bethany to stay with him, to make their arrangement permanent? What did that even mean? That he wanted to marry her? Damnit. Why he ever thought Bethany would stay here for long was beyond his comprehension. He wasn't exactly a loveable man. He was hard, distant, and content with his own company. Not exactly a woman's dream husband.

He hardened his heart against the idea of a future with Bethany and Olivia he had only just started to see. He was sure she would leave to take the job. His heart ached so badly, he wanted to tear it from his chest. He clenched the wood, trying to hold back a tidal wave of emotions threatening to drown him.

What was he supposed to do, wait for her to leave? Pretend that he didn't care about her, that he wasn't so in love with her that the thought of her leaving wouldn't destroy him? He wouldn't be able to go back to his life like it was before he knew Bethany.

The last time he felt this helpless was when he watched Logan drag Joel's body out of the river and he was too far away to help. Or the day his father lay on the ground dying in the pasture. He had held his father in his arms. Just like before, he felt helpless as his world started to fall apart.

"Well, you look like shit," Logan said, leaning against the door of the shop. The sky was growing dark behind him. Logan flipped the lights on and collapsed into a chair in the corner. "The horses are ready. If we get going, we can be back around seven tonight," he said.

"I'm not coming back. I'm camping." Cole didn't think he could handle hearing the news if Bethany was going to take the job and leave.

"I haven't camped in a while. I could use a guy's night," Logan said. He went to Cole's workbench to inspect his tools. "What brought this on? Did something happen with Bethany?"

"No, the weather is nice, so why the hell not?" Cole said.

Logan crossed his arms over his chest. "You don't just camp. Out with the truth." He stood in front of Cole, his towering presence demanding answers. Logan was very perceptive toward Cole.

Cole let out a sigh and stood. "The owner of Deveros, the restaurant Bethany was going to work at, called. They want her to come again."

"I see. And you think she is going to take the job."

Cole glared at Logan and the bastard smiled at him.

"You love her, don't you?"

Cole brushed past him and grabbed his camping bag off the shelf behind Logan.

"It is okay to love someone, Cole. Everyone deserves love."

"Get out of my way." Cole marched out of the shop and toward the pasture where Logan had two horses tied to the fence.

Logan strolled out behind him holding the second camp bag he kept at the ready. Cole mounted the painted mare and took off before Logan could give him a hard time. He rode hard and fast, needing distance from Bethany.

Chapter Seventeen

After a light meal and a few hours to herself, Bethany managed to work herself up really good. So good, in fact, that she was pacing the bedroom staring out the window, praying Cole would come back tonight and not camp. She cradled the sleeping Olivia in her arms, wanting to keep her close. She rubbed her cheek against Olivia's. "I wish you were big enough to tell me what we should do. Making big decisions that affect both of us sucks."

When Bethany was young, she always felt like a leaf being blown by the wind. Always moving. Always searching for something she wasn't sure of. A tear ran down her cheek and dripped onto Olivia's face, causing her eyes to open. Olivia blinked at her.

"It's okay, sweetie. Mommy's just a hot mess. You will get used to it."

A smile tugged at the corners of Olivia's mouth as if she understood, and then her eyes closed again. Her first smile. Bethany fell more in love with her daughter and took that smile as a sign that she was making the right decisions. Bethany loved her travels with her mother and father, but what she had always wanted was to stay still. To plant her feet and see what could grow from time in one place. That was what she wanted for Olivia more than an adventure.

She continued to rock her daughter to sleep. She strolled over to the window to gaze out at the night sky and enjoy the light breeze. The lights from Emma's home glimmered brightly in the darkness of the ranch. Dark clouds were rolling in. A storm was coming.

The ceiling squeaked above Bethany's head. Was Cole home? Had he decided not to camp after all?

After Bethany was certain Olivia was in a deep sleep, she placed her into the crib and tucked her in tight. She ran her hand on the beautiful crib and smiled. Her thoughts filtered back to the day she'd met Cole. He had been so thoughtful and kind from the start. Offering her a job so that she wouldn't worry about being jobless and homeless with a newborn. Not to mention buying Olivia a car seat, a baby swing, and making the crib. After spending three months with him, she now understood how hard that must have been for him. She loved him for it . . . for all of it. Putting her first when he didn't even know her yet. Looking back, she didn't think she'd ever come first to anyone—not even to her parents, even though she loved them. It had always been about her mother and what she'd wanted and needed.

She locked the window. Bethany left the door open so she could hear if Olivia woke up. Quietly, she snuck down the hall and out into the dining room. The room was dark and the house was creaking, fighting to stand against the wind that now bellowed outside.

Pulling in a breath, she prepared for the bravest thing she would ever do . . . or maybe the most foolish. She would find out soon enough.

Bethany raked her fingers through her hair to tame it somewhat. She then pulled at her denim shorts and adjusted her tank top. She was not dressed to seduce, but she had a good feeling this country boy would like it just fine.

Barefoot, Bethany climbed the stairs, working to hear past her speeding heart. Hesitating at Cole's door, she knocked lightly. She heard boards squeaking as he walked toward the door. She felt like her heart was lodged in her throat.

The door opened and a dim light glowed behind a muscular bare chest and shoulders. Her gaze traveled down and noticed he was only wearing loose boxers. Bethany's pulse hammered. There were lines around his mouth as if he had been frowning the entire afternoon. She melted a little. He was sad. She wanted to kiss his frown away, and she would.

"I thought you said you were camping tonight?"

He scanned her critically.

"A storm is coming. Logan didn't feel like getting wet."

She smiled and stepped up to him. He didn't move away. She ran her fingers over the cords of his stomach muscles and went up to caress his tight chest. Flames smoldered in his eyes, startling her as much as it delighted her.

"I needed to talk to you about today." She continued to run her fingers up to his neck and rested her hand there.

Cole gritted his jaw. She dropped her hands.

"I just wanted to say . . ." Her voice cracked.

"What did you want to say in the middle of the night that couldn't wait until morning?" he whispered against her ear.

Emotions twisted her insides.

"Never mind." She turned to walk back down the hall but he caught her arm. She stared at his fingers. He turned and lifted her chin. His eyes were filled with something she'd never seen in him before . . . fear.

"I wanted to let you know that I told Deveros to find someone else."

His eyebrows raised. "Why? Why aren't you going to go? I need to know."

She took his hand from her arm and laced her fingers with his. "I love it here . . . with you. I have never been happier, and I don't want it to end."

Before Bethany could stop them, tears ran down her face. He tenderly cupped her cheek. He stepped closer and pressed his body against hers. He was so handsome that her breath caught in her throat.

"Cole . . . I love you—"

"Shush. Everything will be fine so long as you marry me." He ran a thumb over her lips and trailed a hand down her neck and over her shoulder. He left a trail of fire with his touch. Bethany shivered.

"You want to marry me?"

"Yes."

Her hands went to his lower back and held him tight, afraid to let go. Her blood surged from her fingertips to her toes. She tried to throttle the dizzying current that was racing through her.

He gently gathered her into his arms. His lips were caressing her mouth more than kissing it. There in the hall, she buried her hands into his hair and gave herself freely to the passion of his kiss. She wanted him to feel her love oozing out of her pores for him.

An eternity passed before he released her lips, leaving her breathless and weak. He took her hand and led her into his room, the boards squeaking beneath her toes. This was the first time she'd been inside Cole's room.

Her entire body seemed to be on fire. She took a moment to cool down and surveyed the room. His was the largest room in the house, and it was totally male. There was a queen-size bed with a red patchwork quilt. A rustic bed frame with a matching dresser and nightstand. A comfortable, worn chair hugged the corner of the room, with holes where the stuffing was popping out, and books littered the floor beside it. Cole was a reader. There was another layer she hadn't seen before. It made her smile wider.

He stepped out of her way and studied her as she examined his room. "Do you like it?"

"It's so you." She walked over to the chair and sat down. She reached for a book and read the author's name, Louis L'Amour. Why wasn't she surprised?

"I didn't know you liked to read."

Cole shrugged. "When you're mean and grumpy, people tend to stay away from you. Reading takes me away from all of this." He swept his hand out and around. "Although I haven't been reading much lately." Cole's eyes moved over her body hungrily.

She put the book down and rose to her feet. Walking over to Cole, she pressed her open lips to his. He welcomed the kiss. He lifted her up and she locked her legs around his waist. They moved to the bed and he gently eased her down, his hips brushing hers as he covered her body with his.

He trailed kisses on her ear as he whispered, "Can I make love to you?"

Bethany shivered from his hot breath and giggled. "Of course. Why else would I be here?"

Cole rose to his elbows. She kissed his nose and wiggled against his hips, eager to make love.

Cole smiled a secret smile that curled her toes. She was putty in his hands.

He lifted her tank top, his fingers icy but his palms fiery hot. He pulled it over her head and studied her, his eyes smoldering. She blushed, feeling naked even in her bra. He ran his fingers through her hair and then over one of her breasts. She pushed her head into the mattress, arching into his touch. He lowered his head, kissing her neck, across her collarbone . . .

Cole reached up her back and unhooked her bra. He pulled it away, freeing her breasts. Bethany wanted to close her eyes, yet she loved watching him study her as if she were an award-winning dessert. His tongue tantalized the buds that were swollen to their fullest. Bethany was coming undone from the inside out. He turned his attention to the other breast and a horrible thought entered through the fog of her desire. What if she started to leak milk? She shoved him back gently. She couldn't handle that embarrassment the first time they made love.

Cole's eyes betrayed his arousal. Enthralled by what she saw, she allowed him to continue. Slowly, his tongue made a path down her ribs to her stomach. His kisses were feather soft. His hand gripped the swell of her hips. Again, she pressed into him, all of her nerves taut with desire. She was riding high with pleasure. Thoughts of Cole consumed her.

Cole lightly traced paths over the sensitive skin of her legs. Bethany sucked in a breath, anticipating his next move.

"I have been dreaming of you from the first night we met." He breathed against her soft inner thigh. Bethany closed her eyes. The sound of his voice sent a vibration up her spine. Hunger built.

Cole kissed her thighs. He unbuttoned her shorts and shimmied them down her legs, along with her panties. Bethany lay naked on the bed. Her eyes opened to find Cole sitting back, taking her in. This time, he saw all of her. Desire was flickering in his eyes. She wanted Cole to see how much she needed him and how much she wanted him. Bethany rose to her knees and advanced toward him. He smiled from ear to ear. He chuckled as she hooked a finger under the waistband of his boxers. She moved painfully slow, enjoying Cole's beautiful eyes widen, only to narrow into slits when he realized she was playing with him.

She pulled his boxers down and he stepped out of them. Bethany lay back, waiting. Her core pulsed, and a tightness inside her was begging to be released.

"Finally," she purred, grabbing at his naked body.

Lying on top of her, he took her hands, encouraging them to explore him. Bethany bit her bottom lip.

"Do you want me?" she teased.

"I have wanted you since the day I brought you home from the hospital. I prayed you would be mine."

"Really?" she whispered, tears filling her eyes.

Cole stroked her hair and ran his thumb over her jaw. He nodded, reclaiming her lips, crushing her to him. Joining their bodies together, Bethany found the love she'd hoped for in this grumpy man. There was no one else she wanted to be with.

◡♥◡

Cole struggled to control himself, not wanting to hurt his delicate dream. He wanted her to remember their first time together with fondness and love.

She gripped his back, her nails digging into his flesh. Ripples of pleasure cascaded through her, and he felt her body shudder beneath him. Unable to hold back at the sight of her rapture, he followed.

Bethany's eyes were closed; her face had a look of pure and utter peace. Cole wanted to see that look every night of his life. He kissed her neck, content and happy to be with her at last. He moved to Bethany's side, gathering her curves into the contours of his body. He wanted to hold her all night. He wanted her to feel his love. He pulled the blanket of the bed over them both.

"Cole, I know this may sound abrupt, but I have to go back to my room."

"Stay with me."

"I want to, but I can't. Olivia's alone." Bethany kissed his lips softly. She sat up and wrapped the blanket around her.

Cole watched her as she gathered her clothes and hurried down the hall. They were going to get married. The thought struck him hard and he smiled. Bethany was going to be his wife. *Hot damn.* He hopped out of bed with a new spring in his step. He quickly cleaned up in the bathroom, put on the Sponge Bob pants his nephew, Joel, had given him, and followed his future wife down the stairs.

When he entered the room, there was no Bethany. She popped out of the bathroom in the corner of the room wearing a loose nightgown. She looked at him in surprise.

"What're you doing down here?" she whispered.

"I'm going to sleep with you."

"I thought that's what we just did."

He placed a finger under her chin and kissed her softly. "I want you to fall asleep in my arms."

"What if Olivia wakes up a few times? You won't get any sleep, and you have work to do tomorrow."

"Bethany, she won't bother me. She's my daughter. Let me help. I want to be there for you both. I love you both."

Bethany was quiet for a minute, then she said, "Daughter."

"I think I fell in love with her first."

"Oh, Cole." Bethany threw her arms around his neck and rested her head on his chest. Cole held her tight, resting his cheek on her head. He pulled down the blanket and climbed into bed with Bethany. They snuggled up to one another. He held her close to his heart as she fell asleep in his arms.

Cole looked down at Bethany and then glanced over

at Olivia. He would have never guessed a drive to the hospital a few months ago would change his life so completely. One moment in time had given him the greatest gift: a family.

Epilogue

The music started and Bethany fussed with the train of her white silk and lace dress before stepping out onto the back porch. She looked for Cole. He stood before her, waiting patiently in his tux, looking handsome and distinguished. A knot formed in her throat as she took the first step toward her soon-to-be husband.

Emma looked breathtaking with her hair pulled up, and the pink chiffon dress matched her coloring perfectly. She held a squirming Olivia, who was dressed in the same motif. Next to Peter, Logan held a squirming Abbie. Bethany couldn't have been happier. The joy and the excitement of the years to come converged into the deepest emotion of love she ever felt. She wanted to laugh and cry.

She glanced at Peter. He was very striking beside his brother, yet Cole seized all of her attention. Taking several more steps toward her future, Bethany held back her tears. Cole had changed her life and given her roots. She would do anything for him, go anywhere, and give him her everything. As she reached him, he took her hand. She turned to a bored-looking Joel and handed him her bouquet of flowers. She grinned at her mother as she dabbed at her cheek with a Kleenex.

The music stopped and the preacher stepped up to speak. Bethany didn't hear much. She was lost in the eyes of the man she loved.

Before she knew it, they had said their vows and the ceremony was over. They accepted the applause of their friends and family as they finally faced them together as husband and wife. Emma put Olivia in Cole's other arm, and she touched his face. A smile on her face. Bethany looked at the picture they made and she could no longer hold back her tears of happiness.

Bethany Verbeck. She had a family with roots.

It was time to celebrate.

Unbroken
Dream

Chapter One

Daisy scanned the faces at the wedding reception in search of a short, wrinkly, bald man with a grumpy face. There was no man with that description, though there were two grumpy-looking women sitting at a table near the house. Geez. She hoped she didn't look like that when she got old.

She scanned the area one last time for Bruce Buller, but the effort was fruitless. Frustration accosted her, as well as a pang of grief. She was hoping to speak to Mr. Buller about buying back the land her grandfather, Fred Lewin, had sold to him before she was born. It was a desire that plagued her since his death six months ago. It didn't look as though the task would be accomplished tonight. She held fast against the sharp strike of grief that always followed thoughts of her grandfather.

The outdoor wedding had been the perfect cover to make a trip to Havencrest and casually run into Mr. Buller. What a disappointment the night had been. Daisy blew at one of her loose curls. She hated parties, though she'd looked forward to seeing Logan Miller, one of her dearest friends.

There were ten or so tables set up in a half-circle, with the bride and groom's table at the front. Daisy noticed a middle-aged man and woman staring and pointing at her. Really! Could they be any more rude? She'd become accustomed to being at the center of gossip. She turned her back to the couple, disregarding them. They could stare. Nothing she could do about it. It wasn't a crime.

Detaching herself from the party, Daisy walked off toward the back of the house and settled beside a magnificent willow tree. Long, thin branches with green, finger-like leaves skimmed her ivory skin as they swayed in the soft summer breeze. The sun sank behind distant mountains and cast a soft glow over the Verbeck and Miller lands. She wanted to reach out and touch the beauty of the mountains. The scent of pine, hay, and earth filled her nostrils, conjuring memories of her grandfather's small farm in Elk View about two hours south of here. The scent was such a nice change from the stagnant air in her office building. There was more to life than work. At thirty-three, she should be enjoying life, but work was the only thing keeping her from falling apart over the return of her father and the loss of her grandfather.

Tall evergreens marched across the mountains, shoulder to shoulder. Surrounding the golden plains of the flatland, the trees held the valley captive. Logan and the Verbecks were very lucky to be blessed with such a homestead. You could hide from the world in a place like this, and that was exactly what she intended to do—if she could find Mr. Buller.

As she sipped her champagne, Daisy spotted the oldest Verbeck, Cole, spinning the new Mrs. Verbeck around the dance floor. Bethany Verbeck looked lovely in a silk-and-lace wedding gown. She had class and a subtle elegance. She was positively glowing tonight.

The couple beside them snagged her attention. It was funny to think that a gangly ranch hand could transform into such a stud. Logan Miller was having a great time with his wife, Emma, formerly Emma Verbeck. She was radiant as she glided around the dance floor with her husband, every now and then teasing her brother and his bride. Logan was a lucky man to have attained the attention of such a woman. And a doctor to boot. Daisy shook her head in amused disbelief.

A much younger Logan sprang to mind. Not having much to do over the summers she spent with her grandfather in Elk View, she'd noticed him right away out working Mr. Clay's ranch. His property butted up against her grandfather's small farm. The houses were less than five acres apart, so she'd snuck over to meet him. Only thirteen at the time, Logan stood tall, strong, and dirty. She'd scooted away from him because he smelled of cow poo. When her hazel eyes met his green ones, she saw that they were haunted by a deep sadness. The sadness reached into her and cut open her heart. The next day, she made it her personal mission to befriend him.

It had taken weeks of silly pranks and constant harassment from her before they became friends. Once Logan accepted her branch of friendship, he became the brother she'd never had. After that, she'd looked forward to sharing every summer that followed with Logan. A warm, silly, drunken feeling filled her up. She missed Logan more than she let herself believe, having only a few stolen moments here and there to see him after college.

She lifted her glass to toast him. "Here's to chasing unbroken dreams." She sipped her champagne. She wondered what time it was. Leaving her observation post beside the weeping willow, Daisy headed for the nearest male with a watch or phone.

"Excuse me, do you have the time?" she asked a gentleman in his seventies. She found it more productive to approach older men. Men her age didn't actually listen to the words that came out of her mouth. Especially in such a form-fitting dress.

"Evening. Let me see here." The man pulled up the

sleeve of his blazer and shook his wrist. "Looks to be about eight thirty."

"Thank you so much. Sorry to have bothered you."

He gripped her hand abruptly and kissed her knuckles. "A beautiful woman is never a bother."

Daisy didn't move, and fought the urge to tug her hand away. "That's sweet. Have a good night."

She kicked her heeled feet into gear. Apparently, she was better off staying away from *all* men. She found what looked like a safe spot opposite the dance floor and wondered how long before she could leave without being rude. She ran a hand over her blood-red dress, pressing her matching lips. She didn't want to offend Logan or the Verbecks for so graciously inviting her. She would give it another thirty minutes.

Just then, she felt someone's eyes on her and when she looked up, Peter Verbeck was studying her. He wore a cool smile that radiated arrogance and confidence, exuding a male power that probably drew women in droves. Too bad it was wasted on her.

He was tall and handsome, with a beautifully proportioned body, and Daisy was by no means blind to his sensual allure. When their eyes locked, a tingling sensation fluttered down her back. What poor luck. As much as she wanted to look elsewhere, she held his gaze. She wouldn't show a man like him that he could affect her in any way.

He watched her with a keenly observant eye and then raised his beer bottle to her. She did the same with her glass, doing her best to appear social and friendly. His handsome features sharpened and he flashed her a breathtaking smile. He made his way through the crowd around the dance floor.

Oh no! She drank the rest of her champagne. His eyes clung to her as he approached, but she refused to squirm. When a group of men slapped him on the back and tugged him into an intense conversation about who knows what, she saw his brows draw together in an agonized expression. This is my chance to escape.

She hurried off to the bar in the opposite direction toward the house. She hoped to shake Peter Verbeck off her trail by cutting through a group of men at one end of the bar, all of whom were quite a bit taller than herself. She peered over her shoulder . . . no Verbeck. Satisfied, she stepped up to the bar.

"I'll take a shot of tequila with the trimmings," she told a young, blonde female bartender, who was no doubt the reason for the crowd of men.

Her feet hurt. She peered down at the Saint Laurent Jane sandals. They were so cute with her silk Alfred Angelo dress, but both were made to be pretty, not comfortable. Keeping up appearances and maintaining a social status had been more cumbersome than usual, thanks to dear old Daddy. Her heart hiccupped just at the mere thought of him. An image of his disapproving face made her grimace.

Once upon a time, her father would have wanted her to talk with as many people as possible in hopes of making business connections. Not today—not ever. She didn't care how mad he got. He wasn't her boss anymore, and hadn't been since he went to jail.

The bartender placed the shot of tequila in front of her along with salt and a slice of lemon. A blast of heat pressed against her back. She cautiously looked over her shoulder and was captured by Peter's golden-amber eyes. Ugh!

"You know, tequila's never a good idea. Even at weddings."

"What makes you say that?" she asked, trying not to clench her jaw as she unintentionally spurred him on. Grumbling in her head, she licked her hand, salted it, and took her shot, quickly snatching the lemon and biting down. The liquid heat was just what she needed. "Seems like a spectacular idea to me."

Peter shrugged. "That's what everyone thinks until they're puking their guts out." He leaned around her and got the bartender's attention. "Tessa, I'll take another beer please."

The young blonde whipped around at the sound of Peter's voice and beamed at him. "What kind are you in the mood for tonight?" she asked shyly.

"Something light and blonde." He smiled wildly at the girl.

Daisy rolled her eyes. What a stupid line.

The girl hurried off.

Peter's breath caressed her cheek. A shiver of exquisite delight rushed down her spine against her will. She gripped her shot glass, hating her body at the moment. It had been a long time since a man caused such a reaction from her. It felt wonderful, dreamlike, and extremely unwanted. She bit the inside of her cheek and reminded herself that she didn't have time for men. She glanced at the dance floor. When Logan was done dancing, she would say her goodbyes and make her escape.

The bartender set a Coors Light bottle on the counter next to Peter and slipped a small piece of paper into his palm. He didn't open it, only looked at Daisy. "Ready for a dance?"

Daisy shimmied out between him and the bar. "I'm afraid I'm leaving." Before she made it any further, a large hand wrapped her wrist in a snug hold.

"One dance. It won't keep you long."

Her skin tingled where he touched her. In his eyes was a silent plea. He gently led her toward the dance floor. She paused. Was she really going to yield to this big-headed Verbeck? Logan had told her about Peter seducing half of the Havencrest female population under the age of forty.

He peered over his shoulder when he felt her resistance. His thumb tenderly caressed her knuckles and gently urged her onward. His eyes glowed soft and low. One dance wouldn't kill her.

They entered the dance floor as the music changed. Peter handed his beer to a friend and the next thing she knew, he was singing in a deep, raspy tone near her ear. He could sing, but she wasn't impressed. A ladies' man always had a trick up his sleeve.

Her favorite song splashed a small bit of happiness through her and she moved smoothly with Peter's strong body. She didn't let her guard down completely because she knew men only saw what she could give them: money and power. She doubted Peter Verbeck was any different from the rest. But this was her song, and she decided to ease up for three minutes until it was over. Then she was out of here.

Peter drew her a little too close for her liking. When the song ended, he didn't let her step back.

"One more dance?" he asked.

"I have to go. It was lovely dancing with you, but I must go."

He held her in place, not budging an inch. He grinned as the next song played. This was a slow one.

"Why do you have to go? It's a party." He placed a hand at the small of her back, taking her right hand in his left. He swayed with her in his arms. Her hand felt small in his. Her bottom lip pouted ever so slightly and he stared there for a moment. She pulled it back in. Will I yield? She blew out a breath and rested her left hand on his shoulder and swayed along with him. He stunned her with a smile.

"My feet hurt."

"Take off your shoes. Half the women here already

have."

She frowned. "Maybe I don't want to."

He leaned in, lips brushing her ear. "That's a sad excuse to leave a party." He let her glide out, turned her, and then pulled her back into his arms.

A small grin touched her red lips. "Perhaps you're right—it is a sad excuse to leave, but true all the same."

"Tomorrow's Saturday. You can sleep in and rub your feet," he said in a beseeching tone.

Her eyes narrowed. "There will be no sleeping in or rubbing of my feet."

"And why not?" Peter asked, waiting for an explanation.

"Because I'm not staying, and will have no need to do so."

It was Peter's turn to frown now.

Logan came sweeping in with Emma onto the dance floor next to them. Logan's striking, green eyes could have pinned Peter to the side of the house with that death stare.

"What are you doing dancing with this yahoo?" he said to her. "You know, there are like ten other men who would love to dance with you that I could give a five-star review about. But this guy gets a two point five. I would run away now if I were you."

"Don't listen to him," Emma chimed with cool authority. "My brother is the perfect gentleman . . . when he wants to be."

"Yeah, sure he is. If he thinks he can get laid." Logan released Emma and poked a finger against Peter's chest. "Don't get any ideas with this one or you will be sorry." Logan winked at his wife. "You keep an eye on your brother while I catch up with Daisy." Then he stole Daisy across the dance floor as far away from Peter as he could.

"Logan, when are you going to stop interfering whenever

an irritating man shows up?" Daisy asked, bemused.

"Never." He sent her spinning out and tugged her back in.

Daisy couldn't help but roll her eyes at Logan now. Always the protector. It was nice. She grinned as he spent three songs working to keep her away from Peter. "How are my adopted niece and nephew? They look so big," she asked.

"Great. Ornery as their mother, but as smart as their dad."

She laughed. "I see."

"You should come stay at the house for a few days and hang out with them. Get to know them." Logan pulled back and peered at her. "It would mean a lot to me. I want them to know you."

"Oh, Logan. Don't do that. Guilting me isn't fair. You know things have been difficult since my father's return."

Logan's gaze hardened. "Has he done anything to you since he's been back? I saw him grab you at your grandfather's funeral. It looked too hard for my liking."

She couldn't meet Logan's stare. "Everything is fine. Stop worrying."

"I'm trying." He raised a brow. "I just don't believe you."

They stopped dancing and moved off the dance floor to talk away from everyone. Peter was dancing with his sister. They were laughing together as he spun Emma every which way. It was quite the show. Picking at her nails, Daisy peered up at Logan.

"You know, I didn't go to see my father when he went to jail. And I have done my best to stay away from him at parties since his release, and the funeral. At the reading of the will, I think he was as shocked as I was that my grandfather left his shares of Lewin Land Development to me and the farm in Elk View to my father. I didn't even know LLD was my grandfather's. I just assumed since my father ran it, it was his."

"Wow. Dear old Dad got the farm and you got the company." Logan folded his arms over his chest, putting on his old attorney scowl. "He can't be happy about that."

"He wants the company back in his control. He came to my office with paperwork three months ago for me to sign it over to him. I laughed in his face. I've never seen him look more dangerous. I was completely disobedient." Daisy half grinned. "He was surprised to see me stand against him. Realized really quick I wasn't the same girl he left behind when he went to jail. So he has hired a minion to spy on me. I know when he is watching me. I play it off like I don't know, but I do."

Logan pressed his lips to a frown. "You better call me if anything comes up. You know he isn't a man to play with, Daisy. You should get a restraining order against him."

She gave his shoulder a squeeze filled with warmth and love for her dearest friend. "I will come by before I leave tomorrow to say goodbye. Will you be home?"

He let out a breath. "Daisy, why are you so stubborn?"

"Because I can be."

"Yeah, I'll be home. Or here, cleaning up."

"Tell your wife I said thank you for inviting me to such a beautiful wedding. And giving me the chance to visit."

He shoved his hands in his pockets and kicked the ground. "I miss you."

"I know. Me too. I'll see you tomorrow." And just like that, much later than she anticipated, Daisy made her escape from the Verbeck ranch and back to her hotel.

Chapter Two

Daisy kicked off her shoes, then unzipped her uncomfortable dress and stripped it off. She found a rubber band and fastened her hair high on the back of her head. The tension in her body instantly uncoiled. She put on some comfy clothes and lay down on the bed and stared at the ceiling. An image of her grandfather walked through her mind. He looked like his old ornery self, smiling at her. Being in this town reminded her of him, like she could feel him here. God, she missed him.

Her throat tightened and hot pokers stab the back of her eyes. She wrinkled her nose, trying to stop the burning. The last time she'd cried was at her grandfather's funeral. She touched her left bicep—the bruises were gone, but she could still feel her father's painful grip. His whispering voice cut through her deeply that day. "Stop making a scene. He's dead, he can't see it." It seemed that her father thought a scene was only good if it could be used to manipulate someone. Her father hadn't even shed a tear at the funeral.

Her grandpoo was the kindest man she knew. While her father went traipsing off to do who knows what, Grandpoo showed her what real love was every summer she spent with him; not the conditional stuff her father tossed about. There were times she thought her mother was better off having died when she was born. She did sometimes wonder what her life would have been like if she hadn't passed away. Would her mother have loved her like her grandfather, or seen her as an object to be maneuvered?

Grandpoo told Daisy stories about his life in Haven-crest. He seemed to have loved it here. She didn't understand why he left and moved to Elk View. Her grandfather spoke of Mr. Buller no more than a handful of times when she was a girl. He'd said that Mr. Buller was the kind of man he wished he could have been.

She turned the phrase over and over in her mind, wanting to somehow open the door to that part of her grandfather's life. Grandpoo didn't dwell on the past; he was ready to make new memories every day.

No one would know it to look at her, but she loved working on his farm. Feeding the pigs, getting the eggs, fixing the fences, tending the garden, riding in his old pickup to feed the cows. It was so different than her life with her father and the parties, horse riding lessons, ballet, tutors to finish top of her class, slaps across the face every time she questioned him or disobeyed. That life was about obedience.

She draped an arm over her eyes. If her father knew she was here to make a deal with Mr. Buller, he would be banging on her hotel door. She was taking a risk she never thought herself capable of until her grandfather was gone. He was the light in her life, everything that mattered, and everything good in her life grayed without him. Yet she knew how to stay connected with him.

She kept going over everything she knew about Mr. Buller that could help her cause. It was making her anxious, and that wasn't good. Her heart was beating irregularly.

Mr. Buller was eighty-seven and had no children. His wife passed away ten years ago, and none of his five brothers were alive. Essentially, Mr. Buller had no immediate family. He had lived in Havencrest his entire life and worked in the local mill for forty years, which led her to believe that Mr. Buller was a loyal man.

The only way to deal with a man like that was with honesty. Being the businesswoman she was, she knew honesty was hard to come by. The thought of opening up to a stranger caused her stomach to roll angrily. She couldn't even be honest with herself about most aspects of her life. How was she supposed to be open with Mr. Buller? She pinched the bridge of her nose. Doubt wormed its way into her plans. She felt dizzy. Good thing she was lying down. The pressure she was putting on herself was ridiculous, but it was necessary.

A strange rustling sound came from outside her window. She rose to her bare feet and pulled back the curtain to peer out. A shiver of fear shot down her spine as a dark figure rummaged through her car. The figure stiffened when the light of her room shone on him. A prickly sensation took hold of her body. He stopped, watching her. Waiting for her. He slowly climbed out of the car, closed the door and jogged off into darkness. She let the curtain drop and stepped back. She didn't call the cops. They couldn't help her. This was a message from her father. He would always know where she was. But the why was killing him. And the fact that he had no control over her, or the company, was pushing him to the edge.

Daisy crawled under the covers and curled into a ball. How long was this going to go on, her father trying to intimidate her? She blew out a breath, feeling the weight of her anxiety settle on her chest. She knew the answer to that question. As long as he had to, until he got what he wanted. His company back.

But she wouldn't give in. There was a reason her grandfather chose to will his shares to her to run LLD and not her father. He could try and dangle her grandfather's property in Elk View to get her to sign over her shares of LLD because of all the memories she and Grandpoo had made together there. But if her father had known his father at all, he would have known Havencrest was where his heart had always been. This was where he grew up. There could be people in town that knew him and would have stories for her. This place is where she would stay connected to her grandfather. By buying back his land.

She could still see the article in the newspaper. Daisy Lewin is now president and CEO of Lewin Development, a real estate developer company worth over $10 billion. Founded in 1980 by Fred Lewin, the company owns most of the real estate in downtown Boise, and during the nineties, Lewin Development expanded its reach to the neighboring states in the northwest. Its headquarters are located in downtown Boise. There are over 100 employees, 30 of which work in the downtown office. When Daniel was arrested for hiring a hitman to try and take out a competitor, Daisy stepped in to take over. Her VP, Steven Banks, operates out of Washington state and continues to expand their operations.

After her father went to jail, she wanted to prove that she could do the job better with kindness and understanding, not with fear and appealing to greed. Every land development project she undertook was to improve the local community. She had developed several parks and affordable housing subdivisions for first-time home buyers. She'd been twenty-eight when her father went to jail and she'd been terrified. Armed only with a degree in communications, a stained last name, and her grandfather's support and guidance, she'd secured numerous land deals and held the company together and done well to repair the LLD reputation.

One finger at a time, she released her grip on the

comforter. No. She wasn't going to get her nerves tangled in knots. *There is more to life than my father.* Eyes closing, she forced her mind to wander to more pleasant things.

Peter tumbled from the corners of her mind as if shoved by her subconscious that was only too happy to expel him. It maddened her how easily she'd folded under his golden gaze. He was exasperating, to be sure. Although, there was something in his eyes that intrigued her. A kind of slow-burning fire that could brand her heart if she let it. A brief shiver rippled through her. She could still feel the warm glow of him all over her skin. She was glad she wouldn't see him again.

Chapter Three

Peter Verbeck rolled out of his old bed with a pounding headache. Cole, as usual, nursed a beer the whole night at the wedding while he, Logan, and Emma let loose. Probably too loose, by the feel of it.

With his feet on the floor, Peter sat on the edge of the bed looking around at the bare walls of his room. The closet was empty, as were the dresser drawers next to him. An odd feeling crept up inside him. A few months ago, Cole had found Bethany Heart alone and pregnant in the parking lot at the McClain hospital. He'd managed to get her inside, where Bethany gave birth to a healthy daughter, Olivia. Later, Cole had asked her to become his personal chef to help her out after losing her job and apartment. What still shocked Peter was how hard and fast Cole had fallen in love; but he was happy for his brother.

He'd been waiting a long time to have a reason to move out, and Cole getting married had been it. Cole's death glare from across the kitchen table had been unnerving to say the least when he'd been honest about how he felt toward the ranch. It didn't mean to him what it meant to Cole. This had never been what he wanted. He thought Cole understood that when he'd gone to college in Boise and then the police academy. Running the ranch with Cole wasn't going to happen.

But when Peter had transferred from the police

department in Boise to come back to Havencrest because he missed home, Cole thought he would be more involved with helping on the ranch. Looking back, he should have said something sooner. It would have stopped countless fights. He just hadn't been able to break Cole's heart. After Joel's death, their mother leaving, their dad dying, and having to raise Emma, Cole had taken on the burdens of a life Peter wasn't sure Cole had ever wanted. But Cole had done it, without a complaint.

Peter ran a hand down his face and a small smile touched his lips. He'd never have guessed a small blonde and a baby would change Cole's life, and his. Without Bethany and Olivia's arrival to the Verbeck home this would still be his room, full of all his things. He was going to have to give Bethany a big, fat kiss for making a chance for him to finally live the life he wanted, guilt-free.

Peter got up and stretched. It was strange to think of Cole as married. He'd thought Cole and he would be single forever. But now he was the only Verbeck left who wasn't married, and part of that was his fault. He wouldn't necessarily say that he was unwilling to commit to a relationship, but truth be told, he did scare easily. At thirty-nine, maybe he enjoyed his life a little too much to be tied down; or maybe the right woman hadn't come along. That was why he was a little surprised at how fast his heart raced when he saw Daisy Lewin standing near the willow tree. She looked gorgeous, and so out of place.

Peter hadn't known about Logan and Daisy's friendship until her arrival. He had been shocked to learn Daisy Lewin had spent her summers with Logan on her grandfather's farm, and then they ended up at the same college. Peter had read about Daisy's father, Daniel Lewin, and knew he had a ruthless reputation as a land developer. So much so that to close a large land sale, Daniel hired a hitman to take out his competitor that was working to steal the sell out from under him six years ago. Peter knew the kind of man Daniel Lewin was. He'd seen his fair share of men who thought they were above the law because they had money.

The sun was beaming through the curtains, blinding him as he lumbered to the bathroom. He replayed his and Daisy's dance together, her pressed up against him, his heart drumming, her scent of honey and spice enveloping him like an embrace. He blew out a sigh. Her unwillingness to dance with him sparked a challenge he hadn't experienced in years.

Peter slapped his cheeks in the mirror, trying to wake up. He pulled in a breath, splashed some water on his face, and then wiped it off. Next, he crept down the stairs to make a cup of coffee, hoping to avoid seeing anyone, but he was shit out of luck. Emma and Logan were sitting at the kitchen table when he walked in. With his shoulders sagging, he fetched a cup of coffee and sat in a chair next to Logan, who looked as bad as he felt. Even Emma looked a mess. She hovered over her coffee looking a light shade of green.

"Where are the kids?" he asked no one in particular.

Logan took a sip of his coffee and pushed back his blond hair. "My dad has them. We didn't make it home last night. Slept in Emma's old room." He peered over at Peter. "How the hell did we drink that much and not even notice we were going to pay for it? I mean, look at us. We are old enough to know better."

Emma's cheeks popped out like a frog's. Abruptly, she shot to her feet and ran for the bathroom.

"Oh no," Logan said, face etched with sorrow. "I didn't think she was going to make it without getting sick, but I had been hopeful for her."

Peter chuckled and sipped his coffee, wondering if he

would be next in line to meet with the porcelain god. He one-eyed the strong coffee and then pushed it away.

"So where are the honeymooners?" Peter asked. Then he turned to peer out of the bright window. "Are they cleaning up already?" Peter didn't see any movement outside in the yard. Logan sipped his coffee again and then scrubbed his face, leaning forward like it was a chore. "Nope. Bethany, Cole, and Olivia hightailed it out of town for a day in Boise. I heard something about Bethany's catering business needing supplies for the order she has coming up."

Emma emerged from the bathroom looking pale but at least no longer green. Logan stopped and watched her.

"You okay, babe?"

"Yeah, I'll live. I feel better now. Where is the bread in this place? Bethany moved everything." Emma started rummaging through the cupboards, then went to the pantry and came out with a metal tin of cinnamon rolls. "Anyone want these?"

"I'm in," said Peter.

"Pass," Logan said, continuing to drink his coffee.

"So, Cole made a break for it. Was that his way of making sure we would have to clean up and he wouldn't?"

"Probably," Logan said.

A grin hit Peter in the face.

"Smart man. Knows his family well."

Logan laughed and Peter frowned.

"Yes, he is a smart man. I have no problem cleaning up. But that doesn't mean I have to put it back where he wants it. We can put the tables in the barn. The chairs in the tack shed, and the trash in his room."

"Come on, Peter. No tricks. Think about Bethany. She will have to deal with him all grumpy. That isn't the way to get your new sister-in-law to like you." Emma set a cinnamon roll on a plate in front of him with a fork.

He smirked. "Maybe you're right." He shoved Logan with an elbow to the ribs as his mischievous glow began to match Peter's. One look from Emma put a stop to that.

Logan blurted out, "Fine. We clean up like good little boys and girls."

Emma kissed Logan on the cheek and then took a bite of her cinnamon roll. "So how are you getting settled into the new house?"

"Okay, I guess. I need to paint, buy some furniture, and find places to shove all the boxes. On the upside, I finished the stonework for my built-in barbeque on the back porch."

She let out a grunt. "Because that was a priority over furniture for the house."

Logan peered at Emma like she was a madwoman. "Of course it is. It's summer. The official barbequing season of the year. A man must have priorities."

Emma rolled her eyes again. "Cute, babe, really cute."

Logan grinned, and it was his turn to kiss her on the cheek. It made Peter want to wrinkle his nose at all the sweet, gooey crap, but that was what surrounded him now. It made him think of Daisy. Would she be a gooey kind of woman? Would she want sweet?

"What's the deal with Daisy Lewin? You guys have been friends since you went to live in Elk View," Peter said, wanting to know more about Daisy.

Logan eyed him suspiciously. "Look, man, she has been through a lot. Just let it go."

"What the hell does that mean? I'm only asking about her because she is in my town. Her father doesn't have the best reputation."

"Oh, I see. This is a keep my town safe kind of thing?" Logan leaned back and crossed his arms over his chest, looking suspicious. "She spent summers with her grandfather because her father didn't really care about her after her mother died giving birth. She liked staying with her grandfather more than her father. If she could have, she would have stayed in Elk View permanently."

Peter chewed his food, hanging onto every word. "So why didn't she stay then?"

Logan shrugged. "Her father liked having her around just enough to put her on display when he thought being the doting father would benefit his work. You know, make him look like a family man, though he wasn't."

Emma pressed her lips into a frown. "How sad. Daisy told me last night three clients pulled out of deals because of her father poking around the company, wanting to be back in charge. She didn't know how long it would take before it fell apart completely because of him." She blew out an aggravated breath. "Can you imagine taking over a company because your father goes to jail, you run it for over six years, gain experience, build a good reputation, and then he just wants you to give it back, even though legally it isn't—and never was—his?" She laughed drily. "The nerve of some men. Like she hasn't proven herself."

Peter took the information and filed it away. Finished with his cinnamon roll, He pushed to his feet. "Well, we better get started. I have to go to work soon."

Collectively they groaned, but managed to get up and go outside. They had the tables loaded onto the trailer to take them back to the rental center before Emma puked again, and the chairs before Peter ran to the side of the house and did the same. Logan picked up trash at a much faster rate as he broke out in a sweat and looked green.

Chapter Four

Daisy looked at herself in the mirror for the last time. It was a good choice, going with the black slacks and rose-pink blouse. She didn't look intimidating at all. She hadn't slept well, and when she woke up this morning, her back and neck ached.

Having painted on her favorite red lipstick, Daisy gave her high ponytail a quick brush with her fingers. "You got this. Pull this off and it will be a new beginning."

Why did she feel like a bug about to fly into a spider's web? She gently ran a finger under her eyes. The dark circles had been hard to cover up, but she could barely see them now.

When she left her hotel room, warm air tickled her skin. It was going to be a hot one. She strolled toward her car, which was covered in dust, and saw Cole's wedding invitation lying on the ground. She picked it up and surveyed her surroundings carefully. She prayed her father didn't have his minion spying on her right then. She didn't want him to poke about the poor old Mr. Buller because of her, trying to find out what her intentions were with seeing him.

Once on the road, Daisy kicked into business mode. The GPS took her down long roads with fields of corn and softly rolling hills where cattle roamed. After fifteen minutes, things became a bit more difficult. The GPS stopped working, so Daisy had to pull over in the middle of nowhere and retrieve her paper map. She squinted at it and then up at the fork in the road. There wasn't a sign, and the two roads didn't show on her map. At least the roads were narrow, and with all the dust her car was kicking up, if someone were to follow her, she would notice.

She crumpled the map and shoved it behind her seat. Exasperated, she drove her car to the right. She would either find Mr. Buller's log home or she wouldn't find a thing. Then she could turn around and try the other way. Simple choices, really.

Making her way down the bumpy dirt road, she recalled one of the times Grandpoo described Mr. Buller's property. She looked around the area, praying she would see something she remembered.

On her right, the land rolled with small hills, growing until they were powerful mountains in the distance. To the left the land was flat, with tall, sweeping grass with tips of gold that rustled with the breeze. Moving further down the road, she stopped the car. There, about half a mile away, was a small log home. "Here we go."

As she drove up to the house, she steeled herself. It was very different from her apartment in downtown Boise. Climbing out of the car, she fussed with her blouse for a minute, gathering her courage. She put on her game face and headed toward the front door.

The porch was a bit rickety. Her nerves took hold as she knocked firmly against the wood. After a minute, the door opened a crack. A short, wrinkly, bald-headed man stared out at her with vivid, green eyes.

"Go away!" he said.

"Mr. Buller, I'm Daisy . . . Lewin."

The door opened a little wider. "Lewin? Any relation to Fred Lewin?"

"Yes, he was my grandfather," she said, doing her

best not to sound too nervous.

"Did you hear that, Lucy? Fred's granddaughter," he said over his shoulder before looking back at her. "I suspect he's passed."

"Yes, a few months ago," was all she managed.

"What are you here for?" Mr. Buller's critical eyes raked over her face.

"My grandfather talked about this place when I was younger. I came to town for Cole Verbeck's wedding, and thought it would be nice to finally see it." She gave him the smile she reserved for her grandfather, hoping it would reveal just enough of herself so Mr. Buller wouldn't see her as a stranger.

"We can have some tea on the back porch. Best view is back there." The old, wrinkly man turned and shuffled off.

Daisy followed him, grateful the smile worked. She must have looked as sad and pathetic as she felt for Mr. Buller to let her into his home. She felt blessed to have gotten on his good side so soon. *That's a stretch.*

The inside of the house was a rich, golden honey, with runs of dark maple stringing through the logs that formed the outer walls. Daisy sucked in a breath, awed. The floor was shiny like glass and the ceiling was high, with a large chandelier made of antlers placed in the center.

"You coming?" asked Mr. Buller, looking impatiently from around a corner.

"Yes, pardon the delay. Your home is lovely."

When she rounded the corner Mr. Buller had vanished, so she stood rooted to the spot. The entire back of the house was made up of glass windows. Who could have guessed this log home was such a gem?

"Come, come. Sit!" Mr. Buller said, irritation crested deep between his wrinkles.

He ushered her into a patio chair on the back porch.

Moving rather quickly for an old man, he disappeared into the house. Daisy took in the view and sucked in a breath. Wow. Her grandfather never said there was a small lake on the property. It was stunning, with all the evergreens hugging a portion of the shore. It reminded her of a fairy land where at any moment a winged creature would zip past.

Mr. Buller arrived moments later with two glasses of tea. "What do you think of the lake?"

"Stunning."

"It's more than stunning, my dear. It's the best property in the area, other than the Verbeck ranch. The Miller ranch isn't too bad either."

Daisy saw pride shining in his eyes and she grumbled to herself. Pride was a tough thing to woo.

"I would've had that piece of land too, if it weren't for that Cole who wanted to keep it for himself." He scrunched up his face. "Could be worse, I suppose. At least he's a second generation of Havencrest. The land made him a man. Possibly sooner than it ought to have, what with all that bad business with his brother and father dying and his mom running off."

"What do you mean by that?" A knot formed in her gut. That didn't sound promising at all. Her nerves started to misfire and she set her tea down. She didn't want to show the old man how shaky she was becoming.

"Cole could've sold the ranch to some city slicker when he was younger. Some guy wanted to build a resort with a golf course. Ruin the land; that's what that slicker wanted to do."

Great! Mr. Buller doesn't like outsiders, and he'll only see me as a city slicker.

Wanting to keep the mood light, she asked a question she'd wanted to know for years. "How did you end up with my grandfather's land? He never really said why it was sold."

Mr. Buller regarded her intensely, the green in his eyes darkening. "I think that would be something he'd be keeping to himself. Seeing as it cast your father in a poor light."

So much for lightening the mood. It was suddenly five degrees colder in Mr. Buller's company.

"Why?" she pressed. She wanted to know why Grandpoo sold this place if he loved it so much.

Mr. Buller shrugged. "Guess it makes no difference if you know, now that he's gone. Don't know why he thought it was his fault . . . how your father turned out."

Daisy's jaw fell open. Why was he rambling on about her father? Did her father have something to do with her grandfather selling the land?

"Did Fred ever tell you we were friends all them years back?"

"Yes and no. It was kind of implied. He said he wished he could've been like you."

Mr. Buller frowned into his tea glass, looking misty-eyed. Shit. She hit a sensitive nerve. That could be good . . . maybe?

Out of nowhere, he yelled, "Hear that, Lucy? Fred wanted to be like me!" He glared at Daisy. "A load of horse shit if I ever heard it. You trying to play me, girl?"

Daisy shifted in her seat. "No. Not at all." A feeling of dread hit her. Things were about to go south. She couldn't let that happen. If she did, she would be letting Grandpoo down, and she couldn't handle that. She glanced around the house, looking for a distraction. "Mr. Buller, who're you talking to?"

"My wife. She liked Fred; thought he was good-looking. Teased me a lot, said she married the wrong one. But she knows she got the right one. She just likes to see me get jealous."

Daisy was confused. From her research, Mr. Buller's wife had died years ago. She wondered if he had remarried.

"Why doesn't she join us for tea?" Daisy asked.

Shrugging, Mr. Buller got up and shuffled into the house, only to return with a floral vase. He set it on the table. Daisy was even more confused, and now she was concerned for the old man's mental health.

"Here she is."

Daisy pressed her lips. "Um . . . Mr. Buller, that's a vase," she said as politely as she could.

"I know. She's in the vase." She looked at him, and he chuckled. "Lucy died years ago. Makes me feel better to talk to her like she's still here. Makes the hurt ache less."

"I'm sorry for your loss."

He waved her off. "So, what're you really here for? Did I not sign something right all those years ago? You here to take back my land?"

"No . . ." She felt like a fat piece of meat dangling in front of a wolf. She couldn't shake the feeling that there was more to the story "Not to take it, but . . . to buy it."

Mr. Buller slapped his knee. "I knew it! Didn't I tell you, Lucy, that they would be back to take our home? The daughter of that slimy slicker Daniel Lewin. Here to pick up where he left off." He slammed a fist on the table, sending tea sloshing from their glasses.

"Mr. Buller, I don't know what you're talking about. What does my father have to do with this?"

"Why don't you tell me? How much was he going to offer this time? A million? Two million? I'll never sell my land to a slicker like your father."

"But my father doesn't know I'm here." She shot to her feet, hot at being compared to her father. She was nothing like him. Her grandfather made sure of that with his kindness and love. "I'm nothing like that man."

His eyes narrowed, but that was it. She could see there would be no more talking.

"Get out of my house. Get out now."

"My pleasure."

Chapter Five

Peter had made sure to stay far enough back so Daisy wouldn't notice him in his patrol car. He wanted to witness her actually leaving town. Beautiful as she was, she was still a Lewin . . . or maybe that was what he told himself so he could see her one last time. Once Peter had spotted Daisy at the wedding and recognized her from the newspaper, he was unsure as to her invite. When he had asked about her presence, he found out she was there because of Logan. Peter had bombarded him with questions, refusing to leave him alone until he heard a few stories about Daisy to prove their friendship.

When she pulled out of the parking lot at the hotel and turned right, it was evident she wasn't leaving just yet. Interested, and slightly hopeful for one more day to aggravate a beautiful woman, he tailed her five miles out of town. When she'd turned onto Bruce Buller's property, he stopped on the side of the road about half a mile behind her. What was she doing going to Buller's? You didn't just drive onto Buller's land unless you had an invitation, and he would bet Miss Lewin didn't have one.

Running a hand over his face, he concluded that she just made a wrong turn. She could have been trying to get to the dam. A lot of people turned too soon and ended up on Buller's land. It drove Buller crazy when strangers showed up uninvited. He'd taken to scaring the out-of-towners off with a gun. Buller was a grumpy sort, and everyone in town stayed clear of him. He reminded Peter of his father, hardworking, and a solitary kind of man.

Then again, Daisy could know exactly what she was doing. He gave her thirty minutes and then he was going to be that nosy, pesky sheriff everyone hated.

He sat there, tapping his hands on the steering wheel, going back and forth between rolling the windows down for fresh air and closing them back up for air-conditioning. At one point, he turned on the radio and played a game on his phone. Finally, enough time had passed, so he put the car in gear and headed down the long driveway.

Peter pulled in behind the dusty, black Audi and parked, then meandered up to the porch, doing his best to make it look like his weekly visit to check on Buller ever since the old man broke his hip last year from a fall and couldn't make it to a phone to call for help. If it hadn't been for the mail carrier dropping off a package that needed a signature, Buller could have died. Buller might be a sour-face old man, but Peter enjoyed his company immensely.

The sun was bright and the heat of the day was setting in. All appeared to be calm. Only the rustling of the tall grass could be heard. He'd worried himself for nothing.

Just then the front door flew open and Daisy exploded from the house, with Buller at her heels. Peter stopped her from stumbling down the porch steps.

She jerked as his arms wrapped around her waist, holding her up.

"What are you doing here?" she asked.

"I'm on patrol. I always come by to check on this grumpy old man."

"Oh," she said, frowning.

"You get off my property!" Buller cried.

"I didn't do anything! You haven't even listened to why I came," said Daisy, righting herself.

Peter didn't know what was happening, but Buller's feathers sure were ruffled.

"Why should I care what you're doing here as long as you're leaving!" bellowed Buller. Then he reached for something beside his door and Peter ushered Daisy behind him. When Buller pulled out a rifle, Peter grumbled and placed a hand on his own gun.

"Buller, I wouldn't be shooting her today if I were you."

"And why not? She would look good stuffed and mounted on my wall."

"Yeah, but the mess! Wouldn't be fun to clean up at your age," said Peter, trying to touch Buller's sense of humor.

"Hey," Daisy said, but she didn't move from behind him. Peter could tell she was scared, and she damn well better be. In his opinion, Buller should be in a nursing home so someone could keep an eye on him.

"Hmm . . . you're right. She's kind of thick. I'm sure she would be a bleeder," Buller said, and Daisy scoffed. Peter held back a smile, mainly because the intense look on Buller's face turned to a mask of stone. "She wants my land so she can mow it down and put some resort on it. I just know it. Destroy our home."

"I didn't say that. You're putting words in my mouth!" Daisy snapped.

Peter peered back at her; she was clinging to the back of his uniform. She shook her head. "I never said that. He didn't give me a chance to tell him anything," she whispered, more to herself than to him. Her skin was pale, and beads of sweat formed on her brow. Daisy didn't look so good. How the hell did she make big purchasing deals for property if she couldn't handle an old man?

"He's old and he talks to his dead wife. What did you think was going to happen?" Peter said, and she wrinkled her face. Irritation ate at him. He wasn't a man to be left out of the loop. He was the damn sheriff.

"Get her off my property and I won't shoot her."

"I don't want the land for a resort!" she yelled. Her hand wrapped over Peter's shoulder, causing his pulse to beat faster.

"Oh really? You want to know why your grandfather sold me his land?"

"Yes." Daisy's voice cracked.

As much as she appeared to need the information Buller was withholding, Peter was eager to learn what this exchange was all about. "Why don't you put that gun down, Bruce, and we can talk about this."

Bruce lowered his gun, though he still seemed on edge.

"Some hotshot showed up in town wanting to put Havencrest on the map with some fancy resort and town-houses, and convinced Daniel your grandfather needed to sell his land to him. But your grandfather loved our town just the way it is—a rancher's town. He sold the land to me before your father could get his fingers on it. Fred took the money and created the Lewin Land Development company as a way to keep an eye on Havencrest. Fred got LLD running well, and growing, then let your father step into his role. Fred did his best to keep your father as far away from here as he could."

Buller finally put the gun back inside the house and Peter let out a tense breath. He really didn't want to have to shoot Buller today—or any other day, for that matter. Peter turned and gripped Daisy's elbow, trying to direct her to her car. When Daisy stepped out from behind him, he saw that she was crying. His irritation turned to com-passion.

"I don't want to do that to the property," she said.

"Why do you want it then?" Buller asked. "I know about you. You're a businesswoman like your father. How can I trust anything you say?"

The wind blew, kicking up a cloud of dust.

"You can't." She wiped a tear from her cheek. "I love my grandfather. He's the reason I'm here. Not my father." She lifted a hand and gestured toward the land surrounding them. "Because my grandfather loved this place, I would give all I have to buy it just to feel him close to me again. He was my world, and the only man who ever really loved me." Her head dropped. "I miss him."

Peter knew what it was like to miss someone you loved—his mother, his father, his younger brother, Joel. The Verbecks had their fair share of loss.

Buller's face softened for a second. "Prove it," he said. His voice sounded like rocks in a can.

"Prove what?"

"That this place means something to you because of the memory of Fred, and I'll consider selling."

An invisible force punched Peter in the gut. Did Buller really say he would sell his land? He peered at Daisy.

A fiery determination caused her to straighten. "How?"

Buller gazed at Peter, the wheels in his head turning fast. "Show me you're not a slicker without a heart."

"How do I do that?"

"Get involved . . ." Buller frowned. "With the town. Get to know the people. Show me it's worth your time. I want to see that you understand what it means to be part of a small town, so you won't be so willing to destroy it."

"I do know what it's like to be part of a small community. I spent my summers in Elk View with my grandfather on the land he bought after he left here. Logan Miller is one of my closest friends."

"I don't believe you." Buller folded his arms over his chest.

"You think because I drive a nice car and wear nice clothes that I don't know how to get my hands dirty. Well, I do."

"I don't believe you!" Buller spat.

Her jaw dropped. "I can't stay here. I have a job, a life in Boise."

Buller shrugged. "Guess it don't mean as much to you as you let on." He turned his back on them, ready to shut the front door.

"What do I do?" she whispered to Peter. Fear was etched in her beautiful face.

"What he wants you to do. Buller never talked about selling to anyone. Ever!"

Daisy looked conflicted as she ran her hand over her hair. She shook her head. "Fine," she blurted out. "Fine. I'll do what you ask. I'll stay."

Buller stopped. "Two months."

"What? Two months! You're mad. I have projects to oversee."

"Fine, three months then," Buller said stubbornly, like he was dealing with an argumentative child.

Daisy bit her bottom lip. "Two months. I'll stay for two months and get involved. What do you want me to do?"

"Your time is up on the two months. It's three now. You stay for three months. If what you say is true about Elk View and Logan, your job is to remember how to live!"

⤜♥⤛

Daisy blinked in shock as Mr. Buller slammed his door and locked it. She couldn't believe her grandfather sold his land to a friend to keep it safe from his son.

She knew her father was a piece of work, but this was extremely disappointing. No wait, scratch that. It sounded exactly like her father.

Brushing a hand over her face, she turned her fear to anxiety and the anxiety to dread. It wasn't much of a shift, but it was better than being afraid.

When she looked up, Peter was staring at her. With her hair all over the place and her makeup ruined from crying, what a picture she must have made. Like a half-drowned street cat, that's what. She spun around and rushed over to her car. She didn't have time to worry about Peter or how she looked. She couldn't let her father find out that she talked to Buller. He would ruin any chances at persuading Buller to sell his property to her if he came poking around. Her dread inched up her veins, causing her to scratch. *Shit, all I need is hives to round out the morning perfectly.*

She peered around, checking to see if her father's little minion was nearby. It would be difficult to stay in Havencrest for three months and not have her father find out. If she hadn't worn her Gucci heels, she would have kicked the damn car door. No, maybe a tire. She loved her car. She opened the door and flopped into the seat.

"Well, that could have gone better."

"I thought it went well," came Peter's deep voice. He was hovering near her car.

"What? Did you not hear him? I have to convince him I'm not my father."

"That should be easy. Just don't hire a hitman to take anyone out for three months and you should be fine!"

What a jerk! If only it were that simple. She would never live down what her father had done. It made it diffi-cult to look anyone in the eye.

"He didn't shoot you, and he gave you a chance to get what you want. It's better than a no." Peter smiled, and his honey-gold eyes twinkled. He rested an arm on the car door, getting closer than Daisy wanted.

"If you want to look at it like that, I guess you're right." Daisy allowed herself to relax. "I hope Logan has an extra room I can rent for three months, because I can't live out of a hotel for that long."

"No, he doesn't. But I do."

Daisy glared hard at him. What did he want from her? Was it worth a three-month exploration? His smile warmed her bone-deep. She looked away. No, definitely not. He was a distraction she didn't need.

"Really, and would that be in the same room as you?" she said sarcastically. "I think I can find another arrangement."

Peter studied her before answering. "No. I just bought a house in town. It needs some work. I was going to fix it up and see about getting a roommate."

Well, great. Now I'm the jerk. "How much is the rent?"

"I was thinking four hundred a month. If you want, you can come by and check it out before you make a decision. I get off at six." Peter walked over to his patrol car and got in. He scribbled on a piece of paper, then walked back over and handed it to her.

The paper read: 1131 E. Main Street.

"Come by at six thirty. We can have brats and beer."

"Okay." She wasn't sure about this. She didn't know much about Peter. Maybe she should give Logan a call and see what his thoughts were about renting a room from his brother-in-law.

Just then, his radio cut in. "Verbeck. I got Mrs. Salmons down here at the station saying Bobby Joe from next door stole her cat. She wants to talk to you."

Peter walked back to his car and picked up the radio. "I'll be right there." He gave her a wink.

Does he think I'm going to swoon or something?

"How about I follow you to the main road to be safe, make sure Buller doesn't change his mind and shoot you after all?"

Daisy didn't hesitate at the thought of possibly getting shot. She closed the door and started up her car. At the main road, she pulled off to the side. Peter pulled up.

"See you at six thirty. Small-town duty calls." Peter drove off with a cloud of dust kicking up behind him.

Daisy's head fell back. Three months. How would she survive without Starbucks or Dutch Bros?

Chapter Six

Peter was in his car and had half his uniform stripped off by 6:10 p.m. He made good time following all the traffic signs, lights, and speed limits, although his left eye twitched when Mr. Swift leisurely crossed the road, waving to him and mumbling to his whiskey bottle at the stop sign.

Peter tracked into his navy-blue, one-story house, peered around at all the boxes, and clenched his jaw. *Damn. What a disaster. Why did I say six thirty? I should have said seven thirty.* He ran a hand over his slicked-back hair. He knew why he'd said six thirty and he hated himself for it. The urge to see Daisy as soon as possible clouded his judgment.

A month ago, he'd closed on this house. He'd been eyeing it since Bethany and Olivia moved in with Cole. As much as he had loved Bethany's cooking and seeing his brother happy, Peter felt like he was in the way. It was perfect timing that Cole got married because Peter had an excuse to buy a home and sell off his one-third of the Verbeck ranch to Cole. Ranching just wasn't his thing.

The house was built in the eighties, though it was still in good condition. It sat on a two-acre square lot. The kitchen and bathrooms were remodeled, but the rest of the house needed painting and the backyard needed landscaping.

He had fifteen minutes. He started stacking boxes against the walls in the living room. Next, he hurried to his bedroom, kicked off his shoes, and yanked off his pants and shirt. He quickly put on some shorts, then ran to the bedroom he was going to try to rent out. More boxes. He stacked them in the walk-in closet. He hadn't cared about the closet when he'd bought the house, but he knew it could be something Daisy would like. He smiled.

Strolling into the living room, he glanced around. He only had the basics: couch, coffee table, and an eighty-inch, flat-screen TV. A zing of excitement shot through him whenever he looked at it. Soon he would order more stuff for the house, but it was functional, and that was all that mattered for the moment.

He made for the kitchen and started gathering everything he would need to BBQ. He heard a car door slam. Running to the backyard, he threw everything onto the new, built-in grill he finished building two days ago, complete with a fridge and countertop. He arranged everything neatly, gathered his frazzled nerves, and acted like nothing mattered.

A knock echoed loudly through the house from the front door at six thirty on the dot. He stayed where he was, buying himself some time to get it together, and called out instead. "The door is open! Come on in!"

༘♥༘

Daisy turned the doorknob slowly, wondering if there was another option for housing. After leaving Mr. Buller's, she made some calls from her hotel room. No one in town had a month-to-month leasing agreement, and to stay at the hotel was going to cost too much. Peter's offer was her best option.

The door opened and she stepped inside. "Hello?" she called out, but got no answer. Well, he was telling the truth about just buying the house. He wasn't even unpacked yet. Boxes were stacked against all the walls.

The house was larger than it appeared from the front. The living room ceiling was high, and it connected to an open kitchen. The cabinets were a dark mocha, with shiny, white appliances and a tan granite countertop. It was . . . cute.

Just then, Peter emerged from the door that led into the backyard with an infectious grin on his face. The shock of seeing him half-naked hit her full force. Her breath hitched in her throat. An unwelcome blush crept into her cheeks and flooded her body all the way to her toes. She drank him in. She couldn't turn her eyes away. There was a faint light twinkling in the depths of his golden eyes that made him all the more attractive.

She self-consciously ran a hand over the front of her white, lacy, thigh-length summer dress and tried to think of something to say, fiddling with the brim of a matching floppy summer hat.

"Right on time," Peter said. "Did you want to look around first, or come have a seat and a drink while I cook?"

"A drink would be great."

He turned away from her and she rested a hand over her face. It's only a torso, she chastised herself. *A finely sculpted torso . . .*

She followed him to the porch and was greeted by a huge, green backyard covered with three, good-sized trees. It was clear Peter had good taste in a home.

Peter held out a chair for her and she sat down. He went to a small fridge and held up three different drinks. "Coors, Budweiser, or a White Claw Hard Seltzer," he said. "Emma likes to drink the White Claw. Says she can have twice as many before she has to go run it off, so I keep some around."

Pleasure tipped Daisy's smile higher on her cheeks. She didn't want to admit it, but that was kind of him to think of his sister. She didn't have any siblings. Logan was the closest thing she had. Logan and Daisy had been outsiders in Elk View. They got along well with the other kids in town, but there was a connection of time the others shared that she and Logan didn't.

"I'll give the White Claw a try."

He opened the can and handed it to her, then put six bratwursts, some corn on the cob, and a few hamburgers onto the grill. *How much does he think I am going to eat?* She watched the muscles in his back and arms flex. She took a swallow of her drink, enjoying the view. This was what she needed after this morning's botched meeting.

She still hadn't thought of what she would tell her assistant, but she had time. Her father would be out of town for at least three or four days, since he was in New York. Her father might have his spy, but she also had many others in their business keeping tabs on where Daniel Lewin was and what he was doing there. She was told he was looking for investors to start up a new company. She'd run LLD's marketing and advertising team from the time she graduated top of her class from college. When he went to jail, she had been propelled into large-scale project management of an entire company. The fact that she enjoyed it had surprised her. And that she had run it better than her father ever had, with some help from her grandfather, encouraged her to stick with it. However, with her dad's return the atmosphere had darkened, and she didn't know if she could fix it.

She pushed thoughts of her father away and quieted her mind. The silence grew around her and she soaked it in, letting it calm her. The city never had silence like this. A rural landscape carries a sense of peace.

"What are you thinking about?" Peter asked, tongs in

his hand.

How much of herself was she willing to share? She didn't really know at this point. "How long have you lived here?" she asked, changing the direction of the conversation.

Peter frowned and shrugged. "About a month."

"And you still have boxes everywhere?"

"What can I say? I'm a busy man."

"Here in this town? Busy? You're joking, right?"

He raised a brow, walked over to her, and clicked the oversized barbeque tongs in her face. "You'd be surprised." Peter was close enough that she could smell Old Spice aftershave and sweat.

"How much did you pay for the house? The market has slowly been going up the last three years," she said, taking a sip of her drink.

Peter took a long sip of his beer, then wiped his mouth on the back of his hand. He peered back at her. "I got a good deal."

"Is that your way of saying you're not going to tell me?"

"No, it's my way of stopping boring conversation."

She shouldn't have been surprised by Peter's blunt comment. He was a ladies' man, and they never wasted time with small talk. "Well then, what would you like to talk about?"

"Your hopes, your dreams . . . stuff that really matters. What do you like to do for fun?"

She leaned back and folded her arms across her chest. "I see an interrogation of sorts. Is this how you treat all your guests?"

He flashed her his come-and-get-me smile, and she could have laughed at his sad attempt to charm her. It would take much more than a smile to entice this so-called city girl to do anything she didn't want to do. She had vast experience negotiating purchasing deals with men who tried that crap on her all the time. She let them think it was working until she got them right where she wanted. Then she closed the deal and walked away smiling. Except for Mr. Buller. He didn't fall to her charms. If she was honest with herself, her heart hadn't really been in it this morning. She'd been too shaken by the news of her father's interference in her grandfather's life.

"No, not all my guests. Only the beautiful ones, I guess." At least he was being honest, which was a nice change of pace. She had to keep her distance, though, to be safe. But it was a good beginning.

"Fine. Me first. What do you do for fun around here? Go fishing? Play cards?"

᠆♥᠆

Peter almost grimaced with that comment as he turned the brats and the corn on the grill. Small-town hick; that's what she thought of him. He should have known she wouldn't see past the country boy. Well, he would show her there was more to this farm boy than she imagined.

"I like to run on the trail by the river and around the area," he said. Daisy's brows were raised high on her forehead. What a shocker. A runner in a small town.

"You run?"

"Yes, since high school. It even paid for my criminal justice degree."

Daisy leaned forward and rested her elbows on the table. She was interested. Good.

"Where did you study?"

"Boise State. Love that Smurf Turf."

She half-smiled. "I go to a few of the BSU football games every year for fun. I went to Berkeley for communications with Logan. I'm sure he already told you that."

"No, he didn't. I knew about the summers you spent

in Elk View, but not college, until recently. It's interesting, he never said anything about that. Did the two of you have a fling?" He studied her for a minute, intrigued, then he pulled the brats and corn off the grill and onto a large plate.

Daisy shot him a hard, disgusted look. "No way. He's one of my favorite people. He is the brother I always wanted." She shrugged, then jumped up and took the plate from his hand. She set it on the table and he hurried into the house to get the plates, utensils, and chips, happy to have more information about her. When he returned, she handed him another beer and had turned off the gas to his grill. *Nice. I could get used to this.*

Daisy couldn't help but admire the determined spirit most runners had. They were not afraid to push their body and mind to reach for more. She used to have the same spirit before her father chipped it away in his pursuit of perfect obedience. The last time she ran, she didn't make it a mile before she was sitting on the side of the road with her head between her knees, trying not to pass out. Everything she loved in her life, her father had stained with his disapproval. When she had joined the cross-country team her junior year in high school she could run a 5K in twenty-one minutes. She could have pushed and gotten faster. But running wasn't prestigious enough for him, so he'd made it difficult for her to make practices and she had to quit.

"Running paid for school? Were you on the track team?"

"Sure was!"

Daisy grinned. "Do you still run?" she asked, peering at her bratwurst in its bun. How was she going to get all that into her mouth and not make a mess and look like a fool?

"Once a runner, always a runner." Peter lifted his brat that was smothered in mustard and sauerkraut and shoved it into his mouth without hesitation. The look on his face as he chewed was kind of endearing. What! No, not endearing. Cute. Oh no, he was getting to her.

His eyes were closed, and he chewed like he was eating his all-time favorite. She tried to take a small bite. It didn't work; it was too big, so she smashed the bun flat. When she looked up, Peter was staring at her with a horrified look on his face.

"You killed it."

"Just a little," she said, wrinkling her nose at him before she took a big bite. Juice from the bratwurst squirted Peter in the face.

She jumped to her feet and wiped him with her napkin. "Oh . . . I'm . . . sorry," she stammered with her mouth full.

～❤～

Peter stared in fascination as Daisy wiped his face, mostly in shock at the instinct. It was very motherly of her. He gently grabbed her smooth, slender fingers and held them for a moment. She was beautiful with her full lips in a grimace, her brow wrinkled with concern. She swallowed and her cheeks colored. It was such a turn-on to know he could make her blush. There was hope for this small-town boy. His train of thought slammed into park when she pulled her hand away and quickly sat back in her seat.

They talked about college and the things they did, but nothing else that could help him read her better and get to know who she really was. It was as if she knew exactly how to get around all the questions, stopping just before she could reveal anything significant about herself. At a loss, he picked up their empty plates.

"Want to see the room?"

Daisy followed him into the house. After putting the dishes in the sink, he showed her the two spare bedrooms.

"I was going to make this into an office, but if you like it better than the other room, I can switch."

He didn't wait to see her reaction. He walked down the hall to the other room and opened the door. This time, he waited. As she passed, he caught her perfect scent of honey and spice.

"This room is a little bigger than the other and"—he walked over to the closet and opened the door—"it has a walk-in closet." Daisy beamed, delighted, but then frowned. "What, it's not big enough?"

She glared at him. "No, it's great, but I have no clothes to fill it up with. I only brought stuff for a few days."

Peter swore he could see Daisy's bottom lip start to pout. "I don't think Mr. Buller will mind if you go home to get some things and bring them back."

She bit her lip. "Do you think so? I really don't want to risk him changing his mind."

"If you're worried, I was thinking of driving to Boise to do some furniture shopping. You can come with me and help me look around. Then we can go by your place and get your things."

"Do you think you can tell Mr. Buller for me? Maybe make it sound like a volunteer-slash-charity thing?"

Peter narrowed his eyes. So now he was a charity case. He tried not to get testy with her. The pleading in her eyes told him this was important and she didn't want to screw it up.

"Sure, I can tell him tomorrow. So, what do you think? Want to be my roommate?"

"I don't want to be in your way. It looks like you have work to do."

"Look at it like this: You'll be helping me decide if having a roommate is really for me or not." He hoped that would push her over the edge he saw her standing on.

"I have nothing to lose at this point. Three months, four hundred a month." She let out a long sigh. "I'll have the money for you tomorrow."

"Don't worry about it. I know you're good for it. I'll pick you up at seven. That way, we can be in Boise by the time the stores open."

Daisy went stiff. "Sounds good. Thank you for dinner, and for working out this arrangement with me."

Peter hid his scowl. She walked out to her car without another word.

Chapter Seven

The phone rang and Peter stared at it with distaste. What time was it? He rolled over and looked at the clock. It was six in the morning. Hell, he needed to be out the door to pick up Daisy soon. He stretched out and peered at his phone.

"Hello?" he mumbled.

"Listen here, you pain in the ass. Why did you tell Daisy you wanted a roommate? You moved out of Cole's because you said you were tired of having people around all the time, and now this? If this has anything to do with Daisy being the apple of your eye, I'm going to cut down the whole fucking apple tree. Got it? You keep your hands off her. She's not going to be a notch on your bedpost."

The line went dead. Holy hell. He hadn't heard Logan that fired up . . . ever. Logan obviously felt like playing the overbearing stand-in brother. Well, Logan could be as grumpy as he wanted, but he had Daisy all to himself, and he was looking forward to it.

He was up and showered in a flash. He was dressed and heading to the kitchen for breakfast when the phone rang again.

"Listen, if you're calling to yell at me again, forget it. I'm not listening—"

"Yeah . . . hi, Peter. It's Daisy."

Peter's chin dropped to his chest.

"I got your number from Logan. I hope you don't mind. I was calling to let you know I'm staying at the Havencrest Inn. I will be waiting out front."

He already knew that, but he sure as hell wasn't going to let her know. What a great conversation starter: "I know you're staying there. I caught sight of you pulling out of the inn yesterday and followed you to Buller's." No, he would keep that to himself because it had snoopy sheriff written all over it.

"I'll be there in about fifteen minutes. Is this your cell phone?" he asked.

"Yes." She hung up on him. Two for two. If that was an indication for the day, things weren't looking good. He shrugged and grabbed the milk to go along with his Lucky Charms. There had to be a way to weasel his way into Daisy's good graces. He had to come up with a plan to show her he was a prize.

⋞♥⋟

Daisy sat in the large, 350 diesel truck eyeing the side mirror. Peter was serious about getting furniture. The flat-bed trailer attached to the truck was big enough to move a house in one trip. It had been a long time since she had ridden in a truck like this. It felt rugged and tough.

Adjusting her seat belt, she leaned to the side and tucked her legs up by her bottom. She was glad she chose yoga pants and a running top for the drive back home. She still didn't know what she was going to say to her assistant about working out of the office for THREE months. With her being gone that long, her father could get ideas. She was in the middle of closing three land purchases outside Boise: two in Mountain Home and one in Kuna, to build more affordable housing. She could finish closing the deals on video conferencing and find a notary in town for any signing she needed to do. But she wouldn't be surprised if her father did start up a new company, and he would be out for blood. She was sure he would go after her sellers and try to convince them he could get them more money for their land than she could. She blew out a breath. She didn't have a clue what her life would be like for the next three months but for once, she was excited about the unknown. She only prayed that by some miracle she could pacify Mr. Buller.

"Where do you want to go first? Your place or shopping?"

"Better hit my place first, don't you think? That way, you don't have to drive all over town with a full trailer."

"Sounds logical to me. Where do you live?"

"Downtown, off South Eighth Street. I'll jump out and run up."

"I can park. Are you going to need help with anything?"

"No," she snapped, not wanting help from him. A pang of guilt hit her in the chest. She didn't mean to sound like a shit. It was easier if she did things herself. Other people tended to make things more complicated than they had to be. That was one thing she took away from her father that had been useful.

Peter narrowed his eyes at her.

She hugged the door a little, feeling uncomfortable when she saw that look, even if it was nicely wrapped in hard cords of muscle and good hair. A warning to keep her distance sounded.

Peter regarded her for a moment, then his eyes softened. He rolled down his window for some air. "What did you tell Logan? He called me this morning howling up a storm."

Her jaw dropped, suddenly mortified. "I told him I would be staying in town on business for a while, and that you offered me a room."

Logan always worried about her, and she loved him for it. After he went on to law school and she went to work at LLD, she visited him every chance she could. Which over the years became less and less. She pulled at her yoga pants. She glanced over at Peter, who stared out at the road thoughtfully, and wondered what things could be like with a man like him.

The drive into Boise was peaceful and relaxing, and it had given her time to work out in her head what she would have to do to keep LLD moving along while she was in Havencrest. She frowned at the thought of endless video conferences and phone calls. But she could make it work.

When Peter came into town and drove down the busy streets of downtown without a curse or shout because of the traffic, Daisy's interest in this small-town man continued to grow. Being here didn't seem to bother him like so many others when coming from a smaller town into the city.

Daisy couldn't believe Peter managed to claim an open spot in front of her building, truck trailer and all. That never happened.

"Do you mind if I come in with you?" he asked as they jumped out of the truck.

"Why?" Daisy asked.

"I need to use the bathroom."

"Oh! Sure."

She made for the lobby of her apartment building. Yeah, hers. She'd bought an old bank and a few run-down homes and built some affordable downtown housing with her own money. This was the first project she'd seen completed start to finish all on her own. Her father couldn't get his fingers on it. The tenants didn't know that she owned it, and she wanted to keep it that way.

Peter was at her heels. As they climbed the ten flights of stairs to her floor, he didn't say a word about not taking the elevator. His long, strong legs took the stairs two at a time. Daisy liked to take the stairs after a long day of work. It helped her shake off the day, and it became a habit.

Rounding the railing on the sixth floor, Peter reached his arm out in front of her and grabbed it swiftly to pull himself into the lead. He skimmed her side and set her blood afire as he passed her with a challenging yet playful grin. It reminded her of something a schoolboy would do while teasing a crush. She accepted the challenge with pleasure.

By the time they reached the tenth floor, Daisy busted through the exit door to her floor, breathing hard. They shoved and elbowed the remainder of the way, and Daisy reached the top first. As she stood in triumph, catching her breath, she looked back to find Peter.

She leaned against the wall to catch her breath. When Peter waltzed through the door, he wore a beautiful smile that split his face and brightened his golden eyes. He was barely breathing hard. She inwardly groaned. He clearly had better cardio endurance than her. She straightened, eyes locking onto his. He sauntered over and placed an elbow against the wall next to her head. Gently, he played with her ponytail. And . . . she let him.

Her nerves began to misfire at his nearness. She was such a sucker. He probably seduced women all the time.

"Aren't you just a little spitfire!" he said.

"You started it."

"Yes, and you finished it, didn't you?" Peter rubbed his side with his free hand. "I think I may have been bruised."

Heat worked its way into her cheeks. "Sorry. I got carried away. Sometimes I can get a little too competitive."

"I can see that."

He leaned in as if he were going to kiss her. She didn't know if she wanted him to. She placed a hand on his chest to stop him. Peter hovered inches away from her lips. His chest muscles were hard beneath her fingertips, and every part of her wanted to melt into a puddle of goo.

"It becomes you." He leaned down and brushed a feather-like kiss on her lips. She was frozen, and she forgot to breathe.

Just then, the door next to them opened and Daisy jumped and stepped away from Peter. Branden, her father's assistant—or more like her father's lackey— looked out into the hallway with a confused look on his face.

What the hell was he doing in her apartment? He had just been in Havencrest breaking into her car. Now her apartment. Her father was going too far. Pushing too hard to get what he wanted. She would stand her ground. Her father didn't know who he was messing with. She wasn't the scared, submissive, obedient girl he left behind when he went to prison. When he'd gone it was like breathing for the first time, feeling free to be who she wanted to be. And she wasn't going to let him take that away from her. No matter what the cost.

She did her best not to appear out of sorts, but then she gave Branden a death stare with fire shooting from her eyes.

"What are you doing in my apartment?" she seethed.

Branden's expression grew dark at the sight of Peter.

Unfazed, Peter strolled over and stuck out his hand. "Peter Verbeck."

Branden shook his hand firmly. "Branden Kent, personal assistant to Mr. Lewin."

Peter released his hand, then shoved it into his pockets. "Bathroom, Daisy?"

"Inside, down the hall, first door on the right."

Peter nodded and disappeared inside.

Daisy hurried past Branden to gather what she needed from her room. Branden followed.

"So, what's the deal with the yoga pants and the guy? Don't you have a meeting with Crouch today? That's why I came by your place, to see if I could help in any way to close the deal."

"No, I canceled the meeting." She was irritated that her father obviously knew about the land sale she needed to close to build an assisted living community. She was sure her father had something up his sleeve to complicate the matter. Inwardly she groaned, not wanting to make a scene with Peter there.

Daisy grabbed a suitcase from her closet and plopped it onto the bed, then marched over to the dresser and pulled her underwear drawer out. She peered up at Branden, wanting to see his reaction to her next words. "I'm taking a vacation for a few weeks."

His eyes bugged out of his head. She almost laughed. She grabbed a handful of underwear and shoved them into the suitcase, then went to another drawer and pulled out a few pairs of pants.

"What?" Confusion cut across Branden's chiseled features.

Daisy almost laughed. Clearly, Branden thought he had her pinned down with all his spying, knowing where she went, with whom, and always searching for the why. But not today. She wished she could see her father's face when Branden told him the news. Perhaps if the pair of them really thought she was on vacation, she could get a break from the spying. "I have vacation time on the books and I'm taking it." She peered over at Branden. "Not to mention, it is my company, so I can do whatever I want."

His jaw clenched. She didn't understand why he was

working for her father. She was sure some promises had been made so he thought he had some right to what went on in LLD and he didn't. Neither one of them did.

Daisy tried not to let the chafing irritation of it all grind against her skin. "Why does my father care about the Crouch deal? It has nothing to do with him."

He said nothing, just as she suspected.

She glared at him. "Don't tell me. I'm sure you will be on the phone with my father before you walk out of my place and I don't care."

Daisy hurriedly stashed her pile of clothes into the suitcase. Wariness and an overwhelming need to slap Branden took hold of her. Mustering up every ounce of self-control she had, Daisy marched to the front door, ripping the cell phone out of Branden's hand as she went, and chucked the phone across the hall. "Go fetch, boy. Be the sad, little minion you are. You can call my father, but I'll be damned if you'll do it in my home."

Branden jerked as the phone smashed into the wall. "You little brat. You're going to regret that."

She folded her hands over her chest and pitched her hip to the side. "I don't think so. This is my company now. You might suck up to my father thinking it is going to get you somewhere, but you're wrong. This company is nothing without me. If Dearest Daddy got his fingers on LLD, it would fold within six months because no one would work with him after what he did. Then all your butt-kissing would be for nothing."

Branden's blue eyes narrowed.

"Hand over my key." She shot out her hand. "I don't know how you got it or how you sugarcoated the reasons to get it from maintenance. But it isn't yours." He dug into his pocket and then freed it from the ring.

Branden stormed out and Daisy slammed the door closed behind him. She growled low, hating that sad excuse of a human. She went back to packing, picking up her speed.

Peter stood in the living room listening intently to the conversation down the hall. Pretty Boy worked for Mr. Lewin. An uneasy feeling settled in his gut. To think he managed to get a copy of the key to Daisy's apartment was odd. He was thankful Daisy took the key from the man.

Once the door slammed closed, he sat on the comfy, tan-colored sofa in the living room trying to act casual, even though his instincts told him something wasn't right about that entire interaction.

All the walls were white except for a large accent wall that was painted the color of blue mason jars just like his mother had loved. Dozens of blue mason jars littered his childhood home, always filled with wildflowers picked by him and Emma.

There was a huge mirror with a rustic frame positioned in the center of the wall. He got up and walked over to it. It was perfectly centered. Daisy had a touch of OCD, or as he liked to think of it, perfectionism. At least that was how he justified his own OCD while he was on the job. Every report was filled out perfectly, and with handwriting that could be mistaken for a typewriter. Everything in his office and his patrol car had a place and a purpose. The same as here. Not that his OCD carried over to his own home. He was a bit of a slob on occasion. And he was okay with that. But looking around his current surroundings, he realized his slob tendencies would be put on hold with the beautiful Daisy Lewin moving in.

Under the mirror on an old-looking table was a vase full of soft-pink roses. The effect of this single wall made the rest of the room relaxed and elegant. He noticed the rest of the house was accented with the same shade of blue. It was apparent she was fond of the color. He made a mental note to suggest they paint a few of the walls in his own house with the same shade. Maybe it would score him a few brownie points.

Daisy came rushing down the hall upset, and he didn't like it. It had taken almost the entire car ride to get her in a good mood, and now this.

"I'm all done packing. We can go," she said to him, lugging a large suitcase and a duffel bag with her.

He rose to his feet and rested a hand on her shoulder. "Are you okay?"

"Sure. I'm fine."

"Who was that guy?"

Daisy glanced over her shoulder at the door. "The enemy. He works for my dad. He spies on me for my father. Like I don't know what my father is up to. He wants control over the company again." Daisy's big eyes studied Peter. "When he went away, I was running everything. I thought the company was his and when he got out of jail, he would take it back over. But it was really my grandfather's. When he died, he left it to me. Not my father." She looked worn out. "It is exhausting dealing with my father and his minion. Where are we going to go first? Mor Furniture or RC Willey?" she asked, smiling sweetly.

That smile didn't fool him. He knew women didn't downshift that fast, regardless of the situation.

He placed a knuckle under her chin, staring deeply into her blue-gray eyes. She went still. "Are you sure you're okay? We don't have to go furniture shopping. We can do something else."

She pushed his hand away. Peter took her chin once more and wrapped his other hand around her waist, drawing her closer to him, wanting her near. He could hear the hurt in her voice, even if she didn't admit it. The feel of her body pressed against him sent tremors through his veins. He envisioned her pressed into the wall, his lips ravaging hers.

"I asked if you're okay, because regardless of who that guy is, he upset you."

❧♥☙

Daisy was speechless. Peter was very perceptive. He seemed genuinely concerned for her feelings. So few were—including her father. She leaned into him against her better judgment. He felt so strong, so male. Could a man like Peter be interested in getting to know her?

"I assure you. I'm fine."

He brushed his lips against hers. Her eyes fluttered closed and the most magnificent heat swept from her lips and throughout her entire body, causing her to shiver. Time froze, and there was nothing else but this moment. No spying father. No Mr. Buller. She wanted to wrap her arms around his neck.

As Peter nibbled at her lips, there was a tingling in the pit of her stomach and her heart beat faster. He was dragging her into waves of desire that she had to break free of. So much fog was filling her mind. It took several moments to cut through it. Finally, the question that always arose when a man worked to gain her interest emerged. What did Peter have to gain by doing this?

Because of her father, suspicion of alternative agendas always clutched at her. She had to be smart about this. She couldn't let a physical attraction rule her. She stepped back. Peter was grinning, and she couldn't help but acknowledge that he was a fine specimen of a man. Was it her money, her influence, or perhaps the novelty of a conquest that he wanted? Only time would tell, as it always did.

Chapter Eight

Peter couldn't believe how Daisy looked like a cat who just caught a big, juicy mouse, pleased with her handiwork.

"What do you think? I finished it all today. I hope you don't mind that I unpacked a lot of your boxes, but I had to see what you had that I could work with, aside from the furniture we bought in Boise last week."

Peter scrubbed his chin at all the books stacked this way and that on the six-foot espresso-colored bookshelf. There were knickknacks he made from his childhood displayed on the shelves. The walls were covered with pictures of him, Cole, Joel, and Emma around the Verbeck ranch. His chest tightened. Daisy had blown them up to different sizes and printed them in black-and-white. They were perfect.

"No worries about unpacking. It would have stayed that way for several months. It looks amazing. You've really done a great job." He flopped down into the new La-Z-Boy sofa and Daisy joined him. She had rearranged the sofa, love seat, and recliner for the best TV viewing, and placed the three end tables next to the seating. It looked like a home, not a storage unit.

Her eyes glittered as she surveyed the house. He liked her this way, relaxed, with robin's egg blue paint on her hands and face, her ponytail draped over her shoulder. He wished she would wear her hair down in soft curls again, like at the wedding. He wanted to run his fingers through it. She hadn't allowed him to get close since he kissed her at her home. He wanted that to change but he wasn't sure how.

She smiled warmly at him. "How was your day? Did anything exciting happen in town?"

He chuckled at the notion. "No, not much. A few jaywalkers, but I let them slide."

Daisy laughed. "How kind of you."

"Yeah." He slapped his legs and stood. "Are you ready to get involved in the community like Mr. Buller ordered, my dear?"

Some of the sparkle left her eyes. She touched her hair nervously. "What's on the agenda?"

"A trail race. I signed you up this afternoon."

"Signed me up? I can't run!"

"Why not?" he asked, scowling playfully.

Daisy bit her lip. "I don't think it's a good idea."

"Come on. It's only a five-K, and there's only one hill."

Daisy fidgeted with her hair again and stared past him. "You have five-Ks here?"

"Sweetheart, you'd be surprised at what this town does to dig up some fun."

"Okay . . . three miles can't be that bad." She looked pale.

Peter smirked. "We have to run past Buller's cabin. He likes to yell at us as we pass. He thinks running for fun is a crazy thing to do."

ﻌﯥ♥ﯤﻌ

Daisy was nervous as she stood near the starting line of the old dirt road. She could see Buller's log home. How was she going to show him she was more than a city slicker? For the past few days, she'd been so caught up in decorating Peter's house—and by the fact that he was letting her have full control, which was suspicious. Yet she'd gone all in. It had been a good distraction from thoughts of her father and how he was due back from New York any time. She hadn't thought of a strategy that would make Buller change his mind about her.

Fidgeting with the hem of her shirt, she twisted it around and around. This was a chance to show Buller she was sincere. Taking a deep breath, she thought about the stairs she ran up and down every day to and from work. A renewed determination flooded through her. *I can do it!*

"We'll run a mile down this road, then up and over that hill leading back to town. We'll end at the city park." Peter pointed to the west.

"What's your pace, Daisy?" Logan asked as he lumbered up behind her.

"I don't know. The last time I went for a run was with you after I thought I flunked my Diversity class with Professor Brooks," she replied. "I didn't know you were going to be here." She gave Logan a hug.

Emma strolled up, swinging her arms across her body, stretching. She hugged Daisy next. "Yay, another runner. We need more runners in the world."

"I don't know about all that. Where are the kids?" Daisy asked.

"At the house with Grandpa Miller. They are going to be at the finish line to see us," Emma said, continuing to stretch.

"How fun. I can't wait to see them."

"They made signs for everyone," Logan said, grinning oddly at her. "So, you're not sure what your pace is . . . hmm? Well, I'm a ten, and if I remember right, I struggled to keep up with you back then. I'm sure you already have me beat."

"You're getting faster all the time, babe. As long as you're not whining," Emma teased.

Logan swept her into his arms and kissed her. "Enough, woman. I don't whine. Merely express my desire to stop at regular intervals."

Emma laughed. The sound drifted around Daisy like a sweet song. She smiled at Logan and their teasing. She was happy he'd found the woman of his dreams.

"No stinking way!" Peter shouted.

They all turned around to see Bethany bouncing happily beside a grumpy-faced Cole.

"No way! She got him to sign up for the run. Cole hates running," Peter said, a laugh exploding past his lips.

"Yay, the whole gang is here. And look, so many others from town too," Bethany exclaimed.

Daisy didn't notice the crowd forming around them. There had to be at least sixty or so people.

"You did good, Bethany. Everyone has their shirts on. I can't believe you organized a run and got all the volunteers to help set everything up," Emma said.

Daisy looked at Peter. "Volunteers for what? It's a five-K."

A brilliant smile split Peter's handsome face and butterflies fluttered in her stomach. "You'll see."

She eyed him, wondering what his running pace was if he had been running since high school. "So, how fast is your mile?"

He raised a brow. "An eight-minute mile. Used to be six and a half, but I'm slowing down now that I've gained thirty pounds of muscle." He flexed his wide chest at her and she rolled her eyes.

Logan bumped Peter in the back. "Couldn't be that you're just getting old. I mean, thirty-nine is just a year away from the big four-o."

The teasing banter of the group helped Daisy relax

and put her worries aside. After a few minutes, an old man appeared at the starting line with a watch and a small pistol.

"On your marks . . . get set . . ."

Bang. Everyone took off.

Daisy didn't run next to Peter; she didn't want him to think she was going to try to keep pace with him. Emma came up beside her, as did Bethany. They made running seem so effortless and graceful.

"Logan told me you're going to be in town for three months," Emma said.

"Yes. I'm renting a room from Peter."

Bethany and Emma exchanged a surprised look.

"What?" Daisy asked, feeling self-conscious.

Emma smiled. "My husband seems to have left that little part out."

"I didn't want to impose when Logan said I could stay with you. Three months is a long time to have a guest, so I accepted Peter's offer instead."

Emma waved a hand at her. "Don't worry about it. I understand. I'm just surprised Peter didn't tell me."

"I better double back to check on Cole," said Bethany. "If I don't run with him at all, he will never let me con him into doing this again." Bethany's ponytail flicked as she spun around to find her man.

Emma laughed. "So, are you going to let Peter beat you?"

"What?"

"I saw your face. You're going to try and pass him?"

Daisy's cheeks warmed. "We will see. I'm not sure I can. I'm not much of a runner."

"At the last half-mile, he will make a dash for it. He's not a distance runner. He's a sprinter. He only runs a nine when it comes to distance."

Emma sped up a notch, as did Daisy. She set her pace

with Logan, and Daisy moved in front of them. Peter's body moved with sure strides. Slowly, Mr. Buller's home grew closer. A small figure sat in a rocking chair on the porch.

Daisy's heart beat faster and before she realized it, she was right behind Peter. She hadn't meant to get this close, but it was too late. He looked over his shoulder and smiled.

"Come to visit, have you?"

"No. I want Mr. Buller to see me clearly."

"Oh. Don't let me get in the way."

Peter's brows pulled tightly together, his male ego offended. He opened his stride and pulled away from her with ease.

Really. I'm not going to be able to keep up with that. She focused on Mr. Buller in the distance. As they neared the house, Daisy edged closer to the side of the road. She could see Mr. Buller watching her, and she waved wildly at him.

"A great day for a run!" she yelled. He quickly stood and went inside.

How sad.

Did he really dislike her that much that he'd miss seeing everyone else running? Her spirits fell. No, she wasn't going to feel bad for causing him to run off. He was probably mad that she was doing what he'd asked.

Peter veered to the left, and she noticed a sign with an arrow pointing them onward. They began to climb a hill. The road became narrow and soon became a path. She had to slow down and watch her feet. The ground was uneven, and roots from nearby trees crossed the beaten-down path. Sweat ran down her back and her heart pounded hard against her chest. She was getting worried she was pushing herself too hard and needed to walk the hill.

Peter slowed down and glanced back at her. She could hear feet pounding the ground behind her and she glanced over her shoulder. A look of misery coated a few faces, while some looked determined. She fought a smile as everyone fell into a single file, the line moving swiftly up the hill. She told herself she would be fine and kept moving. This was kind of fun. She knew trail running was a thing, but she'd never experienced it. It was new and different.

A few minutes later, she and Peter reached the top of the hill and started their descent. She was jogging side by side with him now. Sweat ran down Peter's face and chest. He tugged off his shirt and wiped his face with it, then tucked it down the back of his shorts. She couldn't keep her eyes from raking over his body, his chiseled abs and his powerful shoulders. Her heart rate soared. She began to sweat for a completely different reason. Suddenly, her right foot was jerked out from under her and she crashed into Peter.

"Watch yourself!" Strong arms shot out, stopping her from face-planting into the dirt. She focused on her feet. A root grabbed hold of her for a second and she tried to shake it off. Once freed, she stepped off the path so the others closing in on them could pass. She shook her ankle while Peter held her steady.

"Thanks," she panted.

"It's okay." He grinned widely. "We all get distracted."

"With that grin, I would say you did that on purpose. Afraid I would beat you?"

Peter pulled her close, their breath mixing together, his eyes lingering on her lips. A small part of her was afraid he would kiss her again, but a much bigger part of her cried out for him to do it.

"Maybe, but the race is not over yet, my dear." Swiftly, his lips touched hers before he took off as the next runner came over the summit. Daisy blinked hard. There was no one in front of them. They were in the lead. Without thinking, she sprang into action before the next runner could pass her, and she took off after Peter with his soft kiss imprinted in her memory.

Wiping the sweat off her face with her shirt, her body signaled its displeasure as a few muscles tightened just past the two-mile mark. She hit her stride, hating that it always took so long. She pulled up beside Peter, who was once again impressed she'd caught up with him. Actually, she felt great. Her chest wasn't bothering her at all. Her throat tightened for a moment, and her eyes burned from all the sweat, but she was having fun and she was happy. The happiest she'd been in months.

The city park was about half a mile ahead. She could hear music. It sounded like a live band. Emma had said Peter would sprint the last half-mile. Within seconds, Peter's stride opened and she knew he was all in. She did the same, but she moved closer to him as she bridged the gap between them. As their arms brushed he glanced at her, grinning. He was having fun too.

A quarter-mile to go. She yanked her shirt over her head, taking a note from Peter's book of lowdown tactics. He ogled her in her sports bra. She knew the power she had over him, so she grinned and took off with everything she had. She shoved the hem of her shirt down the back of her running pants just the same as Peter had done. She didn't look back until she crossed the finish line. Joel Junior jumped up and down with a handful of colorful signs. *Way to go! Good job!* Little Abbie and Olivia sat at his feet with a grinning Mr. Miller behind them.

The park was crowded with people laughing and clapping. She finished the race in first place, surprised. She waved, trying to catch her breath. She expected to see Peter on her heels, but he was nowhere to be seen.

Where did he go? She started walking back to the side of the trail, concerned. Three people passed by before she saw him limping with Logan and Emma at his side.

Daisy hurried over. "Oh my! What happened?"

Peter wouldn't look at her. He was covered in dirt, and he had scrapes all over his right arm and leg.

"He tripped over his own feet back there a little ways," Emma said, doing her best not to chuckle.

Logan shouldered more of Peter's weight. "Never seen him go down like that before." Logan's eyes were laughing. "Must have been a rock."

Her cheeks flared, feeling guilty for her antics. She didn't think taking off her shirt would discombobulate him, only slow him down for a second or two. Enough that she could take the lead.

"Eat my dust," came Cole's deep, booming voice. Bethany was beside him, her blonde ponytail bobbing. She tried to slow down to see what was happening, but Cole kept her moving. "No you don't. You keep running. This is my first race, and I'm going to beat them all. Keep running."

Bethany grinned. "His first run and listen to him," she laughed, not stopping.

Logan quickly draped Peter's arm over Daisy's shoulder. "I'll be right back," he said, and he took off after Cole. "I can't let him win. It would be a crime against all true runners everywhere!"

Emma rolled her eyes. "I swear. The feud might have ended, but the competitiveness never will. Those two will never change." She touched Daisy's arm. "I better go and make sure they don't start a fight trying to get to the finish line first. You got him?"

"Yes, go. I'll take care of him."

ॐ♥ॐ

Peter liked the sound of that. He limped alongside Daisy, making sure not to put too much of his weight on her, yet enjoying the feel of her tucked into his side. She looked sexy, all sweaty like that. Her sports bra hugged her round breasts, and it was beyond distracting. He was impressed with the restraint he'd exercised over the last few days that this amazing woman was sleeping in his house and not in his bed.

Her hips swayed with every step. This wasn't exactly what he'd had in mind when he wanted to get closer to Daisy, but he would take it. His grip tightened on her possessively.

A minute later, Logan and Cole were racing in an all-out sprint toward the finish line. With elbows, arms, and hands working to offset the other, both men crossed the line at the same time.

He let out a sigh and shook his head.

"Did you see Mr. Buller?" she asked. Peter nodded. "He took off the second he saw me waving at him."

They started to walk once more. His ankle felt better. He gingerly placed more weight on it, letting go of Daisy. Before she could get away, he stole her hand and locked her fingers with his. She scowled at him, but she didn't pull away. His chest swelled with the thrill of the chase.

"Why do you think he ran off like that?"

He lifted her fingers, not afraid to push the limit. He kissed one finger at a time. "Don't worry. He was probably shocked to see you again."

"He told me to stay."

"Yes, but he thinks you're like your father. Would he have stayed?"

"No."

"Be happy. You've only been here a few days, and you've managed to surprise him. There's plenty to get involved in, if you know where to look." He brushed his lips over her fingers much slower this time. Her expression softened and her cheeks colored, causing his body to ache.

"Come on, you two!" cried Logan. "The dancing is about to start!"

Logan, holding Abbie, paused his tickling fingers when he noticed Peter and Daisy's interlocked fingers. Daisy quickly shook off Peter's hand and hurried away, leaving him to hobble to the party at the park on his own.

Slowly, Peter made it to a tree, sat down, and leaned back against it. He smiled as the townspeople milled about chattering happily. Everyone welcomed the event as a chance for people to come out from hiding and mingle. Cole included. Since Peter moved out of the ranch, he hadn't seen much of his brother and sister. He wouldn't admit he missed them. Not out loud, anyway. They would never let him live it down.

Over at the gazebo, Mark's country rock band, The Three Little Pigs, was playing on stage. Mark was an excellent deputy, a compassionate and genuine guy, and Peter would happily take a bullet for him. Mark had been a stand-in younger brother for him since Joel's death. It was difficult to recall what his life was like with Joel in it. He allowed the years to build a thick grime of guilt over the memories that Peter never knew how to wipe away. He'd been fourteen, a sophomore in high school, when Joel drowned. He promised Logan and Joel he would go with them to the river that day, but he had gone to hang out with friends instead. He should have been there with Logan and Joel. Maybe Joel wouldn't have drowned. A few months later, his mother ran off, never to be heard from again. Peter always appreciated his father's hard work on the ranch and keeping their family together. Cole naturally fell into the role of ranching and hard labor, but Peter never enjoyed it. When his father died of a heart attack, Peter moved home after he finished college and entered law enforcement. A world without his father never seemed possible. Work became his sanctuary, with Emma leaving for college and Cole taking over the ranch. Slowly, he had healed, one piece at a time, through his work. He shook his head. He didn't like to look back on the past. It was done and over. He liked to stay in the present.

Peter placed his fingers between his lips and whistled loudly. Mark turned, and Peter smiled and waved. The Three Little Pigs were pretty good. In no time at all he was snapping his fingers, enjoying himself. Nothing beat small-town living.

He sought out Daisy in the crowd. When he spotted her, his eyes took in her beautiful face and her powerful, womanly curves. She was standing next to Logan holding a beer, laughing at his and Cole's dirty faces. Their scuffle to the finish line had been more than entertaining. Her eyes lit up at what they were saying.

It was apparent in her body language that Logan and Daisy shared a deep bond. She was relaxed and unguarded. He frowned. Max, Logan's ranch foreman, was flirting with Daisy, yet she ignored it. She seemed to have no interest in the opposite sex at all, which frustrated Peter to no end. An independent woman, to be sure. He bent his knee and rubbed his sore ankle. When he looked up, Daisy smiled sweetly at him. She strolled toward him, stopping at a vender's booth to grab another beer. She sat down and handed the beer to him.

"I'm sure you could use one of these."

"Thanks."

"How's the ankle? Feeling better?"

He took a swallow of his beer and then rested his arm across his knee. "Better. Thanks for asking." He eyed Logan, feeling a pang of jealousy. "So, what were you and Logan talking about?"

Daisy half grinned. "Nothing of your concern."

"Oh." He took another swallow and looked away from her intelligent eyes. He let his jealousy show and that was never good. Some women would use that and twist it into something cruel.

Tenderly, her fingers laced with his and she leaned back against the tree. For now, this was more than he could ask for.

Chapter Nine

For the next three days, Daisy was thrown headfirst into the deep end of town events put on by Emma and Bethany. Word had spread fast about her staying in town, thanks to them. The exact details of why she was staying had been spared, and Daisy was thankful. The towns-people wouldn't be happy about her reason for getting involved if they knew about her deal with Mr. Buller.

She had no idea how much went on in Havencrest. She didn't remember Elf View being this busy but to be fair, she had only been there a few months out of the year. She found herself at a rodeo meeting on Monday night with Bethany and Cole. The rodeo was going to take place the last weekend she was in town, and they needed help making repairs to the arena and handing out flyers. On Tuesday, Emma dragged her to a meeting for a quilt show because they needed people to sell tickets. On Wednesday, she met with a woman named Fancy who needed business advice to expand one of her rental homes and turn it into an assisted living home for the elderly. Why Fancy had hunted her down, Daisy still couldn't figure out.

All in all, she was enjoying herself immensely, which was quite a surprise. Everyone in town was so nice to her. She didn't feel like she had to keep her guard up around Havencrest the way she did in the office because of her father.

Peter seemed to feature in every one of her thoughts lately. It was getting quite annoying. She hadn't seen him for three days, and she kind of missed him. He was like a pesky cat that belonged to a neighbor but was always coming to you and meowing to be fed. You didn't want to like the cat because it wasn't yours, but it grew on you until you forgot who it belonged to. Her mind hung onto that.

She looked up at the clock. It would be an hour before Peter would be home, and she was cooking tonight. She had just enough time to make dinner and a pie for Mr. Buller. As she pulled out Mrs. Curtis's recipe for Dutch apple pie, her phone rang. She gritted her teeth when she saw it was Mr. Crouch.

"Hello, Mr. Crouch. How are you doing this fine afternoon?" she said sweetly.

"What is this paperwork I received today? I thought we already went over the terms of the agreement if I choose to agree."

"Is that why you're calling? To accept?"

"No. I want to know what has changed."

"Nothing has changed."

"That's not what this document says. It says you want the deal closed by the end of the month or you walk, and that some Lewin Investments would be handling the transaction from here out. Is that true? We've been working together on this for months. We can't close in two weeks. That's not even enough time for the lawyers to look it all over."

Daisy hadn't made any changes to the Crouch deal and Sue, her assistant, hadn't called regarding any issues with work. Her thoughts danced around one another. *Lewin Investment?*

"Who sent you the documents?" she demanded.

"You did. Your signature is right here."

"No, I didn't. I'm not even in town." Her mouth went dry and her palms started to sweat. She leaned against the counter, needing some support. "When did you receive it?"

"Yesterday." Crouch bellowed to someone not on the phone, "Sarah, who brought over these docs?"

"A young man . . . Branden I think he said his name was."

Daisy gritted her teeth. None of this made any sense.

"Mr. Crouch, I know you're upset and confused. I would be too. I'll get to the bottom of this. Please disregard any document you get from Lewin Investments. I don't know who they are and they are not affiliated with LLD. You have the month to decide about selling and the agreed six months to move and build your new house on the parcel of land you're keeping. You speak only with me about this deal. No one else."

"Fine. You get it together. I will not sell my land to a dictator."

"I understand."

Crouch hung up and she dropped the phone onto the counter. Closing her eyes, she pulled in a deep breath. Why would Branden be messing with the Crouch sale? It was the biggest plot of land she'd managed to secure in years. It was going to be an affordable assisted living community, with a park and several sports fields.

She called Sue and was relieved to hear her perky voice. "Daisy Lewin's office."

"Sue, it's me, Daisy," she said in an urgent tone.

"Hi there. Having a good vacation?"

"Yes, thank you. Mr. Crouch called saying documents were sent to his office yesterday, changing the terms of sale for his land and that some Lewin Investments was going to be taking over. Has Branden been in my office or sent out anything? Can you check the shipping account?"

"Sure I can, and no one's been in your office." Sue whispered, "I locked the door."

Daisy frowned. "Why?"

"I always lock the door when you're gone."

"Sue, is there something I should know about?"

"I don't know . . ." She blurted out in a rush, "A week ago, after you left, Branden came in one night looking for you. I told him you weren't here. He went in and sat at your desk. It was only for a moment, but—"

"But what, Sue?"

"I had a bad feeling about it, so I started locking the door so it wouldn't happen again. I'm sorry. I should have told you."

"It's okay, Sue, I'm not mad. But for the love of God, can someone put him on the blacklist? I don't want him getting past the front desk. Tell security." Daisy sighed. "Call me back after you've gone through the shipping records."

"Will do."

She knew Branden and her father were up to something, snooping around her office. Lewin Investments? It had to be her father. Her head dropped and a vein in her neck pinched, shooting pain behind her left breast. *Everything's fine, don't get worked up over nothing. Sue will call me back. It's fine.*

Calming herself down, she tried to think about something else. Pie. She would make Mr. Buller's pie first. It could sit and cool, and she could take it to him this evening. The pain behind her breast eased. Yes, think about something else.

Maybe she'd been looking at this business with Mr. Buller all wrong. She was acting like her father, all business and no heart. She wasn't like that. She didn't want anyone thinking she took after him. Mr. Buller had meant something to her grandfather, and she wasn't going to let him sit in his house all alone talking to his dead wife. Not if she could help it.

She swiftly pulled the ingredients from the cupboard to make the pie. After living with Peter for three weeks and practically taking over his home, she knew where everything was.

She opened the flour to begin making the pie crust. Lost in thought, Daisy realized the crust wasn't sticking together the way it should. The front door opened. Daisy pushed back a curl with powdery fingers and saw Peter entering the room. Oh no! She was a failure. She'd forgotten dinner, and her pie crust was a flop.

Tears quickly filled her eyes. She'd wanted to have dinner ready for him as a surprise. He was going to starve because she'd gotten distracted by stupid work. *Don't cry. Don't cry.* Peter had become important to her. Whoa! Where did that come from? This was big. Peter's eyes held concern and he took her into his arms.

"Babe, what's wrong?" he asked.

Daisy sniffled and looked up at him. "I forgot dinner." She pointed to the mangled pie crust. "I was trying to make a pie for Mr. Buller, but the dough won't stick together." Her throat threatened to choke off her words. Why did she sound so pathetic?

Peter hugged her close and held her for a minute or two. His warmth seeped into her and bit by bit, her misery chipped away.

"Babe, don't sweat the small stuff. I'm just happy to see you here."

He tipped her chin up to him. His eyes searched hers and part of her melted. She loved looking into his eyes.

"I've been missing you for days. Would you like some help with your crust?"

"Yes, if you can."

"For you, baby, I'd do just about anything."

Daisy's heart was in her smile when she beamed up at him. This was the first time he'd called her babe, and the tenderness she felt for him deepened. She was at a loss for words—and scared to death. He had wormed his way inside her heart without her noticing. He was sweet when he wasn't teasing her, he loved his family, he loved his work and caring for his community. He wasn't afraid to let her take control of his home, and he was always there to make her smile. What was she going to do now? What if this was all a game to him?

Peter unbuttoned his uniform, tossed it into the other room, and then untucked his tight, white undershirt. He examined the crust with a critical eye. He washed his hands, then filled a measuring cup with water and poured it over the crust. As Daisy watched him, she realized just how much she was enjoying this side of him.

"Peter!" she cried. "What are you doing?"

He seized a thieving kiss from her lips and smiled.

"All you need is some water, babe." He started to knead the dough. All the dry, little balls she had created dissolved together.

"Come here." He pulled her in front of him and took her hands. "Work the dough until all the lumps are gone. Then roll it out on the counter."

Their fingers worked the dough together as one, and she leaned back against him as his strong arms held her close. He kissed her neck, but she pitched her cheek to her shoulder, stopping him.

"Aha . . . a ticklish one."

"Don't even think about it." She peeked up at him and he smiled handsomely, his male ego interpreting her words as a challenge. She couldn't stand being tickled, so she did the smart thing and tilted her head so he could kiss her neck more easily. Peter's smile quirked oddly.

"Don't want to play I see." He trailed slow kisses along her neck, tasting her. She tried to beat the dizzying current racing through her, but it didn't subside.

"The dough looks good. Let's wrap it in plastic and put it in the fridge. Then I'll light up the grill. We can have burgers." He kissed her neck one last time and took the dough from her fingers.

"Can you set the patio table? It's a nice evening. We should enjoy it."

Daisy dragged her thoughts away from Peter's lips and hopped into action. Oh yes, she was falling for him, hard and fast.

❧♥☙

Peter's body throbbed. He could hardly control his need to take her. She hadn't initiated any physical contact other than holding his hand at the park. Every interaction had been his doing, so was he off base to think that she wanted him? On the other hand, she didn't turn away from his kisses. It would be nice to know if she wanted him as much as he wanted her. He wasn't sure he could stand this situation for much longer. He had to have her.

Daisy fluttered around the back patio wearing cutoff jeans and a fitted, red tank top. Didn't she know how she affected him? The color set off her pale skin, and her brown curls cascaded down her back for the first time since the wedding. He dragged in a ragged breath. How could he make a woman like her take a chance on a small-town guy like him? If he was smart, he would stop mooning over her. After all, she would be leaving in a few weeks. It wasn't like he could convince her to leave her life in the big city and stay with him in Havencrest. He sure as hell wouldn't consider working in Boise again . . . would he? Clenching his jaw at the sight of her bare feet and long legs, he almost lost it. If she wanted him—really wanted him—maybe he would leave the only family he had. He did enjoy his job, but he was under no pressure to work right away, and he could find something in Boise if he needed to. Cole had bought his share of the ranch, and Peter had just under eight hundred thousand sitting in the bank.

Once in his bedroom, he stared at himself in the dresser mirror. He saw the answer to the question he hadn't even asked himself. For Daisy, he would do anything. He would leave his family to have a chance at making one of his own. He let the realization sink in. He had fallen in love with her. Yes, there would be no one he would enjoy irritating more than Daisy.

He changed and went out to the patio, hamburgers in hand. Daisy was leaning back in a chair; her long legs were stretched out and planted on the corner of the table. She seemed lost in thought, but damn, she looked sexy. He strolled over to the grill and lit it. A minute or two after, the meat was on the grill and he was sitting in front of this beautiful woman. Something was off. She seemed distracted.

Not able to sit still for very long, he stood to get a beer. "Want something to drink?" he asked.

"A beer would be nice. Thanks."

"We have a few minutes before the burgers are cooked. Want to play cornhole?"

"What's that?"

He laughed and handed her a beer. "Keep an eye on the food while I set up."

Peter had to keep moving. It seemed the only way he could be around Daisy without ripping her clothes off and blurting out his love for her.

After he set up the two boards opposite each other, Daisy walked over and seemed relaxed. Whatever had been on her mind a few minutes ago was forgotten for a moment, and he had her full attention.

"How do we play?" she asked.

Peter explained the rules to cornhole. Bean bags were flung through the air to try to get the bag into the hole on the board, or at least stay on the board to earn a point.

They took turns flinging bags.

"You're a cheater. You keep knocking my bean bag off the board!" Daisy cried.

He shrugged at the indignant pout on her face.

"I see how this is going to be."

On the next throw, Daisy managed to knock two of his bean bags off the board completely. His mouth fell open. She broke into a big smile and laughed.

"Don't look so hurt, Peter. It's only a game."

"Best two out of three," he said, liking the way she mocked him so openly. Only Emma and Cole had the nerve to do that. Damn, she could mock him all day long if that look of hunger stayed in her eyes when she regarded him. *I wonder what she's thinking . . .*

Time slipped by and before he realized it, the grill was billowing smoke. Peter rushed over and opened the lid. Smoke swallowed him from the chest up. He started coughing, almost choking as the smoke enveloped him. Black and shriveled burgers were left in its wake.

"Do you want to go to Lucy's Diner for dinner?"

"Why? Did you kill our dinner?"

"Technically, it was already dead. Are the burgers inedible? Yes."

"Sure thing, let me go change," Daisy said as she walked past him.

He caught her wrist and pulled her against his body. "Don't change. Just put on some flip-flops."

"But what if the town sees me like this?" She pulled at her shorts.

"Believe me, you look amazing. You'll fit right in at

Lucy's."

❦

Peter was right, Daisy thought as she peered around the small diner. The place was worn out and barely standing. It was clean, but tired-looking. The walls were light yellow with chunks of paint and plaster missing here and there. Peter took a seat at one of the six wooden tables and pulled her down beside him. She didn't resist. She wanted to be near him. He made it easy for her to forget Mr. Crouch's disturbing phone call and whatever shenanigans her father was up to.

From behind the order counter, a red-haired teenage girl emerged with a notepad in hand. "Hey, I haven't seen you in here for a while. Busy with the new house?"

"Sure am, but not as busy as Daisy here. She painted the entire place and decorated it for me. It looks great. Swing by some time and see it."

"Sure." The girl's brown eyes sparkled at Peter, and then she turned to Daisy. "You must be Daisy. The whole town has been talking about you." The girl whistled loudly. "You sure are beautiful, ma'am, but I'm sure everyone tells you that."

Daisy tried not to squirm under the girl's scrutiny. Peter's arm slowly moved toward her and he captured her, pulling Daisy close to him. She worked to control the blush heating her cheeks. Was he trying to stake a claim on her?

"That's very sweet of you to say. I-I hope you've only heard good things about me," Daisy stammered.

"Sure, ma'am. What can I get you two?"

"Two of Bubba's burgers and fries."

"Coming right up. Nice to meet you, Miss Daisy," the redhead quipped before she scooted away.

"She's sweet. What's her name?" she asked Peter, her

head resting on his shoulder.

"Kimmy Swift. She's a good girl. Stays out of trouble; unlike her three younger brothers."

"She doesn't look older than fifteen. What kind of trouble do they get into?" She was curious to learn more about the families in town.

"Well, let me see . . . Blake, the oldest, dumped rocks into Mrs. Mann's gas tank last week. Jack, the youngest, kidnapped Mr. Reilly's hound dog and held it for ransom."

"No!" Daisy sat up, imagining three younger male versions of their sister. Peter gathered her back into his side. "Is that really the kind of stuff you have to deal with?"

Peter shrugged. "Some of the time. What I find hard is keeping a straight face when it comes to those boys. They drum up all kinds of mischief when they're bored, and you can't help but admire their resourcefulness."

"I bet. I don't know what I'd do with three boys of my own getting into mischief like that all the time."

Peter ran his fingers down her arm. "Do you see a family in your future?"

Daisy's heart pounded. A family . . . did she dare talk about her unbroken dream? Wanting a family, becoming a mother, even though she'd never had one. It was the one thing she'd never let her father tarnish by his lack of compassion as a parent. She had protected that part of her that wanted to receive and give unconditional love. That part of her that awakened and was satisfied by being in Peter's arms. Perhaps it was the possibility of that unbroken dream that made her want him so much. She had always wanted two or three kids. She never cared for being an only child. There was no one else that could relate to or understand what it had been like having Daniel Lewin as a father.

"Yes. I want a home full of children. Chaos all around me. Sometimes, when I come home exhausted from work after closing a deal, I think about how amazing it would be to come home to people you love." She bit her lip. "Do you want a family?"

Peter's lips touched her ear gently. "Yes. A big one."

Daisy twisted in Peter's arms, searching his eyes, not sure what she was looking for. Peter claimed her lips. His kiss sent spirals of ecstasy through her, transporting her to a soft and wispy cloud. Daisy gave herself over to him and all that could be possible. She was certain of it now. She could feel the tendrils of her love snaking their way deep into her soul.

"Your food's ready," said a voice from a faraway place.

Peter released her lips.

"Thanks."

Chapter Ten

They finished dinner at record speed. As soon as they arrived home, Peter scooped Daisy up into his arms, carrying her through the door and into his room. He kissed her with all the passion he felt and she responded with the same fervor. She was dragging him under a warm, silky, liquid fire. He would like nothing more than to burn with her.

He placed her onto the bed. She ran her hand up his spine and threaded her fingers into his hair. Her touch set his skin ablaze as her fingertips caressed his skin. When Daisy bit his lip, Peter forgot about everything. He wasted no time devouring her, tasting her, loving the feel of her lips. Sweet, so sweet. He wanted more from her. He needed more. For weeks, they had danced around one another, wanting but never taking more than a touch here, a brush of lips there. It had frustrated and excited him. No woman had held him off so long. He was glad she had. It had forced him to think long term.

"Babe . . . I want you." His voice was rough with need. He pressed his forehead to hers, working to control his desire. "Can I take you?" He pushed out a breath as his muscles trembled, her fingers lifting the hem of his shirt up his back. "It's okay to say no."

She pulled off his shirt and then her own. He waited, not sure what to do. She trailed kisses over his jaw and down his neck. Her lips were as soft as rose petals. He held still. It took every ounce of strength he had. Damn, she was beautiful. Her silver-blue eyes consumed him, swimming with desire. He wanted her pinned beneath him, moaning his name. He closed his eyes and growled low at her. "Can I have you?"

She rubbed her body against his, pushing him to the edge of his control. Her lips brushed his ear. "Yes."

Thank God. He took her soft lips in slow, lazy caresses. He wanted this to last. He wanted her to want him as much as he wanted her. Her hands skimmed over his body, driving him mad. But he wouldn't rush.

⚜♥⚜

She moaned as Peter set her body to flames. The tension that had been building between them for weeks made it hard for slow, burning desire. The hardness of his fingers electrified her. She'd never tell Peter, but she'd dreamt about this the first week she moved in, and it was so much better than her dreams. His lips seared a path throughout her body, devouring her, one kiss at a time. As he unfastened her shorts and shimmied them down her legs, she rose to her elbows watching him. His expression was so intense, she shivered. Peter reached down to unzip his jeans. He reached into his back pocket, retrieved his wallet, and pulled out a condom. He tossed it onto the bed next to her.

"Sure about this? There's no going back once I put that thing on."

She laughed and unclipped her black lace bra. As she let it fall away, Peter's jaw flexed, as did every muscle in his core. He stood, stepped out of his jeans, and kicked them to the side.

She drank him in, her gaze traveling over his flesh. Unhurriedly, he slipped his boxers off and tore open the condom. He was everything she wanted in a partner: gorgeous, kind, hardworking, fun, loyal, and a protector. Peter was a giver, not a taker.

A smile slipped onto Peter's face. "This is going to be fun." He thoughtfully climbed over her, capturing her body. His hands began a mind-blowing exploration of flesh. Caressing the skin of her thighs, moving near to her hot core, but not close enough. He lowered his head and skimmed her belly with feather-soft kisses. She closed her eyes and waves of heat rolled through her. It was as if she were being carried away one touch and one kiss at a time.

He inhaled against her curls, scenting her, and it almost undid her. "I'm going to take you, and I will keep you."

She groaned in her need for him. Her nipples firmed instantly under his touch. Her body quivered and sweat broke out over her skin. He gripped her hips and sank into her. There was only her and him. Together, they found the tempo that bound their bodies together in a rising passion. His kisses deepened, hungry for her. She'd never experienced this much desire. She took what he gave. She was so high she could touch the clouds.

In no time, he reached her peak of desires and they both gave in to the hot tides of passion that raged through them. Peter held her tight. She felt safe in Peter's arms, like nothing bad could touch her.

He brushed a hair off her cheek and she nuzzled his hand. It was such a small and simple thing, but she melted completely. This was everything she could have asked for.

"Thank you for that," she purred.

"You're quite welcome," he said with a big sigh. For a long while, Peter lay there holding her. She felt herself drifting toward sleep when out of nowhere, she heard a faint sound of whistling. She realized it was her ringtone, a whistle sound. Peter sat up and looked around. As the whistle sounded a second time, he grabbed it from off the floor.

Peter checked the caller ID. "Convict," he said. She watched as Peter swiped the Ignore button.

"Not today, sucker."

The screen went black and he tossed it to the floor. Then he was kissing her all over again.

Chapter Eleven

Another week passed in blissful serenity. Daisy was on cloud nine. Making love to Peter was off the charts. Not only did they connect physically, but there was such a strong emotional bond. She thought being in Havencrest for three months was going to be the end of her, but she'd experienced things here that she never felt before, and it wasn't just Peter. She hadn't thought about work or her father all that much. Was this what her grandpoo had wanted for her when he shared his amazing stories about Havencrest? Had he secretly been planting seeds in her head that could one day grow and change her life?

She felt powerful to be able to subdue a man like Peter with her feminine skills. The thought made her smile from ear to ear. If this could happen in just a month, if she could be this happy in such a short time, what else could happen if she stayed longer? She let out a sigh of contentment. Yes, she could love this man—if she let herself.

Then a touch of sadness hit her. At the end of the day, her life wasn't in Havencrest. Peter wasn't a person to fall in love with. She understood that, and somehow, she was okay with it. Her time with him would be something she would always remember with fondness.

She hadn't heard a peep from Mr. Crouch or her father. She'd seen Mr. Buller earlier, but he merely wrinkled his nose at her and asked how the rodeo preparations were coming along. She'd beamed at him unintentionally. "Great! The town is very organized, and everything should be ready in time." She gave him another pie. This one she made all by herself.

He grumbled and went back inside, taking the pie with him.

Now she was off to meet Peter at his office to bring him lunch. It was so domestic, but Daisy vibrated with excitement. She couldn't believe how good she felt. She smiled wildly at the thought. She marched over to the fridge and grabbed two plastic containers with the fresh meatloaf she'd made earlier.

Ten minutes later, she was sitting in the chair across from Peter as he poked at the meatloaf with a fork.

"You sure it's safe to eat?"

"Yes, I followed the instructions. It smells good, doesn't it?"

Peter sniffed the air. "It seems edible." He looked up and whistled for his deputy, Mark. "Try this, will you?" he said.

"Is that really necessary?" Daisy complained, crossing her arms over her chest and glaring out the window, pretending to be mad. She didn't blame Peter for wanting a taste-tester. She had managed to give him food poisoning three days ago. She hadn't known the chicken wasn't cooked all the way. Mark took a bite of the meatloaf while Peter waited.

"I don't think I got a big enough piece. Let me have another one." Mark scooped the container out of Peter's hand. "Thanks, Boss." He turned to Daisy and said with a grin, "Tastes great. You did good."

"Hey!" Peter whined.

"Don't be a baby, here's more." She placed the second container in front of Peter and handed him a new fork.

Her phone vibrated and then came the whistle. Her breath quickened. Fingers ran through her loose hair as she tied it back into a bun, and then she found the phone.

"Hello," she answered. Determination, vivid in the last rays of sunlight, touched Daisy's face. She calmly rose from her seat.

"Where have you been?"

She hauled in a breath, preparing for a fight. "I am visiting with Logan—"

"What about the Crouch deal?"

"The Crouch deal is none of your concern." She glanced over at Peter, realizing her tone was biting. His face became a mask of stone she couldn't read. "Hold on." Then she nodded to Peter and walked outside to her car.

"I know about your little coup with Branden and moving in on Mr. Crouch," she said. "Lewin Investments! Really? I thought you would be smarter than to use your own name to create a new company, with *your* reputation." She paused, waiting for a reaction. There was only breathing on the other end of the line. "Your arrogance is dumbfounding."

Now came a low growl. Daisy knew she was pushing a man that was dangerous, even to her. He had proven that with the lengths Branden had gone to, nosing in on what she was doing professionally and personally.

Daisy's heart beat faster and her chest started to ache. The ache radiated down her arm holding the phone. She rubbed her breastbone. Daisy would hold her ground against her father. She wasn't one for confrontations as a girl, but as a woman working in a man's world, she didn't often back down now.

"I'll have my company back and if you know what's good for you, you'll give it back to me. And Branden will stop following you."

She started to pace, knowing a threat when she heard one. She'd received many of them growing up in his household. She didn't love him; never had. He was just a criminal. The truth was, her grandfather raised her and was who she viewed as a father. Not this man. They might share blood, but that didn't mean she had to love him, or even care about him. Losing her grandfather, coming to this town where she was surrounded by kind, caring people, and being close to Logan again reminded her of what life really had to offer.

"I do love this small-town look you're going for as of late. The cutoff shorts and the purple tank top. Lovely."

Daisy froze and peered around slowly. Branden was here watching her, somewhere. She wasn't surprised, after him breaking into her car and her apartment. Of course he was sneaking around spying on her for her father. She straightened her spine.

"You can have me followed. You can have Branden go poking around my office. You can have him break into my car. You can even have him break into my apartment. But I'll never give you back Lewin Land Development because it was never yours. It was my grandfather's, and he wanted me to have it. He helped me learn everything about that company while you rotted in that prison cell. And he taught me how to do it right, with compassion and kindness.

"You disrespectful child. You will give it back to me. You'll see!" her father said in a low tone.

She clenched her jaw, hitting him with a threat of her own. "Mr. Crouch will never sell to you. He is too smart to be conned by a conman. He called me the second those docs showed up for him to sign. You know why?"

Her father went silent and she stopped in her tracks. A wave of nausea rolled through her.

"Do you know why?" Silence. "Because I do everything

in person. Because it creates trust and loyalty. That is what Grandpoo taught me. Not you. So, feel free to go poking around my clients. They will never work with you."

He whispered, "You're lucky your grandfather loved you and wouldn't let me give you away when your mother died. I never wanted a child."

She didn't hear him anymore. The roaring coming from behind her ears was too much and turned to a deafening ring. Her chest tightened. She bit her lip, almost dropping the phone.

She felt woozy, so she stumbled back into the station. Her hand didn't leave her chest. She sucked in a ragged breath. Peter rushed toward her. She grabbed him. A sharp pain knifed her in the back. Then a squeezing sensation shot up her neck. Her eyes closed.

❧♥☙

"Daisy, what's wrong?" Peter shouted as he rushed to her. Her entire body trembled while she struggled to breathe.

"Daisy, answer me."

She didn't. He gripped her shoulders and forced her to look at him. Unshed tears glistened in her eyes. Her hand was gripping her shirt. Fear iced his veins. Her expression was one of agony. Her body went limp in his arms, her eyes slamming shut. He pulled her to his chest to keep her from collapsing to the ground. He needed Emma. He fumbled in his pocket for his cell and hit the three keys that speed-dialed Emma's cell. On the second ring, she answered.

"Haven't heard from you since a pretty brunette moved in—"

"Daisy's collapsed, she's not breathing right."

"What? Check her pulse. You do know how to do

that, right?"

Peter's brows stitched together. "I'm a cop."

"I'll call the ambulance and be right there."

Peter slipped the phone into his pocket and gently crouched on the ground with Daisy in his lap.

Mark hurried to his side. "What can I do?"

"Go wait for Emma outside."

"Yes, sir."

Peter placed two fingers on the artery at her neck and peered at his watch. She had an erratic heartbeat. Shit. He touched her cheek gently. "Babe, it will be okay. I'm here with you. Just relax. It will be fine. I promise." The tenderness he felt for her expanded into something much more.

What was taking Emma so long? He ran a hand over his head. *Shit.* If something happened to Daisy, he really didn't know what he would do. What was left of his heart after losing his brother and his father screamed for him to hold onto Daisy.

He cradled her to his chest. "Babe, please hang in there," he whispered. "I need you."

He kissed Daisy's forehead and rested his cheek against her hair. He did the one thing that would calm him down and keep him from panicking. He began to softly sing "She's More" by Andy Griggs, which had been playing in his head ever since Daisy moved in with him.

He would never want anyone more than he wanted her, and that scared him. He'd been held at gunpoint several times, almost run down twice, and he survived it all. But her big eyes wrecked him completely. If he didn't get to keep her, there would be nothing left of his heart. He would be a sad, empty shell of a man moving through the days, feeling nothing.

Finally, the ambulance arrived.

Chapter Twelve

*P*eter was a mess pulling out behind the ambulance with Daisy in it. They were taking her to McClain Hospital, which was about an hour's drive. He listened to the radio frequency the ambulance was on so he could hear what was coming through about Daisy. When he was five miles out of town, another call cut in.

"Verbeck, there is a ten-ninety-two in progress at the stinker station on the north end of town."

"Hell."

Peter radioed in. "On my way."

He hit his steering wheel several times and made a U-turn, feeling sick. *A robbery.* This wasn't common in Havencrest, but during summer they had a lot of outsiders passing through for hunting, fishing, rafting, camping, and rodeos. With it came some transients looking for quick cash.

An hour passed before Peter and Mark had the perp in custody, with some help from the sheriffs in neighboring towns. Peter was exhausted and worried about Daisy. He had gotten word Daisy had made it to McClain Hospital, but nothing else. He was going to go home and change, then head to the hospital.

Peter drove past the road that led to Mr. Buller's property and pulled over. Should he tell Mr. Buller that Daisy went to the hospital? What if Daisy didn't want him to know?

He sat there staring down the road, his mind turning. Peter ran his hands through his thick hair and pulled in a few slow breaths and blew them out in an attempt to keep his anxiety at bay. He decided against it and drove over to Logan's to see if he had heard from Daisy yet. Peter knew Logan would be the first person she would call. Emma was waiting in the driveway looking grumpy when he pulled up. She marched up to his car.

"What are you doing here? Why aren't you headed for Boise? Logan is ready to leave any minute. If you want to ride with him, you better go get your clothes."

Peter stopped breathing. "Boise? Did you call the hospital? Is she okay?" His pulse rate immediately climbed.

Emma's brows pinched together. "She had a heart attack and they life-flighted her from McClain to Boise. They have her stable."

It scared the hell out of him when she'd collapsed in his arms. If he ever had any doubt that he was in love, seeing Daisy like that, he knew he couldn't deny it.

"Logan assumed you were following the ambulance."

"I was. Did. But I got a call a few miles out of town. There was a robbery at the stinker on the north end of town."

Emma eyes grew round. "Is everyone all right?"

"Yes. Mark and I handled it. A few other sheriffs showed up to help."

Emma let out a long sigh. "Of all days for a robbery."

"You're telling me."

"Get home and pack some clothes. I'll have Logan pick you up in fifteen minutes."

"Okay."

He reached out the car window and gave Emma a big kiss on the cheek. He pulled out of the driveway and down the road.

❦

Tap, tap.

God that was irritating.

The tapping continued.

Where the hell is that sound coming from? Daisy grumbled to herself. A thick fog filled her mind. Thoughts unable to find their way.

Someone shut that thing up. I'm trying to sleep here!

Tap, tap.

Sleep? Why was she trying to sleep? Disoriented, Daisy tried to open her eyes. They wouldn't open. Her heart rate sped up.

Where was she? She tried to sit up but nothing happened. Her body didn't listen. Fear slowly penetrated her foggy thoughts. What was happening? She concentrated on opening her eyes. With great effort, they opened to slits. Everything was blurry. How long had she been sleeping? She closed her eyes again, gathering her strength before she tried to open them further. Her curiosity strengthened her determination.

When she opened her eyes this time, she blinked the fog away and was able to make out a figure pacing next to her bed. That was what caused the tapping sound. Her stomach dropped. She blinked a few more times and the figure came into view.

The man wore a black suit and a grim expression. She knew who it was. He looked gaunt and pale. She hadn't seen him for months; not since the will reading at the attorney's office. Her chest ached in a way she'd never felt. Where was Peter? He had to be here somewhere.

Hastily, she scanned the small room. Light-blue walls of a hospital surrounded her. There were a bunch of monitors, and a chair sat next to the large window that gave her a view of downtown Boise. A single tear slid over her cheek. She was at St. Luke's Hospital.

A sob welled up inside her and stuck in her throat. She couldn't let her father see her weak. Pulling in a rough breath, Daisy opened her eyes and watched as her father continued to pace the room. His dress shoes tapped loudly on the linoleum floor, not caring in the least if he was going to disturb her rest. His lack of concern was not surprising, but it irritated her just the same.

"What are you doing here?" she croaked.

Her father—no, better yet, Daniel—spun around to glare at her.

"Taking off when you're in the middle of the biggest deal this company has had in years. I can't believe how irresponsible you are." He stormed over to her and shook his finger in her face. "If I lose this Crouch deal because of you I'll—"

Was Daniel really threatening her while she was lying in a hospital bed? Her eyes widened. Mr. Buller had a reason for wanting to shoot her for simply being related to this man. Daniel practically vibrated off the floor with annoyance over a business deal. Not one speck of concern for her well-being.

"You'll what?" Daisy challenged.

He turned away from her.

"What am I doing here? How did I get here? What happened?" Daisy wasn't sure exactly why she was at the hospital, although she had her suspicions. The last thing she remembered was the searing pain in her chest and collapsing in Peter's arms.

"You had a heart attack. Ridiculous, a thirty-three-year-old having a heart attack. Preposterous." He waved a hand in the air as he continued to pace the room, fuming. "It's nothing to worry about. I was next of kin to your grandfather. But seeing how he is dead, the hospital called me when they flew you to St. Luke's."

Her skin started to heat, and she could feel her own anger brewing.

"Don't question me, young lady. I'm your father. If I say it's no big deal, then it isn't." He pinned her with a deadly glare for questioning him.

His reaction roused her curiosity. His concern for the Crouch deal and not her well-being was disgusting. She didn't know what was going on, so she went along with it to see if it led anywhere.

"If Crouch is ready to sell his land, a few days will make no big deal in closing." She waited, watching her father closely. Fire ignited in his eyes and there was something more—something dangerous—and it was aimed at her. It was hate. Daisy swallowed.

"I can't believe you told Crouch to only talk to you," Daniel scoffed.

So, there it was. She was in control of something he didn't want her to have control over.

"I'll call him tomorrow," she said, trying to sit up in the bed.

"No, you will call him this instant." Daniel stormed over to her, thrusting out his phone. "You tell him I will take over since you're in the hospital."

Daisy gathered her strength and moved her heavy legs over the edge of her bed and sat, needing to have some space away from him. "I'll do no such thing. I'll call Crouch when I'm damn well ready to!"

"What?" her father bellowed. "You defiant bitch." He reached across the bed and grabbed her upper arm tightly enough to bruise it. Her chest constricted, making it hard to breathe. He leaned over her, his face inches from hers. "You call him now."

Fear laced its way through her veins. She grew stronger with it, not weaker. She thought about her grandfather, and how he had denied her father the company and his land all those years ago. She could do it too.

"Or what? Why do you care about this property so much?" She sent him a cutting stare, daring to push him over the edge. She tried to pry his fingers loose.

"Call him and close the deal. You'll sign the paperwork tomorrow," Daniel said in a deadly whisper.

With her finger on the call button to the nurse station, her spine turned to steel. "Go screw yourself, Daniel." The hate in his eyes terrified her, but she wouldn't back down.

Daniel ripped her from the bed and slapped her across the face. She spun and hit the floor. She couldn't press the button, but the alarm from her being off her bed sounded.

"I'll tell you one last time: call Crouch and close the deal. I'll have his property, and you're going to get it for me."

Daisy pushed herself up with her elbows, touched her lip and stared at him. Blood coated her fingers. "No." It felt good to say that, even if it came at a cost. She started to laugh.

"You find that funny, do you?" He stood over her, his fists clenched and shaking.

"Yes, I do."

"And may I ask why?"

Nurses rushed in to see what was going on and gasped at the scene.

Daisy glanced up at her father and said, "You just violated your probation."

Daniel's silver-blue eyes locked on hers, burning. Then, he peered over his shoulder. A small, round nurse was pressing a button on the wall and stammered, "Security, room—room 305."

"Looks like someone is going back to jail. Have a nice life, asshole. Because I'm pressing charges."

She finally understood what her grandfather meant

when he said he wished he could be a man like Mr. Buller. He wasn't afraid to go against Daniel Lewin. But her grandfather had been. Daniel was just a sad excuse of a man, and Daisy never wanted to see him again.

Daisy watched her father explode with rage and pulled back his hand one last time. All three nurses screamed, rushed him, and wrestled him to the ground. It was a sight to see. An image she would hold onto.

Chapter Thirteen

The room was dark. The only light was from the nurses' station. Daisy's thoughts were of Peter. She could see him leaning back in his porch chair, smiling sweetly at her. Every part of her body hummed.

Suddenly, the light was blocked out by wide shoulders. She peered over and groaned, ignoring the pain from her cheek. "I didn't expect to see you here," she said to Logan, reaching her arms up for him to hug her. He hurried over and embraced her.

"Daisy, I'm so glad you're all right." He patted her hair and she could hear him sniffle. Daisy buried her face in his shoulder.

"I can't believe all this shit," he said, voice choked. "The nurses told us what happened with your father." Logan pulled back and studied her face. He softly ran a finger over her cheek. "I hope that asshole goes away for a long time."

She hugged him again, not wanting to let go, but did. "I have pressed charges, so no need to nag." A tear ran over her hot and throbbing face. She smirked at him.

"What's that look for?" Logan asked.

"My father has been up to something since my grandfather willed me his shares of LLD. He has been way too interested in the Crouch deal I was trying to close. I knew if I pushed him hard enough, he would step over a line he couldn't come back from. With the assault, he violated parole. No more father to worry about."

"You goaded him even after you had a heart attack?" Logan wrapped an arm around her shoulder. She drew strength from him.

"I've been afraid of my father for a long time, and I was tired of it."

Logan had a sad look on his face. "You didn't have to go to such extremes."

Her heart was warmed by the genuine love she saw in his eyes. "Yes, I did—if I was going to break free and never look back."

❧♥☙

Peter walked down the hospital hallway waiting for Logan to come out of Daisy's room. He had wanted to give them a moment together without him in there. His mouth was dry and his palms started to sweat. As he got closer to the woman he loved, longing and doubt circled one another, ready to do battle. He pulled in a shaky breath when he reached Daisy's room. Doubt was an unfamiliar emotion to him. He had always known his value when it came to women and work. He swallowed hard. But this was unfamiliar ground—and Daisy was different. He had nothing to offer a woman like her except his tattered heart. He felt vulnerable, and he didn't like it.

A dim light from the nurses' station cast just enough light to make out Daisy's bruised cheek as she hugged Logan. He fisted his hands at his sides. *Damn you, Daniel Lewin. How could you do that to your daughter?* If Mr. Buller was afraid that Daisy was like her father, seeing her now would wipe his mind clean of that thought. Her long hair was in complete disarray, sticking out everywhere. She looked so fragile, as if she would shatter into pieces if he so much as touched her. He ran a hand over his face, trying to clear his rampaging thoughts.

Peter was ready to tell Daisy he loved her and risk a broken heart.

He walked over to her bed and kissed her softly, not caring that Logan was staring at him. He brushed her hair away from her forehead and examined the bruising on her face. Driven by the need to soothe her pain, he brushed his lips over her cheek, then pulled her tightly against his body. She sighed and leaned against him. The beating of his heart was so loud, he was sure she could hear it. There was no place he would rather be but here . . . with her.

"I'll go get some ice for the swelling," Logan said, and walked out of the room.

Peter didn't look up. His gaze was locked on Daisy. He sat on the bed. The minutes ticked by, and all he could do was hold her. He pressed his forehead to hers.

"I love you," he said, not daring to breathe.

"Oh, Peter. I love you too."

"You do?"

She cupped his face in her hands. Her eyes brimmed with tears. "How could I not? You are the perfect man to irritate."

Peter kissed her softly as pieces of his heart began to mend.

Chapter Fourteen

Daisy heard soft snoring and slowly tried to sit up. She peered over to find Peter in the chair next to the bed. She turned her body so she could face him.

He was asleep, looking magnificent beside her—and shirtless! His black hair, his dark lashes touching his cheeks . . . she was in awe. Her body was drawn to him like a magnet. He was irresistible. All the emotions she held in check for this man came rushing out and her tears crept down her face, staining her cheeks.

"Are you okay, babe?"

"Yes." She sniffled. "I'm . . . just happy you're here."

A shadow of emotion cloaked Peter's beautiful golden eyes and he wrapped her in his embrace.

"I dreamt about you," she said.

He swallowed hard, and she watched as his expression changed.

"Daisy." He stroked her cheek. His eyes were ablaze with emotions she hadn't seen in them before. He brushed his lips carefully against hers.

"Why do you love me, Peter?"

Peter chuckled and kissed her neck. "Why not? You're smart." Then he kissed her forehead. "You're beautiful." With this last declaration, he kissed her lips.

"Those are not good reasons. There has to be more to loving someone than that," Daisy said. Her entire body yearned for Peter's touch.

He kissed her ear. "I love when you try to hide your grumpiness behind a fake smile. I love when you bounce when you walk if you're excited."

His words surprised her. She didn't know Peter had paid that much attention to her moods.

He skimmed her lips with his once more. "I love the way you taste when I kiss you. I love that you would stay in a small town and ignore your job to convince an old man that you're not like your father."

"Really? Do you mean it?"

"With all that I am."

She pressed her lips firmly against his.

A few days later, Daisy was released from the hospital. Being in her apartment felt oddly cold. Peter's home was cozy, homey, and felt very lived-in. Daisy's apartment was stark. Thankfully, Peter had taken a few vacation days to stay with her.

Daisy touched her chest. The events of the last few days suddenly came rushing at her. The thing she was most afraid of had happened. She let her father affect her life after he was released from jail. She sighed. When he went to prison, she had been afraid and unsure of who she was. Her grandfather had chipped away at her insecurities to help her become the woman she was today.

But that was the thing. Doubts, insecurities, and misbeliefs had a way of worming their way back into your conscious mind if you let them. Though she had held fast against Branden's poking around at her father's bidding, she couldn't hide from the fear her father had instilled within her. He had never been a kind man or cared about her, but she hadn't thought he would treat her like a competitor. She rubbed her chest again. She would have to take care with her heart and make a new beginning. One that had nothing to do with Daniel Lewin.

The next day, a detective arrived on her doorstep asking questions about her father's arrest at the hospital. Three days later, she awoke to the news blaring in the living room. Dragging herself from her nice, warm bed, she fumbled for her robe. Half-awake, she managed to make it to the kitchen, bouncing off a wall here and there.

"Morning, babe," Peter said. He was eating toast and staring at the TV. "The coffee is unleaded."

Daisy wrinkled her brow, filled a large mug, then shuffled to the sofa and sat next to Peter.

"Holy shit," Peter exclaimed.

An image of Daniel flashed on the screen. A chyron ran across the bottom of the screen: DANIEL LEWIN ARRESTED FOR ASSAULT AND FRAUD, AND MONEY LAUNDERING.

Daisy choked on the coffee and it ran down her chin. She wiped her mouth with the sleeve of her robe. "Oh my God!" Everything suddenly made sense. "The paperwork Branden tried to get Mr. Crouch to sign. Lewin Investments."

The news anchor reported that Daniel had solicited investment monies by securing deeds of trust filed with the county registrar of deeds that were to be invested through Lewin Investments. However, Daniel did not put all of the investor money toward the property. Instead, he used investor funds on other properties or on personal expenses where no deeds were filed.

Daisy stopped listening. She felt sick to her stomach. This was just like her father, up to his criminal ways. If this was news, that meant reporters could be downstairs.

Peter turned off the TV.

"I have to call the office."

Peter jumped up to get the phone on the counter. He

handed it to Daisy.

"Sue, what the hell is going on there? I saw the news. Why has no one called me?" Daisy said.

"You had a heart attack. I wasn't going to call you. I called Steven Banks. I mean, that's why you have a VP, to handle stuff like this. Besides, it was your dad. I didn't want you worrying."

"I need the truth, Sue. How bad is it? Are we tied into this somehow?"

"There have been people on it for the last week. Lewin Land Development is fine."

"Thank God. If people lost their jobs because of that man . . ." Anger roared in her. Hot tears squeezed out.

"I got you, girl. Everything is under control. It is all PR stuff. Rest. I will call if something comes up that we can't handle."

"Thank you, Sue. Tell everyone I said thank you. I will be back in a day or two." Daisy hung up and stared at Peter.

He wrapped his arms around her. "It will be okay."

"Even if the company wasn't involved with my father's wheeling and dealing, I'll never save face now. I bet I couldn't even sell the company at this point." She sighed. "What am I supposed to do?"

"I don't know. Give it some time. You'll figure it out.

Chapter Fifteen

Two months later

The next few weeks were a whirlwind. Daisy couldn't believe she had survived it all. Her father and Branden were in jail. And to her surprise, the company was doing better with her father gone.

But she wanted to forget about all of that. Now she was standing on Mr. Buller's front porch. She knew she looked a mess. Her hair was flying all around her face in the wind, her shirt worn and dirty from pulling weeds in Peter's backyard. She was definitely not looking her best. She didn't care. It was a far cry from the first time they met, but she was okay with it.

In fact, she was out of her mind in love with being a dirty mess because it meant she was living the life she'd dreamed about. It was all she needed. Not her grandfather's long-lost land, not the next big deal. Peter was all she wanted for herself, and she was here to let Mr. Buller know that.

"What do you want?" Mr. Buller asked. His face looked extra wrinkled and grumpy. "I thought you left and went back to Boise."

"I did leave."

He narrowed his eyes and stepped up to the edge of the porch stairs.

She walked over to the old man, her spine stiff. She blew out a breath, lifting her chin a little higher. Her father's sins weren't a reflection on her.

"I only came by to let you know that I'm no longer interested in buying your property."

Mr. Buller's grumpy face fell into a sad kind of expression. "Well, why not?"

She looked at her feet, then back at him. "It's not as important as I thought it was. But thank you for giving me an opportunity to own it." She turned her back on him, afraid that the pain in her heart would show in her eyes. No, she didn't need her grandfather's land to feel close to him. He was always with her, living inside the woman she turned out to be. He was in every breath she took and every beat of her heart.

She made her way toward her car, knowing deep down that everything happened as it should. She opened her car door and climbed in. When she glanced back at Mr. Buller, he was smiling at her strangely. She sat back and closed the door.

Mr. Buller tootled off the porch and strode over to her car before she could start the engine. The sun was shining brightly. He motioned for her to roll down the window.

Daisy obeyed and held up a hand to block the light. "Yes, Mr. Buller?"

"I have no one to leave my land to. I would like to entrust it to you. When I die, it will be yours."

Daisy's jaw dropped. "But I didn't do what you asked. I left . . . and I haven't proven myself to you."

He tipped her chin up. "You came back because you wanted to. That's all the proof I need to see that you're nothing like your father." He backed away from the car and waved goodbye. "A pie and a visit every now and then until I die would be nice. That is my only condition."

Tears filled her eyes. All she could do was nod. He

smiled a beautiful smile that took up his entire face and lifted away many of his years. She could see the ghost of the young man he'd once been. He made his way up the stairs and went back into the house with his beloved wife.

Daisy was overwhelmed by his words and the kindness she'd never expected to receive from such a man. She knew that with all the twists and turns in her life, there would always be surprises. This was just another episode until the next one waited around the bend. She glanced at the simple, single diamond ring on her left hand. Her heart filled with warmth. It was time to go home.

About the Author

R.E.S. Tidmore is a defective writer who writes. She has an MFA in creative writing. Being dyslexic, she never thought she could make a living from writing. Writing isn't only about dotting your i's and crossing your t's. It's about storytelling, and doing it in all the best ways. She loves Jane Austen, tattoos, sarcasm, quick wit, gardening, all things Harry Potter, being a writing coach, and a happy ever after.

Check out my other adult romance series: The Awakener series and the Managing Mayhem series.

AUTHOR'S NOTE: For more on the characters you love from all my series, visit my website www.restidmore.com and click on EXTRAS to see my monthly posts.